Beauty of an Undying Love

Book Three

Monica Shantel

BEAUTY OF AN UNYDYING LOVE

FEATHERS & FLAMES BOOK THREE

MONICA SHANTEL

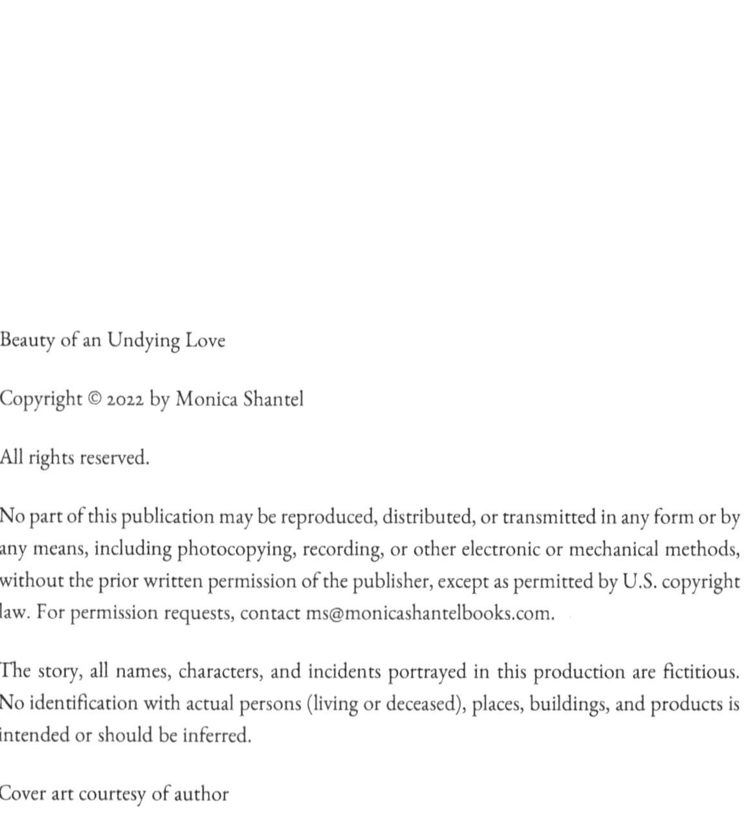

Beauty of an Undying Love

Cover art courtesy of author

ISBN 9781960696977 (Paperback) 9781960696120 (Hardcover)

Second Edition

For those who've had a part of themselves go missing due to trauma—it was never your fault.
And for the people who've been through what Ayden has. His story has helped me heal some of my own.

Hell

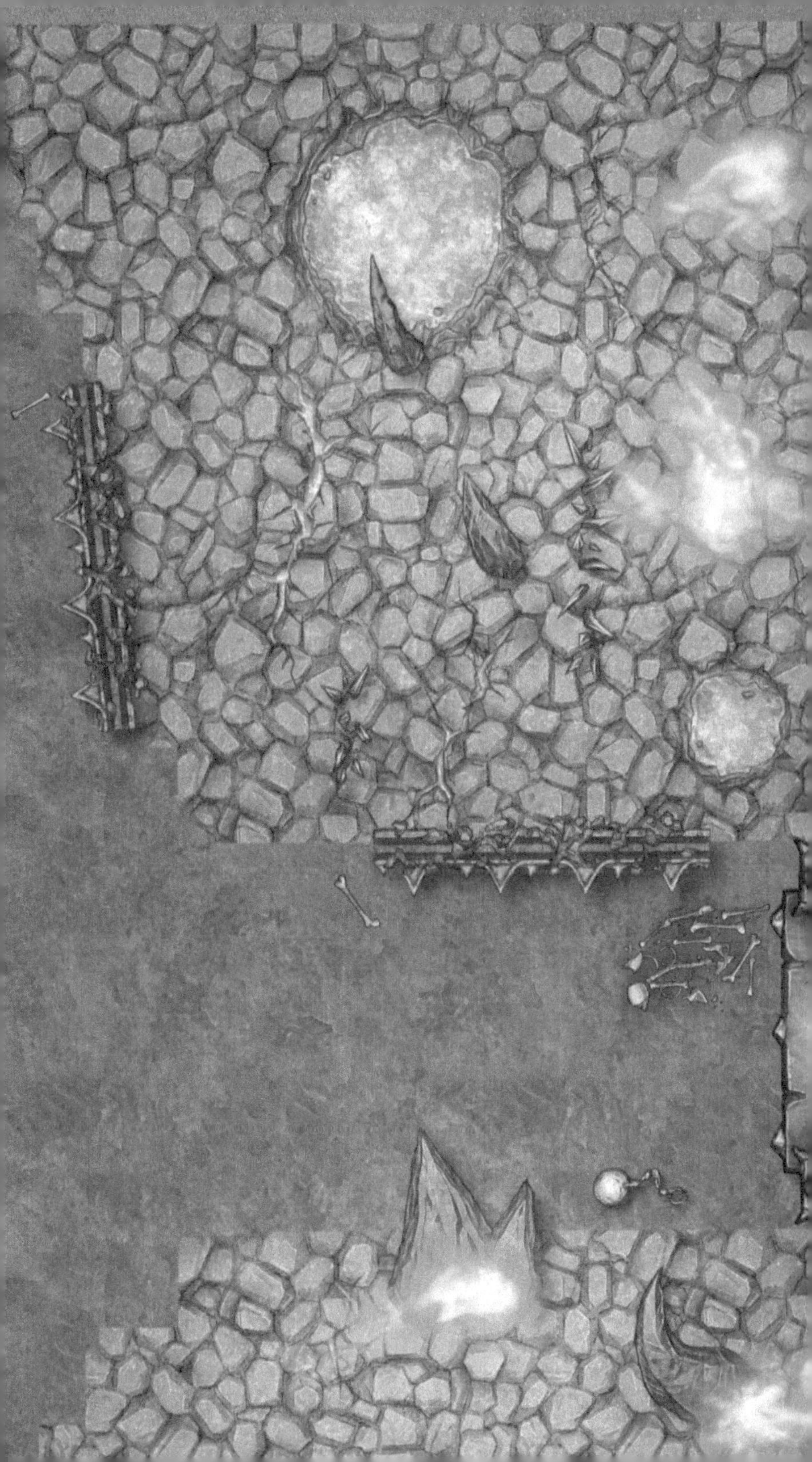

7/30/19
"Lucia

SPOTIFY FEATHERS & FLAMES PLAYLIST

MONICA SHANTEL
A DEAD THERAPIST

Prologue: Dust

Ayden

I was looking out the window when something dark flew by. A demon? No. Fallen angel? Had we not taken care of all these creatures? Liam was dead this time, gone for sure.

But so was Angel.

The pregnancy had taken its toll. The torture. The trauma. Everything weighed her down as if she was worth nothing in this world. And maybe there was a reason as to why. If I could just figure that out, maybe I could fix it. That had been my job—the vows I made at our wedding. In misery and in joy.

It wasn't even just about the vows, though. It tore my heart open to see her walking with her heart dragging along behind her. If I had just gotten there sooner. If I had just protected her better.

"Ayden, are you all right?" Esme asked as she walked by. "I think it'll all be okay now." Would it? In their eyes, they had no idea that my wife was crumbling piece by piece and she was about to turn to *dust.*

"Okay is an understatement," I mumbled. "Did you just see something out there?"

"See what?"

I pointed to the blue sky but in all the sunlight, nothing popped out. "Maybe I'm paranoid."

"You admitting you're paranoid? Bloody hell, she really has changed you." Esme slapped my shoulder.

With a frown, I said, "She showed me the light. It was I who walked into it." I adored Angel. She was absolutely my everything, but I didn't want anyone to think that she fixed me and I was only staying because of the sex. I didn't want anyone to assume the worst, that I called her names or made her feel less than enough. Or that I *hit* her. No, a man who had been fixed by her would not be able to stand on his own and I liked to believe I could.

Now it was my turn to show her the light.

Esme picked up the dishes left behind. They'd had a small dinner to celebrate the end of Hell on earth. It was warranted. "How is she doing?"

As I turned to face her, I helped her pick up a few more. "She's struggling. Mentally and emotionally. But I'm going to help her just like she helped me."

I set the dishes in the sink and imagined her hair running through my fingers, her face tucked into the crook of my neck. She fit perfectly into my arms, and I wanted nothing more than to take away her pain.

"I never thought I'd experience this kind of love," I said. "Never thought I'd love someone so much that I'd give my entire life just to see her smile again. Although I suppose I did do just that." I cracked a small smile.

Esme started filling the sink, pouring soap into the hot water. "We're happy for you. You've grown into a great man, one that all of us are proud to be around. We're happy you decided to allow us back into your life."

She thanked me, but it didn't hit the same. The woman I loved was suffering a fate much worse than death. Everyone Liam had killed was here, fulfilling their purposes.

Mine was clear.

Simple.

My purpose was to love Angel while she didn't know how.

"What if this isn't the end?" I whispered. "What if things are about to get a whole lot worse?" I approached the window, searching for the darkness I'd seen earlier. "What if Angel and I are the last ones left to save?"

FORBEARANCE

Court was dismissed the second the gavel hit the sound block. I stood up with Ayden and we walked out, hearing the chatter amongst other angels. I looked at him, taking in his expression. He seemed calm. How could he manage to be so calm?

He looked at me, grabbing my hand. "We will win this. We've been through enough and we need to have this win."

"How can you be so sure? Everything bad rolls our way." The judge made it clear that letting a human run around without a soul was not an option no matter how much Ayden and I suffered to save Heaven.

"Because I changed. I got into Heaven. You got to marry me. If that's possible, so is this. Our baby will be ours. Nobody is going to take away our child." He tightened his fingers around mine.

Still, I could not agree with him. Our lawyer was going up against another who represented Heaven in this case. The other lawyer made better points than ours, which scared me the most. *Eliana and Ayden Dyer are being selfish, so why do they deserve to keep their baby and let a human run wild,* she said.

A woman ran over, a stack of papers in hand. "We should talk."

By the look on her face, something told me this talk could help our case.

Ayden and I glanced at each other.

After walking down a marble staircase and through a hallway lined with gold trim, we entered a private room. She closed the door and the three of us sat at a table, her across from us.

The room looked small, but the walls were white and airy, making this space feel less claustrophobic.

"What is it?" I asked her.

"We have determined through careful research who the body is. We know who the mother is going to be on earth." She straightened her papers on the table.

I put my hands against my stomach, still holding Ayden's hand with it. It had taken us about two months to finally get our case to court. Heaven was giving us a chance to fight for our child.

"Her name is Lucía Pérez," she told us.

I looked at Ayden. I'd never heard the name before and based on his reaction, he hadn't either. Whoever she was, she was the woman who was getting our baby and I couldn't stand for that.

"The father is deceased. He was a young college graduate, and he was a successful businessman at the end of his life, but he died young." She took a deep breath. "This child that is getting the soul of your baby is the biological child to Liam Brown."

I swallowed, frozen in my place. *Liam.* Our baby's soul would be going to Liam's baby.

I leaned against the counter inside the bathroom of our little cabin.

My eyes lingered on the tiny bump that formed around the soul inside me. I was a soul that held a soul within. It was such a strange concept to understand.

My mind wandered back to Lucía Pérez. She was Liam's lover. She had gotten pregnant with his child. How could I truly let this happen?

After all the plans he made with Lucifer, Liam had time to get down and dirty with a woman, a woman nobody knew about. Did he know we would end him? Was this child his way of living on after his death?

Lucía. He had gone after a woman for whatever reason pleased him. It irked me in ways nobody could begin to understand. He knew what he was doing. This was still his game, even if he was burning in Hell. He got a woman pregnant, and a woman named Lucía as if to laugh in my face that I could never have my baby. He murdered Ayden. He murdered *me.*

I could never regret what I did to him. It was nearly impossible for a woman who's seen what I have to regret what she did to the very man who caused her so much pain.

"What's on your mind?" Ayden asked.

I looked at him through the mirror. "The usual." I lowered my head to glower at the sink.

Ayden wrapped his arms around me and rested his chin on my shoulder. "I'm sorry."

I peeled his arms from around my stomach and stepped away from him, running into the counter. "So am I. I wish I could say I was okay but I'm not. It's going to take time for me to get through this. You know what I went through, but I went through it twice. I'm not the same Eliana you married. You said so yourself." I left the dirty bathroom, brushing past him.

He followed me, walking ahead. "Let me show you something."

I let out a sigh as he led me to a room. This cabin was the same cabin we had stayed in during our war with Hell. Half the steps I made were met with squeaky floorboards and one window was taped off until we could replace it.

Ayden gestured to the room. "I'm making progress. What do you think?"

A half-built crib sat in one corner while the walls were covered in plaster. I leaned against the door frame and shrugged. "What do you want me to say?"

"That you like it? I'm not particularly good at this stuff, interior whatever. I just want to have hope for our future."

"And what if that hope is false?" I laid my head against the wood.

He came over and grabbed my hands. "Then I'll work hard to make it true. We have eternity. We're already dead. There is no expiration for us anymore." He stepped closer. "I will do everything in my power to make you smile."

I dropped my head and stared at my own feet. "You're going to be trying for a long time."

He whispered, "I will. I will try. Your therapist will try. We are all here to support you and comfort you."

Chills ran throughout my soul, causing me to shiver. Ayden was putting in his best efforts, but they were not enough.

"Alex is right. Knowing what we know now, we have a better chance against the court," he said.

When our lawyer, Alex, told us who the father was, I knew that could help us win this battle. They wouldn't allow Liam to steal from us yet again, would they? "Do you believe they will grant us our parenting rights if they find out who is going to be getting our baby? What if the girl he got pregnant is just as nice as Selene? We would be taking away her child because the man she slept with was evil. That makes us just as bad, doesn't it?" I gripped the fabric of my dress to squeeze something to control my anger.

"And what if she doesn't want the baby? As far as we know, she hasn't made a choice. She may not even know. If you're only a few months along..." He looked at my stomach.

I shook my head. "Ayden, don't be ridiculous. We know I'm farther than that. I'm nearly halfway through, I'm just not showing because I am still not human, therefore I won't get as big as Lucía does. She would know by now."

He threw his hands up. "We don't know a lot about her! We know nothing about this Lucía Pérez. We can possibly look for her and talk to her about her plans."

"Yeah, let's just go find the woman whose baby's soul is inside me. She's not going to freak out over what we tell her." I scoffed and turned away from him.

"We have to. We don't know if she's got plans...for adoption...abortion... We have to know what she is thinking. It affects us. We have the spiritual half of her child." Ayden grabbed my shoulders.

I didn't take the time to remove his hands from me. "She's halfway through the pregnancy. I'm sure she's not contemplating abortion at this point."

"Maybe... But we don't know what is going through her head. You're a smart woman. Do you know the statistics of babies aborted in the third trimester or something? Lots of women still do it. I just want to talk to this woman and see what she's going to decide." He wrapped his arms around my shoulders.

"Whatever she chooses, it doesn't work in our favor. If she aborts, our baby doesn't grow. He stays in this stage forever. All of our souls come to Heaven during the moment we die, and we both know nobody grows after death. If she chooses adoption, our baby still goes to earth and to someone else. That makes it even more complicated to fight this because more parents are involved." This case felt hopeless.

He rested his forehead against mine. "We're going to figure this out. We always do."

I grabbed his hands and gripped them. "How? How are we supposed to keep our baby without taking away another? We can't have a soulless human on earth. Everyone knows what happens when that happens. We have enough evil on earth as it is, and a soulless human without a soul is no good. A woman cannot raise her child to be a better human for the world if he cannot make choices without his soul. The soul is what helps us make good choices. The soul is what lives on forever."

"I'm not sure but it'll work out."

I pulled away from his embrace and turned to face him. "You can't keep saying this. You can't. It's clear now that being happy here is impossible. For us, everything goes wrong. I can't listen to your empty promises anymore, Ayden."

"What are you saying?" He furrowed his brows.

I backed away. "I'm telling you to stop lying to me. If this eternity was perfect, I wouldn't need therapy. We would get to have our child without the complications of a soulless human on earth." I shifted my eyes to the floor. "I can't look at you right now." I left the cabin and ventured into the forest.

Birds chirped and clouds floated by. The day was doing fine but I knew I wasn't.

I wished everything would be okay, but this was a reality. Living on earth half the time, we lived by their rules as well. Life on earth was tough, and it sucked.

I sat against a trunk and looked up at the trees and their green leaves.

I wasn't too sure if this could ever work out for us. Everything continued to go downhill even in paradise. When we got a victory, we got shot down following that.

As soon as we were winning against Hell, they kidnapped me and tortured me. As soon as we were pregnant, our baby was no longer ours. As soon as we would get away from Liam, he always came back for us somehow.

"I'm scared. I'm terrified of the end of this tunnel and the only way to ease this fear is to see the end... But it could go either way. We could lose you or live with the guilt of *another* woman losing you." I leaned against the tree and looked at my stomach. "I'm sure you can hear me by now."

I laughed to myself before shaking my head and closing my eyes. "I'm talking to a child I may not keep. I've lost my mind."

Images flashed through my head.

Hot water had burned me. Blisters had formed, covering every inch the boiling liquid touched. Melted flesh filled my nostrils as my soul got stuck to the scorching concrete. Metal rods seared marks into my soul.

I laid my fingers against my stomach, shaking my head. As much as I wanted to have hope, it wasn't that easy. I could never flip a switch and let it be okay. Unfortunately, life didn't work that way.

I wasn't alive but Hell was my weakness. It was the only place I could feel pain, and that included emotional pain. I was mentally scarred more than I was physically.

I had tried to dig myself out of the rabbit hole, but I kept falling back into it. The hole just got deeper and deeper. Every time I tried to climb out, I was pushed back in. It was a never-ending battle with the afterlife. I was at war, fighting for a happy ending after I had a tragic one in my human form.

The worst part of this was the one person behind it all. Every time I heard his name, a *curse* was laid upon our souls. We had done everything to get justice for the shit Liam put us through but somehow, justice was never served.

The last thing I was going to allow was for Liam to get his way and take away our child. This baby was mine. I craved one good thing, and this baby was it. That was all I needed right now to keep myself engaged in this war.

As I sat on the couch, my eyes roamed the room. Plants stood in every nook and cranny, allowing plenty of light to seep through. If I hadn't known better, I would have assumed the couch was made up of the softest clouds known to angels.

At last, I turned my attention towards the woman sitting across from me, her feet placed flat on the floor as she sat in the chair, hands in her lap. She focused on me, and I wasn't sure how I felt about being the center of attention.

"Welcome back, Eliana," she said with a warm smile.

I folded my hands together and lowered my eyes to the floor. "I promised Ayden I would do this if he let me kill Liam. He let me and I must at least keep my promise, right? So, I'm coming back."

Marie nodded. "Of course. Begin speaking when you are ready."

Playing with my fingers was easy. However, releasing my thoughts was not as effortless. "I'm reminded that I'm a bad person just by being here. I'm pregnant and yet I'm spending my time depressed and angry. That affects my baby. This child can feel my emotions and I'm screwing it up. Look at you, judging me. You're an angel, too. You're going to judge."

She didn't appear to be affected by my accusations. "Eliana, I am not here to judge you. You are valid. Your feelings are valid. Your experiences are real. I am here to listen to you. You can tell me what you want to say, and I will be here."

Chills crawled up my arms as I hugged myself. "I have tried so hard to make it better. I am trying. It's just… I have moments where I feel hopeless. I feel like it's never going to work. I'm scared of our future. I want to be happy and have hope that we can have our family, but I can't see the possibility when Liam keeps ruining everything."

Nodding, she said, "Liam is still involved, and it makes it hard for you to see a happy ending."

"Yes. He's dead—and actually dead this time. He's burning in Hell. I'm here, in Heaven, in a counseling room because I can't even cope. I have a wonderful husband who cares about me. I have the chance to raise my baby if we win this case. Ayden and I were never meant to fall in love, and yet I got to keep my job as a guardian angel after God knew about our affair. These things turned out okay in the end… But I still can't bring myself to hold onto hope that we'll get to keep our child."

Silence pierced the air.

"Do you have children?" I looked at her.

"We are here for you, Eliana." She gave me a smile and gestured for me to continue when I was ready.

Redirecting the attention back to me. Exactly like a therapist would do on earth.

I looked at my stomach and pressed my hand against it. "I used to be jealous of women who were alive on earth. They could have babies. I always wanted to have my own. When we were at war with Hell, I had to keep the children safe, and I ached to have kids of my own like that. Somehow, my dream came true. It came true and I was happy to at least believe in the idea that I was having a baby.

"It was ruined the second Matthew told me my baby wasn't mine. I was only carrying the soul of a baby on earth who would be taking *mine* when they were born. Since then, we've gone up against the Heavenly Court because we want a chance to have a child. We just want one child to love. We keep winning battles but the war against Liam is still going on and I'm terrified that we won't survive this one. He's always one step ahead."

I pushed my hair back and looked at my hands, spreading my fingers.

She leaned forward a bit. "I wanted to ask about your other methods of coping. Tell me anything you do to deal with this."

I exhaled, although I didn't need to. "I sit in the woods most of the time and talk to my baby. Other times Ayden and I get into a fight because he always tells me that it's gonna work out, but I hate hearing about that."

"And what brought you to me?"

"Hell. What else could it be? Hell is the only thing that can hurt us now." I sat back, slumping down on the couch. "This is what I chose. When I went to war against Hell, I knew the risks. They were going to come after me again, and they did. They burned me. They whipped me. They were going to cut my baby out. I can never forget the pain I felt down there. It is seared into my brain, Marie. Forever and always," I whispered.

I screamed in agony, gripping the stone that laid beneath me. The boiling water seeped into the fresh wounds on my back, burning the already injured soul. The cuts themselves were beginning to blister while blood dripped down my back.

"Eliana, are you all right?" Marie interrupted my thoughts.

"I'm all right. I just struggle to get these images out of my head. They replay like movie scenes, and I can't make them go away. Over and over and over, the reel spins and never stops." My eyes lingered on the floor for too long.

He pulled the pole out of the fire, watching the orange glow fade. "Beautiful." He put it against my stomach, getting a loud scream out of me.

"Or did he say something else? I...can't remember. My brain feels foggy at times." I shook my head as if forgetting every detail made my story less valid.

"That's normal with trauma. Some details get lost, and others become more vivid over time."

He put the pole back in, looking at me.

I breathed heavily, glancing down at my stomach. A burn mark was now seared into my soul forever, embedded right where my baby resided.

She reassured me, "They cannot hurt you anymore. They have no access to Heaven."

"They don't have to access Heaven to get to me. They already have control of my memories." My eyes shifted to meet hers.

Pain. Burns. Cuts. Wounds. These were what covered my entire soul. There was no possible way for me to focus my energy or mind on anything but the injuries that took over.

Every part of me had been scorched to no end, the heat taking away my ability to think with logic. I needed water. I needed ice. I wished for anything that could make it go away.

My back stung and ached with all of the gashes that had been made hours before. Maybe it had been days. I had no way of knowing how long I'd been down here.

The wounds on my stomach were just as bad, exploding with pain in that area alone.

"Every day, I close my eyes and I relive this event. I remember the pain they caused me and my child. You don't understand what it's like to live every day as if I'm still human. I am an angel and yet, I'm in therapy. The first therapist sucked and now I'm here." I scoffed. "It's really no surprise. You won't last long, Marie. Nobody can fix me."

"Why do you believe this?" Her movements were subtle. A small frown. Shifting in her seat. She thought I wouldn't notice, yet that's all I seemed to notice these days. Every little thing about everyone.

Like the way her brown hair fell perfectly over her shoulders, and the black heels she wore despite being an angel now—most of whom were barefoot. Her beige slacks were too far up her shins, telling me that her height had been taller than what the average woman shopped for.

But it was her voice that always caught me off guard. Soft, and inviting. So warm, and nonjudgmental. With just a hint of an accent, most likely Hispanic.

She deserved a better patient than I.

"You're my second therapist. You won't be my last. I know myself." I shrugged.

Marie nodded before gesturing to me. "I wanted to ask you what your triggers may be. You mentioned earlier that these scenes play like movies in your head. Normally, these things can be started by something in your life."

"Triggers. Triggers..." my words trailed off.

The sofa was nothing like a cloud, but it would have to do. The blankets kept me cozy enough while the outside air dropped gradually. A fire was going to keep the cabin heated.

A sudden craving hit me like a wave at the beach, and my mind was focused only on getting myself some artichoke hearts and tea. It might have been a strange combination of food and drink, but I was pregnant. The baby wanted what he or she wanted.

I made my way to the kitchen and turned on the burner. I poured water into the pan and started to cut up my artichokes. The smell was delightful and my need for this food was growing stronger each second.

I walked over to the pot and grabbed it, dumping out some water into the sink. I screamed out as a rat ran across my feet, and the steaming liquid spilled onto my dress. It never registered with the nerves that did not exist within my soul, but it did hit my memories.

Maybe I could not feel the blazing water against my soul at that moment, but I never forgot the physical pain of what it felt like when they poured it over me. I didn't need to feel the pain to know what it would have been like to be burned. They'd already reminded me.

"Everything. Plenty of things can trigger it. Fire. Boiling water. Heat. Being too hot. Anything red. It's a curse, and it's never going to be lifted. I am destined to live my eternity in the pits of Hell, once known as thoughts of my own," I said.

"Tell me a bit more about your routine. Has your appetite changed? How do you sleep?" she questioned.

Shaking my head, I looked at her, maintaining eye contact. "I never sleep but I have days where I feel fatigued. My appetite hasn't changed. I crave whatever Lucía craves and eat that. My symptoms are in sync with hers, but that is all we share."

A light gleamed in her eyes. Was it for me, or about something I'd said? "How is your job?"

"You mean being a guardian angel? I've put that on hold. I can't go back to this when I've got so much crap going on in my afterlife."

She straightened her posture, recrossing her ankle over the other. "How are the legal issues going?"

"So far, it is stressful, but Alex feels we have hit a breakthrough. She believes the current information that has surfaced will help us with our case," I told her.

"Do you believe it will? You've told me you feel you won't win the war." Her eyes searched mine, prying right where I never wanted anyone to go.

"I don't know. This is the Heavenly Court. They could completely understand why we don't wish for our child to end up as Liam's baby. But on the other hand, they could use the argument that children are not their fathers and deserve a chance to be their own person." I pushed a strand of hair behind my ear.

"How are things with Ayden? How does Ayden feel about your trauma?"

Reluctantly, I answered, "He supports me. He wants to see me get better, but he understands it takes time. He's a great husband but I don't talk to him like he is. I helped him when he needed me and now he's returning the favor."

"So you have the support you need, which is good to hear. Is that part of what made you fall in love with him?"

I smiled a little at the thought of being his guardian angel. "Ayden was stubborn—still is. He won't break even if we fight. He showed me pieces of himself that nobody else saw. He has a passion for baking, and it's so wonderful to see him smile when he is decorating a cake. Ayden always believed he wasn't a man if he embraced his love for making sweets. He would act out. He did bad things. Even in his darkest days, he never hit me. He never called me a name. He wanted to change, and he let me in. I knew I wanted to love him for the rest of my days."

Marie's eyes held a feather-like kind of sorrow in them that I hadn't seen until now. "That sounds very beautiful. You helped Ayden into Heaven. What was your happiest moment with him?"

"Our happiest moment you ask..." I thought back to every experience we shared.

"What the hell is this?" I put my hands on my hips as I looked at Ayden.

"This isn't Hell; it's earth, dear Angel." His lips formed a smirk as

he pulled me against his chest and whispered into my ear, "this is our first date as angels."

He placed a sweet kiss against my cheek and sat down with me on the blanket. "I thought it would be nice to watch a sunset but then I thought that was boring. We can't eat much food because we're dead. However, I thought I would do something I love to create something you love, so I baked this cupcake for you." He handed me a red cupcake.

"Ayden, this is the most romantic thing you have ever done." I took a bite of the cupcake that crumbled in my mouth. "Wow, that tastes like Heaven. And I intended that pun." I gave him my best smile.

He chuckled and kissed me, despite the red crumbs that covered them. "It does, especially on one of Heaven's angels."

My cheeks tinted pink as I looked towards the ground.

He added, "This is not exactly traditional and I'm sorry, but we're dead." Ayden lifted my chin, forcing my attention back on him.

"What do you mean? Angels still go on dates in Heaven."

He whispered against my lips, "They do, Angel, but angels don't have wedding rings." He intertwined his fingers with mine and brushed his lips over my knuckles. "I have no ring to offer you for your hand in marriage. I still want to be with you nonetheless. I wish to spend forever with you, in love and putting up with my shenanigans. Will you marry me and become my Mrs. Dyer?"

Legalism

I drummed my fingers on the table, lost in my own world. A muffled voice called my name.

"Eliana, are you all right?" Alex asked me.

Ayden grabbed my hand, intertwining our fingers. My eyes met hers and I nodded to reassure her that I was just fine. It had been rough since Selene was killed.

That was the beginning of this messy journey into the afterlife and now here I was, fighting for the right to keep my child.

"Angel?" My husband's worried voice broke through the barrier.

I closed my eyes, feeling a tear roll down my cheek. "I'm fine. I'm fine." *But I wasn't.*

Alex didn't say anything, and it was just enough for me to keep my sanity in check.

I looked at our lawyer, folding my arms on the table. "Go on. We only have a limited time before Lucía has her baby and we lose ours. We can't let my problems get in the way of the case."

Alex seemed on edge after that point. "Some points I'm able to make are the fact that you both died so young. You were murdered so you didn't have the chance to make any dreams come true in life and now you wish to fulfill those now."

Ayden's fingers tightened around mine. "Of course. We can also add that Angel was put through hell to help save humanity and fight on the side of Heaven. She deserves something good from the bad. Isn't God about bringing good from the bad?"

She chuckled a bit. "Of course, yes, He is. However, she was pregnant before she was tortured."

He shook his head. "Not the first time. She was tortured twice. I was there the first time. I witnessed the cruel things they did to us. She took on the job of changing me to save my soul, which is what God wanted. He wanted me to be here with every other angel. She ended up in Hell for trying to save me, and she ended up there a second time for trying to save humanity from Satan. It doesn't make sense to take away her chance to have a child. It's something to keep her going."

"Of course, I understand. I am on your side. I want you guys to win this case. We still must look at the arguments against you, and they will tell us that even if you keep this child, it's at the expense of another human—and then some. That is not selfless love and angels are about being selfless. They will not allow a soulless human to run rampant on earth. Souls were created for a reason. They play an important role."

I hugged myself, shivers racking my body. It was so cold and the only thing I could see in my mind was giving birth to a child who would then go to earth.

Ayden grabbed a jacket and placed it around my shoulders.

"Excuse me." I stood and left the room. I needed a moment to myself. This all just seemed overwhelming and hopeless. How was I supposed to make it through?

I couldn't forget what they did to me. I was terrified they would do it again. I could never be safe.

After giving myself ten minutes, I whipped my mental state into shape. Going back inside, I sat down at the table.

Alex continued with her ideas. "Lucía can be one of the big points. It shouldn't be fair that after everything you went through with Liam, your baby goes into his."

I shifted my gaze to meet Alex's. "I have tried countless times to tell myself that this isn't fair, and justice will be served. But what is more righteous to God? Letting us have a chance to keep our child or making sure a human has a soul? It isn't fair that I must lose my baby and to Liam's of all people. His own offspring is taking ours away from us. Liam would've done the same."

"That is what we are here for. We are here to prove that keeping your baby is the better option," she said.

"And how do we make the court believe this? This is how the system works. A soulless human is a worse fate than us losing our child. They are not on my side. They are fighting against us. They are fighting to give our baby's soul to Liam's spawn. Liam did this on purpose to screw us over because he knew we would kill him. I just need to *prove* he did this."

Ayden choked on his words. "No, you don't plan on going back to Hell, do you?"

"I don't have any other choice, do I? I need to face my fears. They ruined me. They scarred me. You really don't think I can do this? Sometimes the best therapy is facing what hurt you and going back may be the only way to help me heal." I looked at him, grabbing his hand to let him know I was going to be okay.

Alex wasn't sure what she was supposed to say. I knew there was nothing anyone could do or say to change my mind. I had to face the darkest parts of myself to stop them from destroying me from the inside out. This was the only way to get back on my feet and get the truth from Liam. I could kill a giant with one stone.

We finished up the meeting with Alex and went back to our run-down cabin. I knew what was about to come. Ayden was ready to fight me on this.

"Look at me." I stood behind him as he tried to fix the crib for our child. He always did this to work off the stress and to avoid confronting me. "Ayden," I repeated.

He stopped and turned to face me. "What do you want me to say? I was there the first time. I watched them rip you apart. I know what they are capable of. You want to go back to the very place that has turned you into this." He gestured his arm up and down my figure.

I was taken back by his words. "Excuse me? Is that what you think of me? I know I'm not the ideal wife, the woman you wanted to marry but this is our reality now. This is who I am. I've been through so much and it is so hard to pretend it's okay. This shit does things to your mind. It changes you. I went through hell and still came back. We are supposed to be a couple and support each other. I was there when you were at your worst. I helped you through everything. If I can put up with you, you better put up with me. There's no backing out now because we made vows."

He sighed. "I'm sorry; that came out wrong. I just don't want to see you, or our baby get hurt. It scares me, knowing what they have done to you. I know that you're dead and I can't lose you physically but I can lose you mentally. They can damage you in ways I never imagined." He came closer, attempting to warm my hands in his. If only. "They did damage you."

"If you had the chance to face the man who hurt you, would you?" I locked his green eyes on me. They were just as beautiful the first day I saw them.

"No. I don't want to see his face. I had nightmares until the day I died. I always feared he would come for me. He destroyed my childhood."

"That's your choice, Ayden. He is the one who hurt you in awful ways. You deserve the choice to handle your problems how you will, and if that means you don't see him again, I won't convince you otherwise. But this is my problem. I make my choices on dealing with it. I choose to face my problem and give us a fighting chance. We need this. *I* need this." I put my hands on my stomach, the firm bump becoming more prominent.

Ayden put his hands on top of mine. "And what about our child? You are putting our child in harm's way. He is still inside you, and I can't keep him with me while you deal with these arseholes."

"I am aware, but I must do this. I can't wait until he is born because then it's too late. I'm going now because I can prove Liam did this on purpose. That is another argument for our case. I can deal with my issue and heal by being more focused on this case and less focused on these images that haunt me." I eyed my stomach.

He shut his to take this all in. I couldn't blame him for worrying and wishing my mind were different. He would have to accept it, however. I was not going back on this idea. Sometimes, the best therapy was to look Liam in the face and tell him he was going to lose. I was doing this for our child in the end. It was our only option. I refused to let Liam win the war.

Ayden pulled me into his arms and made sure to say he loved me. It was all he was able to do since he knew I wasn't backing out. Sometimes, part of being a husband meant supporting your wife even when you didn't want to.

"Do you remember the day I proposed?" he asked.

I smiled a bit. "I always do. It's my favorite memory of us. You wanted to seal our love and that meant everything to me. It's crazy to believe there was once a day where you were not such a good guy."

He chuckled, yet it had hardly any effect on me at all. "Angel, I wasn't the worst guy. You still fell in love with me."

I laughed. "Yeah, and I still have no idea how. They say you can't help who you fall in love with and that much is true. Accepting who you love is the hard part. When I knew I loved you, I didn't want to believe it. You were with Sunny, and she was an absolute mess. The scariest part was admitting how I felt about you. You were so mean about it. When you said you would never love me, I thought it was the end. I believed I could never be happy in this world." My chin rested on his shoulder as my laugh became a sigh.

He pulled away from our embrace and he cupped my cheeks. "You can be. You are going to go down there to fight for our happiness. I admitted my feelings. I changed. We got married. Now, we are pregnant. In a way, Heaven is on our side. They are rooting for us because they know we have a chance to make a difference. Liam is fighting us, but we are still making it through. He killed me and what did we do? We got married. He killed you and you became a guardian angel to change me and love me. He tried to ruin our marriage by releasing Hell's fury on earth and what happened during that? Your dream of being a mom happened. We are fighting and we will not stop until we come out on top."

My gaze fell to the floor as I curled my toes against the carpet. "You're really working hard."

"What do you mean?"

"You're fixing this cabin because you believe in our family. I've never truly had a family before this and it's refreshing to see what it means to you. You have hope for us. This is what a family looks like."

He glanced at the baby's room, a yearning lingering. "I'd do anything for you. You helped me realize who I really am. You've allowed me to be myself."

"Well, I'll let you in on a secret." I leaned in. "Women love a man that can bake. That's what won me over."

Ayden laughed, shaking his head. "If only men were as accepting as women."

"I don't know what it is with humans pushing men to be cold and emotionless. That's not how humanity works. Men have feelings because they're meant to have them the same way we do. And food is a people thing. I'm not sure where the idea of women being bakers came from, but it definitely shouldn't be a feminine thing to do. I'm glad you ignored the rest of the world and embraced your love for baking." I gave him a small smile.

His smile dropped, face straightening out. "Can I ask one thing of you?"

"Always."

"I want to ask you to be careful and extra cautious. You'll be in their territory. I want to see you come back with a smile on your face," he whispered, our faces mere inches away.

"You and this baby will be the reason I fight. I will make it out in *one piece.*"

SLEIGHT

AYDEN

"Mum, Dad. We should talk." I rubbed my hands together, pacing in front of the door. Yeah, that could work. "No, you imbecile. It needs to be more impactful. They have to know this is serious."

The front door opened, and Esme stood there with an eyebrow raised. "Ayden? What are you doing here?"

It was too late to turn back now. "Are Mum and Dad here? I need to talk to them."

"Ayden? Is that Ayden?" Arabella rushed to the door like a child, pushing Esme away. "It is you!" She threw her arms around me. "Come in!" She grabbed my wrist and dragged me inside. Esme closed the door behind us.

"Where are Mum and Dad?" I asked.

Esme walked into the kitchen, coming out with a cake. "They left to get something to finish this. It was supposed to be a surprise but..." She set it down on the table. "You might be dead now, but that won't stop us from celebrating your birthday. It's something we did even after you left the family business."

My birthday. It had been so easy to forget when you weren't

breathing.

"It's your favorite, too," Arabella said. "It's our way of appreciating the fact that you came into our lives. Esme didn't want a little brother, but I did. And I'm glad you're mine." She grabbed some plates. "Do you want some now?"

With a shrug, I said, "I could eat."

The cake wasn't complete, and it had been obvious from the missing words meant to be written in cursive atop it.

Esme shook her head. "Mum and Dad aren't that lazy. They aren't done decorating."

I grabbed a knife, cutting into it. "I'm the birthday boy, Esme. I say the cake is finished." At least this would cushion some of the blow.

Arabella giggled and got herself a slice as well.

Esme eventually caved, grabbing a piece, too. It wouldn't have been long before she broke the rules. That had been how it worked in this family.

The three of us were halfway through when Mum and Dad returned. "Who said you guys could eat without us?"

Mum spotted me. "Ayden, what are you doing here?"

Right. The real reason I was here. "I think you guys should sit down."

Dad nodded, but Mum hesitated. Dad assured her it was okay, and so they both sat together.

There hadn't been an easy way to prepare, or any right way to say this. "Do you guys remember when grandpa went to prison?"

Mum looked at Dad, nodding. "Of course. It shocked everyone."

"You remember why he was arrested?"

Dad leaned forward. "It's not a secret, Ayden. When your father gets arrested for child pornography, you don't forget."

Child pornography. It was a serious crime, but nobody ever suspected it got worse than that. Because I never said anything. So, he simply got *help* for eight years, in prison. He hadn't been an abuser. Yet.

Because of that event, my parents wanted to uproot our lives and take us back to England. But we fought hard to stay.

I put my fork down, unable to take another bite. "Do you remember if they ever investigated it further? Did they ever find any victims?"

Mum furrowed her brows. "Ayden, this was so long ago. You were just a little boy then. Why does this matter now?"

I clenched my jaw, offended that she wouldn't give me the chance to speak. "Answer the question."

"No, there weren't any. They asked all of us and we asked you, but you all said he never did anything."

My chest deflated. I'd said that? I never even remembered telling my parents. I also didn't remember seeing him get arrested. There were certain memories that overshadowed others.

"I lied."

The room fell silent.

Someone had the courage to speak, finally. "What do you mean you lied?" Dad asked.

I set my plate on the table, refusing to look at anyone. Even after twenty years, I still felt the shame. I knew it wasn't mine to bear, but did I have the choice? "I mean when you're a child who barely understands anything, you lie. You don't want to get into trouble. So if you asked me then if he did anything, and I said no, I lied about it."

Mum didn't move. I wanted her to say something. Was she angry with me? I couldn't tell.

"You mean you lied as in..." Arabella couldn't finish the words.

Mum swallowed, looking at my sisters. Whatever she was thinking, she wasn't about to say it now. She faced me. "What did he do? No,

I don't want to know." She balled her hands into fists.

A big part of me never wanted anyone to know. It was shameful. It made me feel less like a man. Maybe the other part of me didn't want my mother to have to hate her father. I had destroyed a bond for good.

"It makes me angry! How could I let this happen?" She shot up from the couch. "No, I need to confront him. I have to."

"Mum, no!" Esme grabbed her hand, making her look at her. "It is not your place to confront him. This is about Ayden right now."

She stopped and looked at me. It seemed to dawn on her for a moment that it wasn't the time to be angry. She circled the table and sat beside me, pulling me into her arms. "I'm so sorry. I am so, so sorry."

I didn't know what to say, so I said nothing at all. It was good to get it off my chest, yet now I got all these pitiful looks. Now they'd see me differently. I didn't like the thought of that.

I sat up, making my mum let go of me. "Do you need therapy? We should get you into therapy."

"Mum, stop." I shook my head. "It's not about what you want. I don't need therapy. I spent over twenty years healing by myself." A small part of me wanted to go to therapy, but I didn't want to keep talking about the trauma. It made me feel sick, like a victim and nothing more. I just wanted to forget about it.

It'd been so much easier to bury the event in the back of my mind and relive it in spurts against my will.

"Twenty years... That is such a long time to suffer on your own." She grabbed my face, forcing me to look at her. "I'm sorry if I made you feel like you couldn't confide in me."

"He made me feel that way. It was never you." It wasn't the whole truth. My parents had always been so occupied with the business. They had been so sure of making sure I knew when it was and wasn't a good time to show emotions. They never thought to teach me to stand up for myself, nor did they bother teaching me about the danger of abuse. Stranger danger was a bigger deal, but the real danger always came from inside the home.

Dad stood and went to the kitchen, because he wasn't sure what he could say at this point. Esme followed, and I could faintly hear the question, "Did he do something to you and Arabella, too?"

After I left my parents', I decided to distract myself with some shopping. Well, it wasn't much of shopping without money. Angel wouldn't mind, right?

I stood in the baby aisle, trying to decide between two outfits.

"Is your baby a boy or a girl?" a woman asked.

I glanced at her before facing the clothes. "We aren't sure yet, but I'm hopeful." I picked up a pink onesie. "Do you think women like this? I can't decide. My wife is having a hard time and I'm trying to build the nursery, but I know nothing about babies. What else do babies need besides cribs and clothes?"

She laughed, putting the outfit back. "Let me show you." She led me to some furniture. That wouldn't be easy to steal. "They need a dresser for the clothes, as well as a changing table and bottles. Have you gotten a breast pump yet?"

I crossed one arm while the other one was stroking my chin. "Breast pump. How sexy are those?"

The woman grabbed one. "They're not. They're for your wife if she wants to store bottles for future use. I assume this is your first child."

I glanced at her, grabbing the breast pump. How did this work? "We didn't plan to have a baby, but it happened. Although I guess that's what I get for teaching her to love sex as much as I do."

She pulled the breast pump from my hands, putting it back. "How about diapers? A diaper bag is also a must."

"Diapers. How often do you change a diaper?"

The woman let out a sigh. "Oh, dear child. You are so clueless."

"How often do babies sleep? And how often do they need to eat? I also heard you can tell each cry apart. How is that possible?" I looked through some baby shoes.

She pulled the pair from my hands. "You should wait to find out the sex before you buy a bunch of shoes." She put a hand on my shoulder. "Listen—"

"—Ayden—"

"—I think your heart is in the right place, but you need guidance." Her smile looked oddly familiar. "You need so much guidance and I know your wife is not going to want to put up with a lot of it. Why don't I help?"

I should have been asking my own mother, but I had no way to break the news. They didn't know Angel was pregnant. "You'd offer to help me build a nursery?"

"Well, it's the least I could do." Her smile faltered, but she made sure to fix it. Something made her sad, but I couldn't be sure what it was. "Where do you live?"

I scratched my neck. "That's the thing..."

"You have a house, right?"

"Sort of?" I laughed nervously. "I mean, it's a cabin. An abandoned cabin that we found. We don't have any money."

She stepped back. "You're having a child where you have no money? Could you not afford condoms either?"

"We didn't think we needed condoms."

She gasped. "Everyone needs condoms." She shook her head and grabbed my hands. "Listen, I have plenty of money and no children to spend it on. My husband certainly wouldn't mind if I helped you and your wife out. Let me help."

The idea of having a middle-aged woman help me wasn't too wonderful but I had no choice. She knew more about this that I did, and I needed a woman's touch to make this nursery just right

"Okay, but we can't tell my wife. Angel would be pretty angry with me if she knew I asked someone to spend money on us." She'd been angry a lot lately, which had been understandable. But part of me wondered...

Her comforting smile appeared again as she patted my hands. "Of course. It will be our little secret."

We spent a few more hours picking out some neutral baby things to get the nursery up and running. She drove us up to the cabin, and I sank in my seat when she saw the sight. "Oh dear." She got out of her car. "This is your cabin? This will certainly not do." She shook her head. "Let me find you a real home."

I got out of the car as well. "No, please. Mrs..."

She cleared her throat. "Please, call me Diana."

"Diana, this means something to me and my wife. We love the location, too. It just needs some work."

"All right, show me what we're working with." She gestured to the front door. I took Diana inside and she almost fainted. "This is not some work, Ayden. This cabin needs much more. It's falling apart! You cannot raise a child in this environment."

"I know. Please, don't take it from us. I found this cabin and it's the one thing that shows my wife I can provide. I want to fix it up."

She placed her hands on her hips, giving me the side eye. "Fine, I will help you. They say that the most expensive part of renovating is the labor, and if we do it ourselves and just buy supplies, we might be able to save this place."

I grinned. "Thank you, Diana. And you can be our baby's grandmother as a thank you."

She laughed. "Oh, I was already going to be if I'm paying for everything. But I'm glad you joined me on that page." She patted my back, scanning the living room. The structure was stable, but the wall needed to be fixed. "Where do we begin?"

As I stared at the woman, she reminded me a lot of Angel due to her kindness. My thoughts began to run wild, but the one that caught me off guard the most was about Angel's soul. I feared she was missing a piece of herself—broken and bruised like a trauma patient—and she had *no* idea.

The walk through the woods was long and eerie. I knew what was in store for me, but I chose this option. I came upon the door that led to Hell—invisible to the human eye.

I had an angel's blade with me to keep myself safe the whole way down. They were sure to try tricks, but I was not falling for them this time.

"What is it that you seek, Eliana?" an angel asked. Of course, this angel's wings were *black*.

"I am here to speak with Liam. That is all." I was truthful, being from Heaven and all. However, no truce could stop the creatures down here from aiming to hurt me. They knew I wasn't lying but that wasn't the problem. They were the bad guys, and they would try anything whether they believed me or not. It was in their nature to bring harm.

The fallen angel let me through the gate and as soon as he moved behind me, I stabbed him with the angel's blade. He dropped to the ground, all that was left of him leaving his eyes. Motionless. I needed him to let me inside, but I didn't trust him to stay alive.

The stone beneath my feet was scalding and the heat surrounded my entire soul. As hot as it was, it was the least of my concerns.

I came upon the archway that led to the cells where each soul was tortured. I had been tortured down here but angels were tortured in separate areas from actual souls that had been condemned to Hell.

Each door had the letters of the alphabet on them. When I found the door with L, I knew I was close.

Walking inside, I glanced at each cell as I passed by and watched the souls beg for mercy. I approached the cell of a soul that looked all too familiar. “Liam.” I stood on the outside of the bars, peering in at the man who’d ruined so much.

To say it was satisfying was an understatement, watching him sit in the corner and apologize a million times. It amazed me that so many people believed in Lucifer and Hell, yet they sided with him anyway. Did they think Lucifer was going to make them second-in-command? No. That wasn’t how he worked. They were his bitch every single time.

“Elli…” he whispered.

“Don’t call me that.” I showed no emotion. I wouldn’t let him have this. “I’m here to talk to you about something.”

Liam didn’t move a muscle. He was probably worn from all the torture on his soul.

“You remember this, no?” I smoothed my hands over my stomach, defining the bump under my dress.

His cough was dry. “Yes.”

“Do you remember a Lucía Pérez?” I watched his eyebrows shoot up. “So you do. You must know she’s pregnant.”

“What about it?”

“She’s having your child. I’m sure Lucifer told you that our babies are just souls of the living. You knew. You intended to get her pregnant so we would lose our baby to you. You just don’t know when to quit." I narrowed my eyes on him.

"I suppose my cries for help are useless if I've pissed off Eliana Wilson." He sighed.

I scoffed. "It's Dyer now. Pity yourself all you want. It's your fault you're here." I pointed to him.

Liam didn't respond to that.

"What was the purpose of destroying our lives? I want to know why. Selene loved you so much. We trusted you." I shook my head.

He lowered his head. "What do you want to hear?"

"The truth. I want to hear the truth. I know there's more to it than losing your mom."

"I did love Selene. It's the truth. I loved her so much. When the time came...something switched. We were at a party one night, where everyone else was. You weren't there. You hated parties. I saw her. She got drunk and she kissed another man. She was supposed to be my girlfriend. How could I trust her if she would do that to me?" He looked at me, and something I'd never seen before flashed. Genuine pain.

I clenched my jaw. "You killed her because she cheated on you during a night of drunkenness."

He nodded. "Even after that night, that stupid boy would follow her and ask her for more. She would tell him to keep his mouth shut. But I knew. I already knew and the damage was done."

"You're disgusting. I don't condone what she did, but I don't condone murder just as much. You killed her, Liam. You killed her instead of breaking up with her or keying her car. You *killed* her. You killed me. You killed Ayden. You have been actively fighting against us since." I gripped the bars, ignoring the sizzling sound of my soul against the metal.

He leaned back. "God killed the one person I needed in my life, and the other person I had learned to love cheated on me. Yet she got to have the perfect home. It wasn't quite fair, Eliana. It wasn't fair that Selene got to live this beautiful life while my mom died from cancer. She didn't do anything wrong." Standing from the concrete, he came closer, meeting my eyes. "My mom was innocent. I was innocent. Yet, we both got fucked over. Selene got away with her sins. I had to take matters into my own hands because God wasn't doing anything about it."

I loosened my grip just a bit. "You killed my best friend because you felt life was unfair."

"No, I killed her because God was unfair. He took my mom, making me capable of murder. He gave me a girlfriend who would then go to kiss another man. I gave Him the middle finger right back." He cleared his throat. "I didn't mean to kill you, but you were beginning to figure out the truth. You got that article about the suspect, and I knew you were going to figure it out. Once I killed Selene, I had no reason to stop. It was easy to kill you. I killed Ayden because you were going to turn me in. I couldn't allow God to punish me when he made me this way. So, I kept killing and things escalated. It was always about revenge on God, Eliana. You were just the pawns in the way." He shook his head.

"You didn't want punishment?" My voice got louder. "Revenge? What about our lives? You destroyed our lives, Liam! You murdered us and took away our hopes and dreams. You are still doing just that! You don't get to say shit about your life being destroyed. You deserve to rot here," I spat at him.

"Don't pretend you're better than me. You're not. You've murdered. You've done terrible things. I've watched you." He leaned forward. "I know things you wouldn't think I would know."

I swallowed, shaking my head. "Don't turn this on me. I didn't kill innocent people. I killed you."

"And Sam." His eyes grew darker.

The memories were quick, like a passing storm. I vowed to forget that Sam ever came into my life.

He continued, "They're not innocent. They've sinned. We all have. None of us are innocent. Babies are, though. You want to take away my innocent child's soul because he's got half my DNA." Liam shrugged. "How does that make you better than me?"

"I want to take away the pleasure of you getting your way. I want to have a chance to raise my own child." I wrapped my arms around my stomach. "You took that away when I was alive and now, you're trying to do it again."

He leaned against the wall, slowing his head to fall back. "Humanity is a shitstorm."

"Tell me something I don't know."

"That's why I released Hell. I had to. It seemed like the perfect way to make humans pay for being the worst creatures to live on this planet. They cheat. They steal and *run* red lights. They defend bad people. Humanity is a terrible group. I wanted to make them suffer for every bad thing they've done. It seemed so perfect. You took away the chance to make them change." He folded his arms across his chest. "Revenge on God was the ultimate goal, but He was too scared to punish His own creation. I killed two birds with one stone."

I glanced at the hallway. "No. You can't change them by unleashing demons and shadows. You can't change people that way because all it leads to is a lot of murder and destruction. You must approach it differently. That is what guardian angels are for. We protect and change humans. We are here to spread good. Do not take on our position and undermine our work."

"What good does it do?" He laughed without a single drop of humor in him.

"What good? I've changed so many people. I changed Ayden. Do you not understand how many lives we have saved and how many souls end up in Heaven?" I shook my head.

"Justin? He died. You didn't save him."

"He had cancer. I couldn't compete with his fatal disaster. I can't be God and save everyone. I'm still just a guardian angel. I can only do so much." I rolled my eyes.

Liam locked his fingers together, laying his hands in front of his crotch. "Letting Hell loose would've changed more people than ever. If people see the truth, they will be more likely to believe. I was showing them that it was real. *I'm* real."

I tilted my head. "Do you not think God would have done that if that was His plan? He doesn't want to show everyone all at once, because then that negates the whole purpose of having faith. Faith is important. It shows that we can put our trust in what we can't see. Sure, we all could easily go to Heaven if we just saw the truth for our own eyes to believe. But that's not what our journeys are meant to be. Our walks are different, and we all have to figure it out somehow. Just as we trust in God, He puts trust in us choosing to walk by faith and not by sight."

"He didn't trust Ayden. He sent you to change him because Ayden needed sight to trust in a higher power and afterlife." He shrugged once again.

"Yeah, well, I trust in His plan. I would never trust yours. You killed Selene and Ayden. Don't assume for even a second I'll ever be on your side." I dropped my hands at my side, subtly feeling the recording device taped to my leg.

"Is this why you're here? You're here to tell me how much you hate me?" He cocked his head. "It's pathetic, don't you think?"

"I want to see you pay for what you've done to us. I know it was your plan to get Lucía pregnant. It just amazes me that you would push to hurt me more than hurting Selene. Now you're fighting to take my baby away." I began to pace.

Liam scooted close to the metal, peering right at me between two bars. "You did kill a friend of mine. I say you're not as innocent as you play yourself to be. You're guilty. You're not the quiet nerd. You're a killer."

"Did you see the part where it was defense, or do you choose to see what you want to?" I turned to face him, waiting for his answer.

"What's the difference between you and me? Maybe I killed Selene out of defense." He shrugged for the third time.

I choked on a laugh. "She hurt you emotionally, not physically. You went out of your way to kill her. Sam was an accident. I only wanted to get him away from me." I crossed my arms. "Is it true? You planned this whole thing? You got Lucía pregnant on purpose to take away our child."

"And what if I did?"

"The joke is on you, Liam. You being the father of our baby's body makes it much easier to fight against you." I backed away from the cell. "Sounds like it's time for them to torture you again."

His demeanor switched. "No, Eliana. No, please. I'm so sorry, take me back with you. Please. Have mercy. Please, don't let them do this. I'd take it back if I could. I'm sorry I was taking your baby from you."

"You're not sorry. You're just sorry you're the one left to deal with the consequences." I walked out of the hallway of cells, leaving him behind as he screamed for me to help him.

I stopped the recorder as I left the gates, heading back to the cabin. I had what I needed.

I walked into the living room, instantly craving whatever Ayden was baking. "What is that smell?" I moved into the kitchen, seeing chocolate chip cookies sitting on the counter.

"I made something to help you when you got back from your trip. How was it?"

I snatched a cookie, taking a bite. "I was right. Liam planned everything."

Castaway

Going down to Hell had become a regular thing. I'd go down just to check each hall of souls and see who was locked up for eternity. Maybe I had been sick, or maybe I had my own problems to sort out. Either way, something inside me had been begging to see who else might have been down there.

I made it to the B hall today. The A hall took me a lifetime to walk through with all the A names that existed.

I passed by a cell and stopped. This soul seemed all too familiar, but she didn't recognize me. Of course. I had no wings and now I wore red instead of white.

"Wait, I remember you," I said as I searched my brain. It hit me all at once. Booze. Loud music. Sweat. Half-naked women. *Halloween.*

"What, you're here to laugh at me?" She pulled her knees to her chest.

I frowned. "That's not right. I thought I had gotten through to someone. I remember you agreed with me. You wanted to change for the better. Why didn't you change for the better?"

She wanted to lash out, but her anger quickly dissipated when she knew the effort it took. “Do you take pleasure in watching us suffer?”

“Pleasure? You think this is fun for me?” I glanced down the hall, avoiding the other souls. I approached the bars and pulled my dress off. It fell to the ground while I covered my breasts with one arm, and my vagina with the other hand. Turning my back towards her, I waited for the gasp but there never was one. The one scar Matthew could never erase was the indent from my wings. They had been permanent and removing them was just as irreparable. “None of this is entertaining. But somehow, someway... This is a form of therapy for me. Facing my trauma is therapeutic. It’s not about pleasure, but about trying to do what’s best for my baby.”

“I tried.” She released a sigh. “I did try to change. I thought I had.” As I turned around to face her, I saw the failed attempt of crying. She had no tears to shed anymore. “I was doing so well, and then that drunk driver came out of nowhere and I woke up here. I don’t understand.”

While pulling my sleeves up, I furrowed my brows. “You did change? You didn’t drink or sleep with random men?”

“I got sober. I was going to therapy and classes. I was doing everything I could turn it around. I hadn’t slipped up and then...a drunk driver hit me. How ironic is that? A drunk driver kills me because I stopped drinking. It’s not fair.”

I stepped forward. “What’s your name?”

“Becky. Becky Maslow.”

If she had been telling the truth, then I had to get to the bottom of this. I’d have to talk to Matthew or God Himself and see why she was in Hell. It didn’t seem right if she was truly doing better. Ayden had made it, so why didn’t she?

“I have to go,” I said. “But I’ll come back. I promise.” I hurried out of the hallway and then the portal. I found myself in the elevator that they made for me to get to and from Heaven. I needed answers, and she deserved to hear them, too.

When I made it to Matthew's office, I didn't bother to knock. I had been polite too many times, and now I had no wings and a baby to fight for. Did I have any reason to spread courtesy? Not for the angels who made no effort to help me in my times of need.

"Eliana, it's always a pleasure to see you." He looked up from his desk with his eyebrows knitted together. "Is there something I can help you with?"

"Becky Maslow." I sat down in the chair that faced his desk. "She's someone I helped when I was first assigned to change Ayden."

"What about her?"

"She's in Hell as we speak. And I want to know why."

Matthew leaned back in his chair, tapping his fingertips together. "We can't give out that information."

I needed incentive. Matthew wasn't going to just tell me, nor would he hint at it. Somehow, I would have to make him subtly let the truth slip. "Right, of course. But you do know her? Am I able to see her file?" *So vague.*

Matthew smiled. I couldn't recall a time when he had ever smiled, at least not around me. "Eliana, I can't give you what you want."

Since I had ruined the route of trying to discreetly get it out of him, I'd have to take a different door. "You never could."

His smile dropped in an instant. "Excuse me?"

As I placed my hands on my small baby bump, I shrugged. "You never could give me what I want. But I suppose part of that is because it's not supposed to be about me. That's selfish—am I right? I was assigned to Ayden, even after being told that I would fall in love with my guardee. I was told to put aside all my feelings for him, just to focus on saving his soul. I didn't want to be a guardian angel when I found out Liam was alive, and yet I was tasked to save the world. I lost my wings because of it. Now, I'm pregnant, and that means I must fight the Heavenly Court just to keep him or her. It was always about putting everyone else first, right? So, if you truly believe that's the person I am, you'll let me see her file. After all, this is about putting her soul first. I'm doing this for Becky. It's not for my own benefit."

"You are questioning the decisions of Heaven. If she's in Hell, she's there for a reason. It is not your job to be the judge."

"Do you truly believe that, or is that just what you say so you don't have to look like the bad guy? Isn't it our job to ask questions? Does God not encourage curiosity?"

Matthew sat forward. "Curiosity, yes. Questioning his judgment, no."

"I want to speak to Him myself."

Matthew gestured to the door. "Feel free."

I exited his office with less confidence than I went in with, but I wasn't going to give up. Something felt wrong. I knew within my soul that Becky did not belong there.

Upon entering the Hall, I wanted to run. I wanted to hide. However, I also wanted to scream and cry and ask *why me.* Instead, I stood still.

"What's on your mind?" He asked.

"Everything," I whispered.

"What does everything entail?"

"Becky Maslow."

He nodded. "I know who she is. You met at the Halloween party, and she promised to change her ways. You helped her. In fact, she changed her entire life around. It was a miracle, Eliana. She did better for her daughter."

"Daughter... She didn't mention a daughter."

"She didn't have a daughter at the time, but she was pregnant. Neither of you had any idea but that same night, she found out. And between the positive test and your words, she turned around. She has a daughter who she loves very much."

With a hand over my heart, I looked up into His eyes. "Why did she end up in Hell?"

God frowned. "Becky is not dead, Eliana. She should be alive."

This sent a shiver down my spine. *Alive?* She was supposed to be alive?

"No, God, she isn't alive. I visited Hell, and I know I shouldn't have but I did, and she was locked up in a cell. She was just as confused as I was as to why she had ended up down there. She said she got hit by a drunk driver."

God snapped his fingers and her file appeared in front of Him. He opened it up, studying every detail. "Eliana, I am certain she is alive. There is no mention of a drunk driving accident. She doesn't have a body, nor a grave. No death date. These files are never wrong."

Arguing was no longer an option. Something was going on, and I needed to figure out what it was.

I thanked Him and left the Hall. I could have gone to Becky and asked her more questions, but that wasn't going to do me any good. She was as confused as I was. God didn't have answers, which meant Matthew certainly wouldn't be keeping secrets. Someone knew, though, and I needed to figure out who they were.

I could have gone home, but that was too easy. It was painless to give up and let Ayden talk about hope. It wasn't in my name to take the simple journey.

I found myself at the library, reading and searching all books about Hell and souls. They mentioned the most obvious answers, souls and death—and how the soul was eternal. It needed a place to go after the heart stopped beating.

An idea occurred to me, and I rushed back to Hell until I came across Becky.

Immediately upon seeing me, she hurried to the bars. "What did you find?"

"Something isn't right, and I don't think you're the only victim. God said you're not dead, which means I need to find your body. Where did the accident happen?"

Hope drained from her face as she let go of the bars. "I remember I had been on a windy road by the mountains. I can't remember the name anymore, but it was there. I had been driving to..."

"I know you have a daughter."

Her eyes went wide, and she shushed me. "Don't let anyone hear that. She has to stay safe." She darted her eyes between other cells. "I don't trust anyone down here."

"Everyone else is locked up, too, and a lot of these people might be like you." I glanced at the cell across from Becky. "I'll get to the bottom of this."

Before she could protest, I left. It didn't take me long to find a windy road by the mountains, since they had been so close to the city. Ayden and I found a cabin in Salt Lake City, and that's where we would stay. It had been where we met, and where everything happened. It didn't make sense to drift so far out.

Unfortunately, it took me longer to find the source of the accident. Without any wings, I had to walk along the road like a hitchhiker. It wasn't my finest hour.

I came across skid marks, following them down into the trees where I spotted a car. I ran over and found a man who had been long gone. Blood covered his head but had dried up long ago. His skin had already sunk in, telling me he was well into decomposition.

I kept searching for another car, and another body. I found the car just a mile down, but I didn't find the body. Becky's body was missing, and I had a sneaking suspicion that she wasn't the only one.

Why had her body been kidnapped? It was obvious that she hadn't gone through the windshield, which was still intact. She could have walked away, but that didn't make sense. She left her phone behind, and if she had a daughter, she never would have abandoned it.

Who was kidnapping vessels, and why? Why did they take Becky's, and why hadn't they taken the drunk driver's?

"I know, I should tell Ayden but if I tell Ayden, it no longer stays just my mission. I miss leading everything. I miss the thrill of solving a murder mystery." As wrong as that sounded, I couldn't deny it. The psychology behind it all had me intrigued. Why would people do what they did? What was their motive? What triggered them?

"Okay, I promise I will tell him," I told our baby. "But not now. Not quite yet."

Reform

I almost tripped over my feet. "Ayden, I swear I will cut your balls off if you don't tell me where we're going right now," I demanded. My sight had been taken from me when he had tied a blindfold around my eyes. I hated this. Ayden knew full well I was not into blindfolds for kinky sex. The idea of having my senses removed just put me on edge, and far more than I was willing to handle.

"Okay, okay." Ayden stopped us, pulling my blindfold off. My hair stuck out everywhere as I scanned around us. "How do you like it?"

"What is all this?" I dropped my arms at my side, in awe at what I was seeing. This was the same place we had our first date as angels. This was where he asked me to become his Mrs. Dyer.

"I know things have been rough and you deserve the world. I want you to relive the best moment." He sat down, helping me sit next to him. "I just want to show you that I made a commitment to be your husband for eternity and I don't regret a single second."

I fixed my hair and glanced at our intertwined fingers. "You mean that? Even if I'm moody and fat?"

He chuckled and put his hands on my stomach. "You have every right to be moody. Although I would appreciate a little more love from my wife," he joked. "But don't think that. You're not fat. You're doing us a favor and carrying our mini-Ayden. Or mini-Eliana. You're carrying our angel, and let's just agree on that."

"Okay." A small smile formed. "Of course." I looked at the basket and my eyes grew wide. "You brought food?" I opened it up and peeked inside, pulling out a cupcake. My mouth would have watered had I been alive. I couldn't believe my eyes. "You're the best husband ever." I bit into it, frosting rubbing off it and onto my upper lip and nose. I continued to devour the treat, feeding into my craving for sweets. I moaned at how perfect this tasted. Only a baker could be this good at adding flavor to a simple cupcake.

"Bloody hell, Angel. You're gonna get fat if you eat like that." He shook his head with a smirk on his face.

I choked on the fluff of the cupcake, turning to face the man I married. "You're so romantic."

"I got you to marry me, so I do agree on that." He leaned back and took a bite of his. "I had a question."

"Shoot."

"Are unicorns real?"

I choked. "Well, of course. What makes you ask?"

He leaned back. "I saw a unicorn one day, in Heaven. I didn't think they were real."

"Unicorns weren't just made up. Most people miss them, but they are in the Bible. They were too busy goofing off to get onto the ark with Noah. Unicorns went extinct and people began to assume they were made up, because a horse with a horn? That's absurd. But it's not crazy when you really think about it." I flashed him a small smile. "God loves unicorns, too."

With a chuckle, he rubbed his thumb across my bottom lip. "You have the best answers."

I peered out at the horizon, watching the sunset. The array of colors ranged from orange to red and it was by far the most stunning sight I'd ever seen. We sat at the top of a grassy cliff, overlooking the ocean.

I laid my head on Ayden's lap, feeling the cool breeze brush against my back. My hair tickled my soul and a shiver drifted down my spine. Ayden pulled the blanket over, covering me.

The air smelled of a fresh meadow where thousands of flowers would blossom. The appearance of summer with the scent of spring. How lovely. Utterly perfect, really, with all its luscious green wonder and the shorter nights. Crickets chirped while stars twinkled.

I could still taste the cupcake I had finished a few minutes ago, and it was fitting to eat such a delectable thing on such a sugary evening. Cupcakes were the right kind of baked goods to have on a reinstalment of our first date.

The waves below us rolled against the sand, gently moving back to the ocean. The birds were quiet during this time and the wind whistled a soft tune for us. Between the waves hitting the shore and the serenity lingering in the air, I forgot about all the problems worrying me as of lately. This was the beauty of creation.

Ayden's fingers gently moved through the strands of my hair. The gesture was soothing to my soul, something I desperately needed. These months had not been kind to me or our child. I was on the journey to recovery, and it was long, but I was walking it. If we would win this case and raise our child, I had to be there for our baby and that meant I had to heal. I had to heal for Ayden and our little angel, but most important of all, I had to do it all for myself. It was just easier said than done.

He caressed my cheek, and I was ready to take a nap forever. All I needed was the green light.

With my eyes closed, I pictured our future, one that was filled with joy and hope.

Our baby in our arms, smiling at us as we smiled back. He made little noises and reached up, wrapping his little fingers around mine and Ayden was careful as he stroked his thin hair. We were the happiest little angel family in the world.

I had always pictured having more than one child because being an only child was the death of me. But if our baby was the only child, that was more than enough. In this state, I was grateful that I had the opportunity to get pregnant after death.

I would be a hundred times more thankful if we won our case and they let us keep him. I needed that more than anything else. I just desired to be able to raise *our* child.

"What's on your mind?" Ayden whispered.

"What shall we name our child if we keep him?" I turned to look up at him, mesmerized by his smile. Everything about him was golden—radiating the color of his heart. His green eyes shined bold and full of so much color. It fit his personality so well. His smile could light up a room and make my day. I'd do anything to see it. His hair had been just the right length, enough for me to run my hands through it. His small beard topped it off, making him look more masculine. I'd never change a single thing about him.

I knew deep in my soul, nobody else was better made for me.

"I'm not sure. What do you have in mind?" He continued to stroke my cheek.

"I was wondering if Skylar would be cute. She comes from the sky after all. For a boy, maybe Connor, since you conned me into loving you." I laughed.

He shook his head. "I did no such thing. You loved me all on your own. I was with Sunny, in my defense." He put his hands up.

With my smile fading, I rested my hands on my stomach. "When did you fall for me? I need to hear it. It had to be before I confessed."

Ayden moved his gaze towards the sunset. "It was. I can't quite pinpoint the moment it happened, but I remember when I realized it. I knew when you confessed, I felt the same way. Knowing how bad I was, I couldn't begin to taint your good soul with my rotten one. I had to reject you. It was by far the worst decision. When I saw you run away crying, it stung. I did that to you. They captured and tortured you because I had done it first. It was the hardest thing I've ever had to live with."

"Hey, don't think that way. It's behind us. We aren't meant to dwell on the past. You've been forgiven and we got married. It didn't stop me from loving you. Nothing can take away the love I have for you. I would do anything for you, Ayden Dyer. I would go through hell again if it meant I was guaranteed to see your happiness forever." I put my hand against his cheek.

He pressed his hand on top of mine, leaning down to kiss my nose. He began to lick the tip. "You still had frosting on you." He chuckled and licked my upper lip before his expression turned serious. His lips pressed to mine.

It had been too long since we kissed like this. Not ordinary, no. It was something special and we shared it together. Our emotions had been exposed to the highest extent.

He pulled away, laughing to himself. "If we kiss again, I do not want to be hunched over like this."

I sat up, facing him. "Problem solved." I wrapped my arm around his neck, bringing him closer and breathing him again.

I jolted as the ground beneath me seemed to move. I screamed out as the cliff broke away and I fell. With panic setting in, I had no time to remember that I was already dead.

Despite my stupidity, Ayden flew down, grabbing me and landing us back on the cliff, away from the broken edge. His eyes darted to what looked to be a demon at the bottom of the cliff, using something to split it apart. "That monster is going to Hell." Ayden gritted his teeth as he threw a rock at the demon. It wouldn't do any good.

The demon had no more than one goal in mind. Although part of me question why a demon could stand beneath us, outside of Hell. We'd sent them all back. And why exactly was this demon after us? Liam was dead. Lucifer had no need for us now. That was a mystery for another day.

"Ayden, please. Forget the stupid thing." I grabbed onto his arm, pushing him away from the edge. "Let's just finish our date. This is the happiest I've been in a long time."

He pushed my hair behind my ear and nodded as he took a deep breath. "I can't just forget. They hurt you. They're still trying to ruin our happiness."

I leaned close, grabbing onto his shirt. "Don't let them," I whispered.

He opened his mouth to speak but I cut him off with my lips. It didn't take long for him to respond and lose thought of the creature. He was deep within my trance.

My fingers found the buttons on his black shirt, undoing them and exposing his chest. I pushed the shirt off his shoulders and went for his pants.

He grasped my hands, stopping me. "Angel, do you want to do this?"

"I know what I want. Don't take that from me. I want *you*, Ayden. Do you want the same?" I asked.

He chuckled. "Do I want myself? No."

"Damnit, don't ruin the mood." I groaned in frustration.

He cupped my face. "I'm being serious. I need to make sure you're okay to do this."

While his hands held my face, I unzipped his pants and removed them along with his briefs, turning him naked. "You're my husband.

I am positive that I'm okay to do this with the one man I love. You have stood by me and supported me. I want to give you something in return, something that makes us both happy."

He grabbed my dress, pulling it over my head. His lips hovered over mine as he said, "I am always happy to do anything that involves you."

"Then lie down." I pointed to the ground.

His eyebrows shot up as he cleared his throat. "Bloody hell, you are so hot right now."

"Just do what I say. Do you want to have sex or not?" I crossed my arms, keeping the *girls* covered on purpose.

"Well, when you put it that way..." He quickly lay back on the grass.

I shook my head and looked at the trees as if they had the answers. "Who the hell did I marry?"

He was beginning to grow impatient with the waiting game and I knew it was fun to prolong his suffering. What more could a wife do if not offer sex and be slow to come through?

Giving in, I sat down on top of him. "You started as a broken man with so many issues. I did not fix those but with my help, you were able to heal yourself. We've been through Heaven and Hell together and I wouldn't do it differently if I could. Although, I would probably change the fact that I went to Hell twice. Or three times. Okay, so I would change most of it. Is that bad?"

"Why are you giving me a speech? Are we having sex or not?" His hands rested behind his head.

"Mind your manners, or I will lose my appetite for you and your friend." I shook my head. "Sometimes we must deal with the rough patches, but we do it together. I am completely in love with you." I leaned down, planting a kiss on his lips with my hands splayed on his chest. I placed a few more kisses along his jaw, ending at his neck.

"Tonight, we celebrate one stone turned and a new path paved."

Much like the effect he had on me, I'd turn him into my little follower. Who'd do whatever I asked of him.

My nails dug into his chest. Why did he have to make it so hard to let him go? That was what I wanted to ask. That was it. The question burning in my mind.

Regardless, this time wasn't rough. It was slow. Much more gentle. Like he knew the question and was answering it by saying he was going to give me whatever I wanted.

He always did.

He knew that there had been nobody else out there like him. Nobody else who could love me. Nobody else who could understand my specific needs. He taunted me by making promises.

And after another minute, I let him. I gave up that fight. Maybe from exhaustion. Maybe because the way we moved made my body dance with joy. It could have been a number of things.

But I gave in.

While giving Ayden every piece of me even in my darkest days, I realized a day without him had been much harder to survive than one with. That's why it felt different now. Better, even. And I didn't even care if sex was what made me realize it. I begged for more, allowing him to see the most vulnerable side of me.

I was in love with him, deeply, and that's why I had pushed so hard against his help. I was afraid of hurting him, because I loved him too much.

I'd been terrified of dragging him down with me.

Ayden relinquished all control to me. I'd be the one to stop when we were ready. But I couldn't recall when I did. I just relished the feeling of him, in case something bad ever happened.

I didn't want something bad to ever rip him away from me. Not again.

And I feared it might.
I'd been the death of Ayden Dyer.

Prophecy

I relaxed on the couch, looking everywhere but Marie. "He was perfect. I won't disclose the private details of what we did following the date, but I will say the beginning was romantic."

"It sounds like it was a wonderful and well-needed moment between you." Her smile flourished.

I lay back on the couch, resting my head on the arm. "It was. It felt like I had my husband back and he had me. It was like our first date all over again, without the sex part of course. We also saw a demon. It tried to ruin our date, but he refused to let that happen. That's why I love him so much. He knows how to make me feel better. I know I'm here because he can't be my therapist, but that night was truly spectacular. It meant so much that he did that."

She nodded. "What else can you tell me about your relationship?"

I looked up at the ceiling. "When I was assigned Ayden, I was also informed that he was going to be in a car accident that day. I knew ahead of time because God told me so. He said that I was being sent to change him. Of course, since Ayden could've died that day, it was a wake-up call for the rest of us to help him make Heaven."

Walking across the clouds, I met up with Matthew. "Can we talk about Ayden before I go to meet him?"

Matthew gave me a look and sighed, waving me to follow him. We went to a separate area where no other angel could hear us.

"What is it that you wish to know?"

"What am I dealing with?" I showed him Ayden's file. "Ayden will be in a car crash at approximately 11:34 tomorrow. He comes from England and has two older sisters. Is there anything else I must know about him? He mentioned that Ayden will be my toughest human yet."

He grabbed onto my shoulder and leaned close. "I was not supposed to mention this, but Ayden is your toughest because we know something you don't. We know that you're going to fall in love with him."

I couldn't contain the laugh—loud and obnoxious it was. "Love? You believe I will fall for a human?"

He didn't even bother to amuse me as he replied, "We know for a fact. God told me you will fall in love with Ayden Dyer."

My smile faded, worry beginning to settle in. What did this mean for me? God was never wrong. He was God. *"But He still assigned him to me. If it's forbidden, why is He giving me Ayden Dyer?"*

"I don't know why God does what He does but I know this is your task at hand. Don't fail us, Eliana," he said.

I swallowed, dropping my gaze to the puffy cloud beneath my toes. I was going to fall in love with this man and everyone knew before I had even met him. I had to stop this. I had to make sure I never fell for Ayden. I had to lie to him and keep my identity secret. I couldn't let him know who I was a lifetime ago.

It had never been an issue in the past to tell our humans about our previous lives. It helped them connect to us. We still went by our earthly names in Heaven, mine being Eliana Wilson. But no matter how true that was, I had to tell Ayden otherwise. I had to lie *to him and keep myself masked to make sure I never loved him. I was not going to fall for Mr. Dyer.*

Eliana Dyer? That name sounded terrible. I was Eliana Wilson, and no human was going to win me over. I was only here to win them over to the good side.

"I knew from the beginning that I was going to fall in love. I tried hard to stop it. It was not something I could stop. We can't help who we fall in love with, and no amount of hiding could stop the inevitable. Do I regret trying to keep myself from falling in love? I'm not sure. It was bound to happen no matter what I did, and I can confirm that I don't regret it. Ayden is the one person who keeps me sane in a world of insane beings." I met Marie's eyes. "What were we talking about again?"

She gestured to me. "We were talking about your love for Ayden and how he's been helping you on your journey to healing."

I put my hands on my stomach, rubbing it. "Ah, yes. To this day, he has no idea I knew I would fall for him."

"Why would that be?" She tilted her head a bit.

I furrowed my brows, wondering why I never told him. "I guess it's because I never thought to tell him. It wouldn't change anything. We would still be together forever. Whether he knows what I knew before or not, nothing changes."

"Did you ever question if you could truly keep your identity a secret when you first saw him?" She leaned forward.

"I did. When a guardian angel gets the file of their next guardee, we know almost everything about them. We know their address. We know their past. We know why we are sent to them before it happens to them. We don't get pictures of them. We go to their address and wait for them there and that's when we first see them. Their appearance holds no purpose to the file, so we don't take it into account. I knew I would love him, but I never knew if he would love me back. That was the scary part. I had to worry if he was going to return the feelings."

"What went through your head when you first saw Ayden?" she asked.

I smiled. "Where do I begin?"

Standing in his apartment, I took a quick look around to see how messed up this man was. I was supposed to love this man? How could I fall in love with all of this?

I walked to his room and looked through his things a bit before a door opened. I dropped the boxer briefs in my hands and rushed into the closet, peeking out of the sliding door.

The footsteps grew closer before he entered the room and looked through his clothes.

This was the man I was supposed to fall in love with. Ayden Dyer.

He grabbed a new shirt and threw it on. He ran his fingers through his hair to fix it up, then he touched his beard before deciding to keep it for the night. He shoved some condoms into his pocket.

He heard his phone ring before picking it up. "Bloody hell, I told you to stop calling me." He hung up before whoever was on the other end could argue with him. His accent was still thick, and it was obvious that he hadn't been in America for too long.

If one considered two decades not too long.

I followed this man to his next destination: the bar. It was no surprise that he loved his beer.

I stood in the corner, masking my appearance so that I was invisible to the human eye. A small part of me wanted to walk over and run my fingers through his hair. The other part of me wanted to slap some sense into him. I couldn't listen to either side. I had to stay hidden until we were both ready. For what? I wasn't entirely sure.

The leaves of the small trees around me moved in the slightest breeze. "He was a beautiful man. From the moment I saw him, he wasn't an eyesore. I won't tell a lie, Marie. From that first day, there was a tiny part of me that always wanted to see what it would be like to kiss Ayden. I may not have loved him for a while, but that doesn't mean I didn't wonder what it would've been like to be with him. I believed I could change him and that was the Ayden I wanted to be with."

She asked, "What was it that you wanted to change about him?"

"I wanted him to do something he loved and be at peace with his family. I wanted to change the part of Ayden that believed he wasn't a man if he loved to bake. He just had to be a better human being and make some better choices. I needed him to believe in his own self-worth. He thought he didn't deserve Heaven. He was right. Nobody deserves Heaven. That doesn't mean we shouldn't try. We were given the chance to make it here and I wanted him to be with him. It would've been harder to be in love with a soul locked up like Liam was. Don't even get me started on how much harder it would be to marry him and fight for our baby if he was in *Hell* this whole time." I sat up and faced her.

"I guess I'm just thankful that Ayden came around. We get a fighting chance. It would not have worked out this way had he been burning in Hell. When Liam killed him, I was scared that I had lost him forever. I was scared he would go to Hell. Someone pulled me out of the car and held me close and I had no idea it had been Ayden, but I should have. He had made it to Heaven, and I was relieved to be with him once more. He still wears all black, but I love that about him. No matter what, he is Ayden. His personality stayed the same.

"He brings a smile to my face every time he makes a joke. It shows me that nobody can change who he really is. I love that about him. He's strong in keeping his basic traits. He's sarcastic and funny. He's got some perverted comments, but we're married so it's not like it's bad. They're always made towards me and what kind of wife doesn't want to hear her husband want her as much as he wants me? Some women worry about growing old and not being beautiful. With Ayden, I have no doubt that I will always be beautiful to him. We are dead, after all. I will look this young for all of eternity."

With a vibrant smile, she stood. "Thank you for taking the time to talk to me. If you ever need to talk outside of our sessions, I'm always available. Just ask for Marie and I'll be here. You can even press the button by the door, and it'll alert me that someone is calling for my help."

"Thank you." I left the room. I took a deep breath, feeling a bit of the weight lift from my shoulders. The least I could do for myself and the ones I loved was to not let Hell control me. I was going to get better for everyone.

I walked back to our cabin, listening to the sound of silence. I walked to our baby's room to check on Ayden. He wasn't here at the moment, but the room was coming along. It was a neutral color palette consisting of gray, white, and yellow. The yellow was a mix between a mustard yellow and a pale version of the same shade.

There was a chair in the corner, next to the half-built crib where some stuffed animals sat. A simple dresser stood against the wall, and across from that was the box of a changing table yet to be opened.

Tears began to fall from my eyes, and I couldn't help myself from the emotions that flooded me. Ayden did all of this because he loved us, and he had hope. How could I show him my appreciation? He was a better husband than I was a wife.

Today I stood in front of the door labeled *S.* I'd been grateful that I knew Selene wasn't down here. No, she couldn't have been. She was in Heaven.

I stepped inside, chin held high. I had begun asking the souls about their life before to decipher who belonged here and who didn't. I had come to the conclusion that the ones that told the truth died in an ironic way, and they could be trusted.

Becky had been hit by a drunk driver after struggling with alcohol in her previous life. It hadn't struck me as odd at first, but eventually the pieces fall where they may. Every soul that didn't belong here had been killed in the manner that they struggled with in life.

Someone didn't want to see these people change. They didn't want these people to believe they could, and so they had stolen them from earth and locked them up here. They had been jealous in some sick way.

A gasp echoed in a cell, calling my name. "You have to help me!" she yelled.

My heart shattered at the sound of her voice, and I uttered a word I never said in life, "Fuck." As I turned to face the redhead sitting in the cell, my eyes watered from what little they had left.

Sunny Smith.

"Are you here to save me?" She reached her fingers through the bars, touching my hair.

She had once been my charge, and I knew full well she didn't belong here. Yet another victim, but who was the villain? It seemed so obvious. Lucifer, sure, but one of the angels. Lucas, maybe. They all despised me.

"Sunny, how did you die?" I asked in a quiet voice.

Her eyebrows furrowed inward as she recalled the memory. "I was driving across a bridge, and I noticed a man standing on the ledge."

Goosebumps covered every inch of my soul. Someone did not like to see me win.

"You stopped to help him, didn't you?"

"Of course, I couldn't leave him. But he took me with him."

"Sunny..." I grabbed hold of her fingers. Finding her body in a river with a fast current wasn't an option. I knew, though. Deep down, I was well aware that she was just like the rest of the souls.

"I didn't mean to. It all happened so fast."

Fast was an understatement. Whoever did this had to have been going at the speed of light to be able to steal her body before she hit the water.

She let go of my fingers and lowered them until she was touching my stomach. "I didn't know angels could get pregnant."

Glancing at her hand, I nodded just the slightest. "Ayden and I both were surprised."

Something flashed in her eyes, but I couldn't quite grasp it. Was it jealousy?

"How is he?" She pulled her hand back.

Remembering the kisses that sent butterflies to my stomach, I could tell her he was great. We both were. But that was a lie. As hot as my soul got when he touched me, it wasn't enough for a lie. "Ayden is fine. He's been helpful, trying to make me feel better." And certainly he did a great job some days.

"He was always good at that." She smiled a bit, although it never reached her eyes as they fell to the floor.

I couldn't let this feeling linger. It had been nagging at me since I noticed it, and it was now or never. "You really love Ayden."

Sunny's cheeks tinted pink as she scratched her head. "Love? No. I mean, he's your husband. And I was only using him to fill the lack of love from my father."

Her lies were amateur at best. Part of me wanted to slap her, but I knew full well that you couldn't choose who you fell in love with. "I wish I could believe that."

"You're married and having his baby. The last thing you want to hear is that I, your friend, am in love with your husband."

"You're right." Her gaze met mine. "But wasn't it a certain redhead who told me to look after my mental health?" I reached through the bars and fixed a strand of her hair. "I kept my promise, and now I'm in therapy. It's my job to help you again. So, when did you realize you love him?"

She hesitated for a moment, knowing I didn't want to hear this. Maybe I was purposely trying to get myself worked up, but I'd use my anger to fight for her freedom. It would be used for good. "Shortly after I found out you were married. I hadn't tried to think about him, but I found myself wondering what if. What if I had been able to keep him? Maybe I wouldn't be dead." I had no heart to tell her she wasn't dead. "I got a little upset." She showed me a scar on her palm. "I shattered a glass because I wondered why he married you and not me. I quickly realized how wrong I was. You're a better person than I could ever be. He deserves you."

I followed her line of sight, frowning. "He didn't choose me because of my breasts." Sure, it seemed a little coincidental that he broke up with Sunny after I admitted I loved him.

"I didn't say that."

"You were staring." I crossed my arms over my chest. "I don't want these. I had planned to get a breast reduction, but I never got a chance. Now, it doesn't make a difference since I can't feel the back pain."

"You don't like having big boobs?"

"I never did. It's all everyone sees, but they hurt. Or they did. That's not the point." I shook my head. "I came here to promise that I'm going to get you out of here. Even if you do love *my* husband."

Sunny nodded. "Thank you."

Before I said another word, I left. When I walked in the front door of our cabin, I closed it behind me, falling against it. Sunny *loved* Ayden.

"Angel, Love, what's wrong?" Ayden asked as he exited the nursery.

I couldn't tell him. He didn't know I kept going down there. He didn't know about the souls or the bodies, and if I peeped, he would force me to stop for the safety of our child. I couldn't do that for him. Finally, I felt useful. After a long while of contemplating everything I'd done, I had a purpose again.

"Angel?" he asked again.

I pushed myself off the door and grabbed his hand, pulling him to the chair in our living room. I sat him down, keeping my knee between his legs so he wouldn't try to stand back up. "Don't speak."

His expression changed and every part of his soul relaxed. "I can follow that order."

Tangling my fingers in his collar, I smashed my lips against his. Everything about him sent my senses in a spiral. His scent. His passionate touch. His irresistible appearance. His thick English accent. And just the mere taste of *him*.

Ayden groaned, not daring to say anything about it. He returned the kiss, but before he could slip his tongue in my mouth, I found my way to his neck.

A sliver of my conscience tried to guilt me for this. For loving my husband. What did I have to feel remorse for? *No*—I wasn't the least bit ashamed.

He leaned his head back, exposing more of his neck. "I love this side of you."

I pulled my lips off him, looking him in the face. I could have yelled at him. I could have accused him of so many horrible things, but that wasn't the route to take. We both knew this had been part of me all along—and now that I had the freedom to do with him whatever I pleased, I was discovering these hidden parts of myself.

I liked this feeling. I liked being the leader. I *liked* taking control.

When I removed his shirt, I ran my fingers through his messy waves of hair. "Can I let you in on a little secret?" I whispered, nearing his ear. "I do, too." I nibbled on his lobe, earning a moan.

Ayden rubbed his hands on my thighs, pushing my dress up. "Don't stop," he breathed.

Kissing him again, I unzipped his pants. He pulled my dress over my head and paused. Before I could tell him what bothered me, he lifted us both so we could get his pants down. Angels didn't need to wear any underwear, or boxers, or bras. However, Ayden still wore boxer briefs out of habit. We took those off him, too.

A knock echoed, and I gritted my teeth. Who was coming to interrupt at this hour?

"Do you need me to make them go away?" Ayden asked, chest rising and falling quickly.

I grabbed a blanket off the beaten couch and wrapped it around me. "Let me." I answered the door. "What do you want?" It came out harsher than it should have, but I couldn't apologize now. Women had fragile sex drives, and mine was running wild. I had to chase it before I lost it.

"Did I interrupt something?" Selene looked at the blanket.

"Yes."

"Oh, I'm sorry."

I glanced at Ayden in all his glory. When I faced Selene again, I closed the door more. "Come back another time." I shut the door. Guilt gnawed at me, but I ignored it. It felt good to say what I wanted.

Fingers brushed across my shoulder and neck, sending shivers down my spine. "Let's keep going," Ayden whispered in my ear.

I loosened my grip on the blanket, allowing him to pull it from my body. I spun around and kissed him. "You weren't supposed to move."

He wrapped his arms around me, squeezing my butt. "Have you ever known me to follow the rules?"

With one hand in his hair and the other on his back, I deepened our kiss. "I had a special something in mind for you."

He moved one hand up to the small of my back. "And maybe I have something in mind for you." He let go of my butt, lifting my chin so his lips could show my neck some affection.

An inner battle started. One side begged me to let him take full control. She argued to just enjoy the moment, and as badly as I wanted that, the other side didn't. She wanted to take full control. She wanted to run the show.

His lips were soft against my soul. *Too* gentle. Ayden was still afraid to unleash the extent of his desires with me, and it drove me crazy. I wanted him to be rough. I wanted him to show me how desperate he was to be with me.

Instead, I needed to show him how much I ached.

The other side of me won.

"Ayden, sit your ass on the chair." I grabbed his hands with more strength than I anticipated. "Now."

He slowly nodded, backing up and falling into the chair.

I leaned over him, hands on both sides of the chair. "Do you realize how much of a pushover I am? Everyone takes advantage of me. They insult me. I always just take it because that's the kind of person I'm *supposed* to be." I pressed my lips against his, holding his face in place. "I don't want to be the follower, Ayden. I want to be the leader, too. I want to take *charge*."

He swallowed. "You can have as much control as you please."

The corner of my lips tilted upward. "I plan on it." I traced a finger down his chest, slipping onto my knees. "You're afraid to hurt me, and I understand that. But it pisses me off." I forced his knees apart. "Where's the fun in marrying a bad boy if he won't give me what I want?"

Ayden's eyes closed as he gripped the arms of the chair. "I thought you married the baker. Bakers are gentle."

That was everyone's first issue. "I married Ayden Dyer, the man with a dark side. I don't just want the baker. I don't just want the bad boy. I want all of you. Every single inch."

"What are you asking of me, Angel?" He groaned from sexual frustration.

I glanced up at him, slipping my fingers up his thighs. "I'm asking you to bring out my dark side."

WITTY

Ayden passed me a shirt, but before I could put it on, he placed kisses on my shoulder. His eyes locked with mine, and he lifted his head. "Sorry, I forgot." He laid a hand on my thigh, squeezing. "You want less gentle and more..." When I looked at his hand, I put mine on top of his, attempting to grab him. "Wild."

"Unrestrained."

He smirked, leaning closer. "Yes, unrestrained. And maybe the best way to attempt that is restraint." His fingers traced my inner thigh. I could let him try it out, but I knew I wouldn't like that much. It would feel like torture.

"You're doing it again," I whispered.

Ayden's eyebrow shot up and he grabbed my chin, rubbing his thumb across my lip. "Doing what, exactly?" Just as I brought my knees together, he pulled them apart.

I pulled the shirt over my head. "You're being too gentle. It's like you're afraid to be in complete control." I stood. "I get that I'm supposed to be this good girl, and I'm supposed to like it that way. But sometimes I don't." Shaking my head, I released a sigh. "I'm tired of always being the good girl. Everyone looks at me and thinks I'm boring. That I follow the rules. That my life has no meaning, and I can just be walked on."

He grabbed hold of my hips, pulling me back onto his lap. He pressed his lips against my neck as I leaned my back against his chest. It was exhausting at times, trying to be nice to everyone. I was always pleasing them. I gave them what they wanted. What about what *I* wanted?

He pushed my hair to one side, pulling the shirt off me. "You are far from boring. Bad boys don't fall for boring girls." He put his hand on top of mine, intertwining our fingers. "You asked me an important question, Angel." He placed a kiss along my shoulder. "You asked me to bring out your dark side." He rested our hands on top of my thigh. "I need you to answer me something."

"Anything."

Resting his chin on my shoulder, he wiggled our fingers a bit. "Have you ever touched yourself?"

I choked. That wasn't what I expected him to ask me, so what could I even say? "I know you have, Ayden, but... I haven't. Not everyone has." I swallowed. "It's kind of...taboo."

"Why?"

"Because... I can't quite explain it well but when you're single like I was, you're supposed to be this good girl. You're expected to never put yourself first, and that includes masturbating. It sounds stupid, but that's the truth."

"You're right. It is bloody stupid." He chuckled, pulling our fingers apart. Ayden guided my hand between my legs. "I might not always be around, and you should know how to handle that by yourself."

I didn't have the heart to tell him that me vs. him controlling my hand were two different feelings. There was just a different kind of pleasure that ignited within me when he touched me. I could never replicate that.

Before I could close my eyes and relax in his embrace as he took the lead, Ayden dropped my hand. I thought maybe he was going to tell me to try it on my own, but he lifted me off his lap and set me on the bed beside him.

"Ayden, what's wrong?" I grabbed the blanket, pulling it around my chest.

Something swirled around in his eyes. Whatever had been in there before had vanished. Now, pure hatred was left behind.

"He fucking ruined it, Angel." He stood, grabbing his briefs off the floor. He pulled them on. "That..." He closed his eyes and exhaled. "That position was the same position I was in as a child."

I cupped my fingers around my ear, pushing hair behind it. "I'm sorry. I didn't know."

He grabbed a pillow, *ripping* it apart. "That fucking dickhead has tainted what's up here." He repeatedly hit his finger against his temple. "That is how he used to touch me. And I will never put that horrid memory in your head, too."

I stood, pulling a shirt over my head, then putting on some of his extra briefs. I didn't have underwear or pants of my own. "Listen to me." I grabbed his face, making him look at me. "You don't have to worry about me. Worry about yourself. If you're not comfortable with certain things, I won't force you to relive the nightmares."

He gulped, looking away from me. "I *am* afraid."

"What?"

"I'm afraid to hurt you, the same way he hurt me. He did it in ways that it felt like it was my fault. In a sick way, he made it look like consent. That's absurd considering I was just a little boy. But to me, that's how it felt. I was the one who asked my parents to go over to his house. I was the one who made that choice."

I reached down, wrapping my fingers around his. I brought his hands up to my lips, kissing his knuckles. "No, Ayden. You didn't make any choices. You had no say. You were confused. You were lost. He used you and none of that is your fault."

He rested his forehead against mine as tears slipped from his eyes. "I don't want to do that to you. You are so..."

"Do not say innocent."

"*Pure*. You're so full of love and kindness and you're not a pushover. You are a beautiful person." He slid his hands from mine, cupping my face. "You have not seen what I've seen. I don't want you to see sex the way I do."

A ping bounced off my heart. "That's not going to happen. Not with you." I wiped away his tears. "I promise. When I have sex with you, everything is raw and real. It's loving. There's no way you can destroy that. And I won't let him ruin your view of it, either. He can't take this away from us."

He backed away, pulling his pants up. "In a way, he already has."

Biting my tongue, I kept my mouth shut. I wanted to yell and scream that he was wrong. I wanted to show him that it didn't have to be like this. However, I had no place to do so. I didn't know what it felt like to live with those memories. I had no idea what Ayden was going through, and I never would.

I understood being afraid to an extent, but my fear stemmed from a half-stranger. His came from a trusted family member. They were not the same.

To change the mood that drenched the air, I sat down on the bed, saying, "I should tell you what I found."

This got Ayden to stop in his tracks. "Tell me what?"

"When I went to visit Liam, I decided to keep going back. Not to see Liam, but to see other souls. You won't believe what I found, Ayden, but I found a bunch of souls down there. They don't belong there."

"What do you mean?" He threw a shirt on.

I rubbed my palms against my knees. "Sunny is down there." I was going to keep her love for Ayden a secret. He was married to me. He didn't have any right to know how she felt.

"Sunny? My ex-girlfriend Sunny?"

"The one and only."

He slowly sat beside me. "Why?"

"She said she was trying to stop a man from jumping off a bridge. She's not alone. There are so many souls, and they keep growing. And that's not even the weird part." I turned my head to look at him.

"What is?"

I closed my eyes, taking in a deep breath. "None of the bodies can be found. They're all missing—missing from the scene of the accident like they just walked away. Like someone kidnapped them."

When I opened my eyes, Ayden seemed to be lost in thought. Whatever was on his mind, it had to link to something I hadn't thought about yet.

I said, "I've been gathering all their names and how they died. Or, how they think they died. I talked to God, and not a single one of their files has a death date. According to Heaven, these people are alive. But they're all in Hell. How is that even possible?"

"I might have an idea."

"Which is?"

"Whoever is behind this is angry. They're clearly working from Hell, and they're angry that we won, right? So what better way to hurt us than to steal bodies? They can't be pronounced dead officially without a body to be found." He got off the bed and ran a hand through his hair. "But they can only truly scar the soul, so somehow, they are ripping souls from their physical bodies and stashing the bodies somewhere no one knows."

I furrowed my brows. "Ripping souls... You really think someone is ripping these souls out? Why not just kill them?"

He shook his head as he crossed his arms. "You and I both know killing someone doesn't send them to Hell. Not if they are already set to go to Heaven when they die."

As I stood from the bed, I walked over to the window. "If Sunny and Becky didn't do anything to end up in Hell, then they couldn't be killed. But somehow, someone has learned the art of tearing a soul from its body and preserving the body so God can't officially declare them dead and wonder what's going on." I dug my nails into the wooden sill. "They want to destroy their souls, souls that *we* have saved." As to where these bodies were that even God Himself couldn't find—that was another mystery.

I jumped as a pair of hands grabbed hold of my hips. "We have to save them again, don't we?" he asked.

I spun around, facing Ayden. "I can't leave them down there. That is wrong on so many levels."

"Remember when you asked me to bring out your dark side?"

"This is not the time. I am not going to let something this big happen under my watch. Do you want to help me? Then let's do this together, and we will save them. Maybe this will show Heaven we would be perfect parents."

Ayden threw his arms up, banging his fist against the wall. "You don't get it! They keep doing this! We keep getting stuck with the task of saving the world and I'm sick of it," he yelled. "They are not going to let us keep our baby anymore. This is some game to them. It's meant to keep us distracted but their answer won't change. They know what they're going to choose." He grabbed my wrist, pulling me closer. "Don't let them win this time. You were in Hell, twice, and you lost your wings. What's the most they've done for you as a way of saying sorry? An elevator? Fuck that, Angel. Fuck that!"

"I don't have much of a choice! That is who I am! I help people, and that's never going to change. Do you remember Daniel? He fooled me, and I am still absolutely humiliated by it. You saw him for who he was, but I never did. How could I not see it? This must make up for the wrong I've done."

"Daniel was his own set of evil. You're not to blame for what he did. But to feel obligated to make up for the wrong you've done?" He placed his hand against the wall beside my head. "Then what? You get tortured a third time? How much do you think your soul can take? How much do you think you can handle before you realize you might not even be a whole soul!" His eyes screamed rage, and something inside his head was turning. He knew what I didn't know.

"A whole soul? What are you talking about?" Tears pricked my eyes.

He released a sigh and rested his head against his arm, closing his. "Angel, I don't think you are whole. I think you're missing a piece of your soul."

Where had this awful thought even come from? Was his entire goal to tear me apart from the inside out? I was the one who had told him about broken souls in the first place, and now he was using my words as a weapon against me.

"Why would you say that?" I clenched my jaw, attempting to push against his chest to get him away. "How the hell could you say that about me?"

He didn't budge. "I'd been pondering on it for a while." He held my chin between his thumb and forefinger. "It's not your fault and you couldn't know, but it's worth a thought."

"Screw you," I grabbed his wrist to swat him away. However, with the swipe of a hand, he caught my wrist instead and pinned both above my head.

"There's that sinister side peeking through," he said with a small smirk. "Why don't we hold onto this anger for a little while?" He kissed me before I could respond, and between the fury of those helpless souls and Ayden accusing me of being like them, I allowed him to use it to fuel our agony.

CAREFUL

I ran my thumb across the inside of my wrist, pressing it right in my palm and squeezing my fingers around it.

"Angel?" Ayden knocked on the door frame.

Barely glancing at him, I clenched my jaw, but the tear expressed my emotions better. "How could you say that? Do you really believe I'm missing a piece of my soul?"

He walked into my view, pulling my chin up. "It wasn't to hurt you. I would never hurt you." He studied my eyes before wiping away my tears. "Do you think I love you less? I would never." Grabbing my face, he cupped my cheeks. "Why does this hurt you? Tell me."

Was it worth a conversation? An argument? "You're so certain that this isn't me. You believe that I must be broken because you can't accept that this is who I am. Do you not love me?"

Confusion flooded his face. "What? No. I mean yes. I do love you, but no, I'm accepting who you are." He stepped back. "Listen, do you remember when I asked about souls breaking apart? You asked me if I thought I was an incomplete soul."

"What does that have to do with me?"

"I didn't think I was incomplete. I thought you were."

I wrapped my arms around my stomach. “I’m pregnant, Ayden. We know that now. We don’t need to question my behavior anymore.”

He sat beside me, stealing one of my hands. “You told me that people lose pieces of themselves. Memories. Trauma. And whatever happened... I think something deeper happened. You can feel it, but you can’t remember it.”

I yanked my hand from him, walking away. “No! I remember everything.”

“Your hatred for Liam is beyond anyone else’s. Have you ever wondered about that? I know he’s done awful things, but even Selene and I don’t despise him as much as you do.”

Even Selene and I don’t despise him as much as you do.

With nowhere to go, and nobody to turn to, I walked into the river nearby, screaming into the green abyss. Ayden’s words had scrambled everything I knew. Every thought I originally had—he took it, ripped it apart, added his own pieces, then proceeded to give it back to me.

I feared I may have believed him.

What did that mean? If he was right, I had never been a complete soul, and yet I felt whole.

The scariest part of it all was that I never had any idea if a piece of me was missing, and simply because I had lost a memory. How did someone lose a memory and not notice? It wasn’t possible.

When I came out of the river, everything appeared dry. My hair, dress, and eyes. I had no tears to cry.

As everything else failed, I took a trip to the one person I shouldn’t have wanted to see, but the only person who may have understood.

"Is there something I should know about?" I grabbed the bars, showing Liam that I wasn't afraid of him anymore. I had no reason to be.

He shrugged. "What is there to know? I'm not hiding anything at this point."

I pressed my face between each bar while ignoring the sizzling pain. "Did I...forget anything? About us? About you? Why do I hate you so much?"

Liam laid his head against the wall, too tired to bother arguing. I was beginning to reach the same point. "Isn't it obvious? I killed your best friend and your boyfriend."

"Husband. He's my husband."

"He was your boyfriend when I slit his throat."

"That's not the point! Do you really believe that I could hate you this much?"

A sigh. "I believe anything is possible when you lose the only people you love."

Love. Was that it? Neither Ayden, nor Selene had ever watched me die. None of them had the baggage of losing a loved one. I did.

I looked around at the other cells, making sure nobody was keeping too close of an eye. I pulled a pin from my hair while bending down and picking the lock. Marrying Ayden taught me something useful, and if we were going to free those souls, we needed useful skills.

Liam straightened his posture, eyes fixed on the pin. "What are you doing?"

I made it inside his cell and locked it behind me. I couldn't be too careless. "I'm coming to you because I need the truth." I sat in front of him. "But don't bother to attack me, because everyone knows I'm here and they will find you."

"And kill me?" He chuckled. "Relax, I have no strength to fight.

Not anymore."

With my eyes glued to the floor, I inhaled, then exhaled. "Tell me, Liam, what I'm forgetting between us." Oh, no, that had come out wrong.

"Nothing. I can't answer your questions." He shrugged and lifted his head as an angel came by the cell. "If you want to stick around for my daily dose of torture, I think it might ease some of your worries."

I glanced back at the fallen angel, scowling. "He's all yours." I stood and left the cell, and before the angel could grab me, too, I shoved the blade into his abdomen, watching him drop to the ground. "Looks like your medicine is out of stock today." I shot Liam a look before I left.

I asked Selene what I may have forgotten, but she couldn't give me answers. Nobody could give me any answers, and that all led me back to the big question: was I really missing a piece of myself?

Without anyone to confirm a lost memory, I thought maybe Ayden was wrong.

I told him I wanted him to bring out my dark side, and this was not what I meant. Well, I decided to pay a visit to Esme and Arabella, which wasn't too difficult. I found them both working at Dyer's Bakery. Maybe another woman—or two—could give me some answers.

"Angel, come in." Esme waved me in and pulled out a chair. "How are you feeling?"

The question was directed at my pregnancy, but that wasn't what I was here for. I guess Ayden had finally spilled the big secret. "I'm fine. I actually came to talk to you and...Arabella. About Liam."

Arabella came out of the back, smiling when her eyes landed on me. "Hey!" She sat down at the same table and rested her arms on it. "How are you?"

That question was beginning to get on my nerves. "Not too

great, all right?" I slammed my hand against the table. "Ayden said something that pissed me off, and I need your input."

"Oh no..." Esme's expression turned sour. "Ayden always screws up."

"He suggested that I'm missing a piece of my soul, and if that's true, then I can't remember it or what...and he thinks it has to do with Liam. I talked to Liam, and he said I haven't forgotten anything. I talked to Selene, and she said there's nothing I forgot." I looked between them both. "Is there anything that could make me hate Liam that I forgot about, yet nobody knows I had this memory?"

Arabella tapped her fingers. "Well, it has to be something personal, right? Did you ever have a crush on him? Wait, you wouldn't remember."

I imitated gagging. "I would never. That is repulsive. I remember that I was friends with Liam, and that's only because he was dating Selene."

Esme gave Arabella a look. "She has a point. You despise Liam with a passion, correct?"

"I mean, yeah."

"Only something of equal passion can bring about such emotion of the opposite feelings." She leaned forward. "What is something that only you knew but would have forgotten? Something big enough that would make you hate Liam as much as you do?"

I growled, standing up. "Are you suggesting I was in love with Liam?"

Arabella reached for my hand. "It's not your fault if he made you feel a certain way before he showed his true colors."

"No!" I ripped it from her. "I know my feelings well. I would never be as stupid as Selene to fall in love with that prick." I spun on my heel and stormed out of the bakery.

People went about their business in the city. It was as if the war had never happened. Nobody around me noticed my presence, and maybe it had to do with the fact that I had no wings. They would never know I was an angel.

I did something idiotic. *Reckless.*

I went back to Ayden's old apartment.

The apartment had been cleaned up and emptied since his death. Now it stood vacant. The memories created here began to drift away as if this apartment was losing a piece of itself.

I visited his bedroom, taking in all the voices. It spoke to me. The room told me about how much had changed. Too much had become something else.

It wasn't that I wasn't happy about where we were now, but I wanted to rewind the time and do it over again. I wanted to go back to the days before we ran into Liam on the streets. If I could have seen him before he saw me, we could have avoided him, and none of this would have happened. I'd still be Eliana.

Eliana Bree Wilson was dead. Murdered. Throat slit open on Christmas. She had only lived to be twenty years old. She never had a boyfriend. Never kissed a boy. Never had sex. She was known simply as Selene's roommate.

Eliana Bree Dyer was barely alive. Not breathing. Wings chopped off in Hell. She had no expiration date and no real age anymore. She was married and pregnant, and famous for saving the world.

This was the room where everything changed. What she decided to tell Ayden would be what led her to become a whole new person. I couldn't decide if I liked this new version.

When I told him I was in love with him, my world shattered. I knew it would happen, but I never predicted that I would confess my feelings and have them returned. I missed those days. I longed to go back and hold Ayden close. He used to push me away, and a part of me liked that. He didn't trust me, and he had every right not to.

Most of all, I missed the Ayden I fell in love with. And that made me a horrible wife.

I approached the indentation of his bed, stopping on the side of the rectangle they formed. He first kissed me right here, and it had been wonderful. He caught me so off guard. The spontaneous decisions were part of who he was, and they made me love him more.

I craved more of that kiss, and at the time, Ayden had no idea how I felt. I wanted more than anything to tell him to undress me. To kiss my body. To love me like I had never been loved before.

Every day I asked myself why I loved Ayden. It seemed so simple to me then, but it became far more complex. I loved the raw parts I saw and the man he grew to become. However, it was deeper. *Much* deeper. I loved Ayden because he brought out the parts of me I had always been afraid to face.

Never would I consider going down on a man until I met him. Never would I get married or break rules until it was for him. Never would I have seen behind the locked doors inside my head, catching a glimpse of the things I had always craved. Ayden taught me that I yearned to step outside of the box. He had shown me so many pieces of myself...

As I stood where our passion blossomed, I closed my eyes. Could it be true? Was there a time when I had loved Liam the way I loved my husband now, or was this all a hallucination? Illusion. Delusion. Call it what you may. No matter how asinine their suggestion sounded, every figment of the imagination stemmed from a small dose of reality.

Over the course of a few hours, I used the community in the city to listen for Halloween parties. It wasn't difficult to track one down. It was Halloween night.

So I went to one.

There'd been a time when I used to chase Ayden down at a

Halloween party. I never wanted to be there, but I was, for his sake. And yet, tonight, I came on my own accord.

I came for me.

To have a little fun.

I slipped through the bodies, ignoring the comments I got on my boobs. Every single body in this room was coated in sweat, except mine. It might have been freezing outside, but it was a boiler inside this house.

Alcohol saturated the air. I could just about taste the salt from everyone's skin, but what stood out the most of all were the half-naked bodies surrounding me.

It didn't slip my mind that I was married or pregnant. I wasn't here to have sex. I came for a different experience. When I was alive, I never once considered a party. But one couldn't hurt, could it?

The escape would remind me of what I didn't miss out on after my death. Or maybe I did miss out all along.

I found myself in the kitchen, pouring juice into a red cup. I knew it was spiked with alcohol. And drinking alcohol had never been wrong. It was simply about how much one drank. But I intended to drink it all.

After the first cup, I leaned against the counter with my palms flat. A body pressed against my backside and hands slid down my arms before holding my hands down. "Not really your scene, is it?" he whispered in my ear.

"But it's yours," I glanced back at him.

Ayden grabbed the red cup. "You've never drank alcohol before. Why now?"

"Rhetorical question." I turned around to face him, but he didn't move. "And I've had alcohol. You just never saw me drink it."

"We should go home." He attempted to walk away.

"No."

Ayden halted. "What?"

"No. I don't want to go home. I want to be at this party tonight. I want to forget about everything wrong in my life. Liam. The souls. Our baby." That came out wrong, but I never tried to fix it.

"Angel, we need to go home. These kinds of people aren't fun. I would know."

"Then let me figure that out for myself." I approached him. "Don't you miss this? At all? Is it not comforting?" I brushed my fingers up his arm. "Now we can enjoy it together."

He leaned in closer, wrapping his fingers around my wrist. "I want to go home."

"And I don't. You can go home, or you can stay. But I'm my own person, and I'm staying here." I pulled my wrist back and disappeared into the crowd.

I didn't make any trips back to the punch bowl, but I made a few to the bathroom just to give myself peace and quiet for a second. This brought back many memories. Becky Maslow. The Halloween party of 2020.

Life had been simple then. Pure. Full of hope.

Now I wanted nothing more than to forget about it.

I almost fought back as Ayden spun me around, pressing me against the wall. Whatever I had in mind dissipated the moment his lips hit mine.

Rough. Begging for more. Hunger.

One small movement and he had my wrists pinned to the wall. "Don't move."

I didn't disobey his orders.

"Am I still a rose?" I asked, breathless. I missed the feeling of being human so much. I ached for that.

"What the bloody hell are you talking about?" Ayden began kissing my neck.

Right. He'd been drunk.

"Am I *your* rose?" I asked again.

Dragging his nose up my jaw, he hovered over my lips for a few seconds before kissing me again. I craved every last ounce of him. Whispering, he lifted my legs and wrapped them around his waist. "My beautiful, fragile rose with thorns that *bite*."

With Selene and Ayden behind me, I led them to the portal to Hell. We had weapons in case of anything, but the least we could do was get a few souls out. This wasn't right and it was up to us to stop it.

"Selene, you take hall M. I'll take S. Ayden will take B." I pointed to the halls. "And Ayden, don't forget Becky Maslow. Please." He shot me a look, promising that he wouldn't forget. He went down hall B, and Selene took M as soon as we approached.

When I arrived at S, my chest ached. Everything about it was nerve-wracking. If we failed, everything could go south from here. Our baby could go to Lucía, whoever she was.

My steps were slow and steady, and I made sure to keep my eyes forward. I had one mission. Every now and then, I stopped at a cell to let them go. "You can try to make it out of here now, but the reality is they'll catch you. You have no defense, and your body is still stored somewhere. I say you stick with me."

Most people listened, following me as I released more souls. Some were too eager to leave, and they made a break for it, and it had cost them. As bad as I felt, I had warned them. I couldn't risk the rest of the souls for others who had made their choice.

"Thank you," Sunny whispered as I picked her lock.

I had freed the souls I could, unfortunately not making it to the end of the hall. It was impossible with how many people had lived over thousands of years.

"Eliana Wilson." That voice shook me to my core.

Sam.

"It's Dyer now," I corrected him. I barely glanced in his direction.

"How's Liam?"

"Dead."

"You kill him too?" He chuckled.

I spun on my heel, grabbing hold of the bars while clenching my jaw. "You don't get to make jokes. You deserve to rot here."

He frowned. "Aw, you can't lie and say you didn't like the idea. I mean, here I am..."

A hand landing on my arm. "We should leave."

I sent a glare at Sam, grabbing Sunny's hand. "Yes, let's."

"You always did have the biggest boobs!" he yelled.

Before I could get far, I faced Sam once more yanking Sunny's hand in the process. "You always did have the smallest dick."

Sunny pulled me away before things could get further off track. As soon as we left the hallway, Ayden had been waiting for us with his group of souls. My anxiety faded away as Becky's face appeared among the crowd.

However, I hadn't thought about this moment. When Sunny saw him, she slowly made her way over as if she'd been a lost lover.

She was.

"It's been a while. Last time I saw you, you were saving the world," she said.

"We both saved the world," I mumbled.

Ayden smiled. "I'm like a superhero."

Selene came out of the M hall, looking at both Sunny and Ayden. "Ah, this is always a fun little run-in. But we should get out before they notice." Her eyes darted my way.

I nodded, taking the lead. For Hell, they sure had been empty a lot lately, but with all the souls being taken, I understood they had more out stealing them than they did worrying about guarding them.

"How's Mason been?" Ayden asked.

"Not sure, but I hope he doesn't think I committed suicide."

"He doesn't," I said. "He doesn't even know you're dead." It had come out harsher than I anticipated. "Nobody does. Not even God." I spun to face her, walking backwards. "That is why I set up this mission to save you."

Sunny tilted her head. "What happened to your wings?"

Whipping back around, I worked with Selene and Ayden to get everyone out of Hell.

There were so many of them, and without a body, they weren't safe. Our cabin was far too small. Only one place was a haven for all of them.

Using the elevator, we took groups up a few at a time. The first few groups made it up unnoticed, but after many dings from the elevator doors, Matthew came to check out the constant usage. "Eliana, what is the meaning of this? What are all these souls doing here?"

"You refused to tell me about Becky Maslow, so I took matters into my own hands. Had I not investigated, I wouldn't have discovered that Hell is stealing souls from their bodies. That's why they aren't showing up as dead so they can go undetected on earth and in Heaven. I'm saving them." I gestured to the souls. "And until we find their bodies, they need a safe place to stay."

Matthew eyed the group, but he knew he couldn't just turn them away. "All right, I can keep them in a room for now. But this isn't permanent. We don't know which of these souls is going to end up here or not."

"I'm well aware." I went back down and gathered the rest while Matthew took them all somewhere safe.

I walked back towards the elevator and stepped inside, pushing the button. The doors started to close but a hand stopped them. Sunny followed, standing beside me. "I figured it was my turn to save the world. Or at least save a few souls."

"I would never ask you to do this." My eyes shifted her way.

She smiled. "You didn't. I offered."

Looking back on it now, I saw how silly it was of me to be jealous of Selene being around Ayden. But Sunny? She was his ex. She loved him.

Sure, I trusted Ayden, but could I trust Sunny? I had to make it clear that Ayden and I were together now. She no longer had a chance.

When we touched the ground, the doors opened. Ayden lifted both eyebrows upon seeing Sunny. "What's she doing here?"

Sunny crossed her arms. "You still have an attitude I see. But I'm here to help."

"I do not have an attitude."

"Mhm, and I suppose not asking me yourself was just sparing my feelings?"

"I am not going to deal with this right now." He shook his head, running a hand through his hair.

I closed the gap between Ayden and I, grabbing his wrist. "You do have a bit of an attitude." I tugged on his wrist until he wrapped his arms around my waist, and I put mine around his neck. I pulled him in for a kiss meant to be innocent, but the taste of his lips intoxicated me.

He kissed back but was the first to break away. "I see you like that attitude."

"I don't mean to interrupt, but maybe we should find my body,"

Sunny said. "I would love to get my life back."

He nodded and turned to walk away, but before he could make it far, I grabbed his hand and intertwined our fingers. Maybe it was petty of me to act this way, but I couldn't spend my time trying to justify my actions. I had souls to save.

"Where do we search?" Sunny asked.

"I think there might be one person who we can ask," my husband answered.

We didn't say another word until we approached a familiar door. Sunny kept her distance, afraid of what the outcome would be. Ayden knocked, and we waited.

The door opened and revealed the one person Sunny had been afraid to see. Mason—her brother. "What are you guys doing here?" His eyes landed on Sunny. "Sunny?"

She lifted her hand to wave. "In the flesh. Well, not really. It's a confusing story."

I took a step towards Mason, getting his attention. "Sunny's soul was ripped from her body, and now we need to figure out where that might be. We think you can help us."

"I barely remember you, I'm sorry. What's your name again?" He rubbed his eyes.

Ayden choked on a laugh.

Sunny scratched her head and turned the other way.

I lifted my chin, scowling at him. "Eliana, but everyone calls me Angel. I used to be considered Ayden's therapist, and we both know that's never what I was."

He nodded a little. "Right. I don't know why you're just..."

"Easy to forget?"

"Not ringing a bell," he finished.

Sunny came between us. "She's one of my good friends. Even if she is married to Ayden now." She flashed me a smile.

"Oh, Ayden's wife." Mason let us all inside.

Ayden's wife? That's what I had been reduced to?

"So, what really happened?" Mason asked as he hugged Sunny. "You just disappeared from the face of the earth. They found your car, but you were nowhere, so they assumed..."

"I committed suicide," she said, nodding. "But I didn't, Mason. I wouldn't. I stopped on that bridge because I was trying to save a man from jumping."

I cleared my throat. "And somehow, they stole her soul from her body, taking her body somewhere else. She would have been too confused, assuming she hit the water and died before that happened. She never questioned it." I narrowed my eyes at Mason. "I'm the reason this whole mission is even being started." I was more than Ayden's wife.

"Excuse us, Mason," my husband said. He grabbed my hand and pulled me outside. "Are you okay?"

"What ever do you mean?"

"I mean you're...being rude."

Widening my eyes, I stepped back. "Rude? He called me Ayden's wife! I told him my name and he didn't even bother with that!" I pointed towards the house.

He frowned. "What's so wrong with being my wife?"

I rolled my eyes as I laughed. "You don't get it, do you? It's one thing to be your wife, but another to *only* be referred to as your wife. I'm not here to live in your shadow. All of this?" I circled my finger around everything. "This is all because of me. I introduced everyone to this world. I'd like the credit, not Ayden's wife."

He wasn't sure how to respond. He wanted to, but he decided against it.

"Tell me what you're trying to say."

"I was just going to say, you've gotten a lot more selfish." He chuckled. "It's interesting."

"Interesting? What does that mean?"

"It means you've changed a lot."

"And you don't love me."

"What? Where the bloody hell did you get that idea?"

"You don't like me anymore. I've changed a lot."

"That doesn't mean I don't like you. I was just making an observation. Am I not allowed to do that?"

"We both have changed." I shifted my eyes to the floor. "I used to be reduced to just the good girl. But people use that as an insult. They assume I have nothing to offer. I'm boring. I don't want to be that woman anymore. And you were once just the bad boy. It was an insult, and something women loved. Now you're changing that."

Ayden's shoes came into my view. "Is that so terrible?" He used two fingers to lift my chin. "We're learning to be better people."

I never got over the shade of his eyes. *So emerald.* So mesmerizing. "You are. I've been learning to be worse."

That didn't stop the smirk that tugged at his lips. "I like to think of it as balance." He kissed me slowly. "We're teaching each other." He trailed his kisses down to my neck. I wanted to say something, but I was far too lost in his touch. "Tell me when to stop," he whispered.

But I didn't.

He had been right about my selfishness. He'd been teaching me to be more like him, and now we were standing on a front porch while he got me all hot and bothered.

"Are we still looking for my body?" Sunny asked from the doorway.

Ayden pulled away as I lowered my head, and we both turned to look at Sunny. I wanted to feel guilt. Shame. Remorse. I wanted to feel like I had exposed mine and Ayden's private life.

But I didn't.

“We are,” he answered. He grabbed my wrist and pulled me inside behind him. When I glanced at Sunny, I saw a mixture of jealousy and longing in her eyes. She wanted Ayden as much as I did.

Fog settled in every pore, clogging the air like a humid day in Florida. I'd left Ayden home tonight. After sex the other night at the party, I'd gained a new taste for the way we used to be.

I stood outside of the library he broke into when we first met. Sure, it was closed for the night, but it didn't stop me. So, I walked right through the glass door.

Getting into the computer was easy. Technology had been my forte in a previous life. When your parents left you to fend for yourself, you became the tech whiz. What a wonderful title that was—sarcasm intended.

I searched the database for anything on Ayden. Anything new I could find. But I knew everything from his file. There was nothing more I could learn now that he didn't already tell me. So, I turned and left the library.

The fog grew thicker with every passing second.

By now, the streetlamps were hardly visible. And in some odd way, I hoped that the fallen angels would come out and liven up my walk. But they didn't. Not now. Not anymore.

"What are you doing all the way out here?" Ayden asked. "More danger?"

"I want what we had," I said before I could catch it. Facing him, I took in his appearance all at once. Utterly sexy. "Let's have sex. Right here. Right now."

"On the street? I've had sex in some odd places, but this is not one of those."

We had sex at the party, and now he was refusing. Why now?

I pushed him against the side of a building, kissing every inch of his neck. "Why don't you want me?" I slipped his belt out of the buckle.

"It's not about not wanting you." He grabbed my hands, pushing them away. "Stop."

I stepped back. No matter how hard I tried, he'd never want the old Mr. Dyer back. He'd never want *us* again. I was left to live with the past and reminisce over what had once been. "Come find me when you want to screw your wife." I backed up some more, turning on my heel and vanishing with the fog.

Endamage

Matthew folded his hands on top of his desk, giving me that pitiful look. "I thought you knew."

"If I had known, I would have been searching for my missing piece long ago." I wouldn't have become a guardian angel, but then I never would have met Ayden. "Every guardian angel has to take that test, so how could I have known?"

"No, Eliana, it's not every Virtue. Only those with missing pieces must take that test. But that missing piece didn't affect you at all."

"It's affecting me now, isn't it?" I stood up and left the office, scowling. Why hadn't anyone said anything? Ayden was right on the money when he told me I was missing a piece of my soul.

As if my plate wasn't full enough—I had to save souls, keep our baby, and find my missing piece.

Although, I wasn't sure about that second one anymore.

Nothing changed the fact that I had been a broken soul all these years. Whatever piece was missing, I had a feeling it had to do with Liam. I needed to find it, to remember what really happened.

I visited Liam's place first. New people had moved in, so I needed to mask myself. But when I searched the place high and low, I knew it wasn't here. I wasn't sure exactly what I had been looking for, or how to tell that it was mine.

This led me to the library in Heaven next, where I researched more about broken souls. It didn't say much about how to find them, or how you knew it was yours. If God knew, why would he keep it from us? Did we not deserve to be whole?

"What's that?" Sunny asked.

I closed the book, swallowing my pride. "I'm...broken."

She sat beside me. "We all are. It's nothing to be ashamed of."

"No, Sunny. I am *broken.*" I pushed the book to her. "A piece of my soul is hiding somewhere. It's out there in the world, and I don't know where to look. Whatever it is, it took a memory with it. I need to find it."

She opened the book, turning pages. She skimmed a few chapters. "You don't talk much about your life before this. What happened?"

Where did I even begin?

I decided to start with my childhood, telling Sunny that I had been that rich girl. I had a nanny for some time, before my parents got rid of her. At that point, I was left to fend for myself. No siblings. Parents had always traveled for business.

Being the good girl wasn't easy. People thought maybe it had been, because I had everything. But I never had a family, and that made it harder for me to want to do what was good for me. I could have gone and slept with boys. I could have turned to alcohol or drugs. I could have ended up pregnant, or in jail. But that would not change how my parents felt.

Choosing to be the good girl was my only way of sticking it to my parents. I wouldn't let their screw-ups affect my future. I wanted them to feel guilty, and I didn't want them to take credit for how I turned out. How I turned out was all me, because they were never there to help shape who I became.

I never had friends growing up, and that was my decision. Having been alone so long, I enjoyed it. I took to books to help distract me from this world. It was a wonderful way to escape loneliness.

I happened to mention college, and Selene. She was dating Liam, but that all turned sour. It went downhill from there.

"I'm so sorry." She reached out and wrapped her fingers around mine. "I'm sorry for loving Ayden. You deserve him, and he deserves you." She squeezed my hand. "I haven't been oblivious to it. You've been more affectionate with him, and I get it. Another girl comes into his life, in love with him... You want me to know that he's your husband and he's not available. I was never going to take him from you. You're my friend, too."

"It's easier to think otherwise. I shouldn't have, but you had him first. I always fear there might be some buried feelings on his part, too."

She laughed. "Um, no. When Ayden and I were together, he talked about you. I was too desperate to care, but looking back on it now, you were the topic of conversation all the time. Granted it wasn't good, but it was about you."

I turned my head to face her. "What would he say?"

"He was annoyed. Mostly. You came into his life. He didn't want you around, but he didn't have much of a choice after the accident. He said it drove him crazy that you were always too nice about everything. Too calm, as he put it. I think he wanted to kiss you."

Tension fled my soul as my shoulders relaxed. "Kiss me? How do you think that?" Yet I knew it. We had made a bet, and he won. His prize was a kiss from me, which he never wanted when he was with Sunny. After they broke up, he practically begged me for it.

She shrugged. "Whenever he kissed me, it never lasted long. And damn, he is such an amazing kisser. But he always pulled away, and that was it."

I couldn't disagree there. The first time Ayden kissed me, I knew right away. I never needed to kiss a boy to conclude that he had lots of experience kissing girls, and thus, he was fantastic at it.

She flipped through pages, trying to help me find any information I needed.

"He's amazing, by the way."

"Hm?" Sunny barely looked up.

I closed my eyes. "Ayden. You asked me how he is in bed. He's amazing."

This time she looked directly at me. "Really? I mean, I know that's private. And it's probably weird telling me that since I...ya know...love him."

I shook my head. "If you don't mind, I don't mind."

Sunny spun in her chair, facing me. "Okay, then, what's he like? I mean, aside from amazing."

"He's certainly not shy, nor inexperienced. He knows exactly what he does to me." I glanced at the table. "It makes the wait worth it. I think a lot of people thought I was crazy because I didn't have sex with anyone. But if that's what I had to wait for, it was worth every second."

"That good, huh?"

My laugh permeated the air. "That good." I cleared my throat. "Hey, can I ask you something?"

She faced the book. "Anything." She skimmed through more pages.

"Is Ayden...a boob guy, or a butt guy?" It was an odd question, but I was curious to know which asset should have been used more.

"I think sometimes he comes off as the boob guy, because every straight man has to have some attraction towards boobs, whether it's a sliver or a whole tree, but... I think he's an ass guy. When we'd makeout, his hands would grab my ass before they ever touched my boobs."

Nodding, I traced the table. "And how would I use that to my advantage? I think we both know that I'm blessed in the boob department more than the butt."

She glanced at my body. "Well, this might sound wrong but if you want your butt to be the center, you need to find clothes that cover your cleavage. Without cleavage, eyes won't automatically go there. I also suggest jeans. Accentuate the bottom half."

A T-shirt and skinny jeans. That had been far from my style, but it was worth a shot.

"Ass guys like it when your back is towards them more. Boob guys like the cleavage, and they certainly love it when you bend over and shove it in their face. But with ass guys, it's the opposite, right? Butts are on the backside. So back to him more times than not."

I pushed a strand of hair behind my ear, chewing my lip. "Does that mean Ayden is into..." I couldn't even say it without embarrassing myself. "We've tried oral, vaginal..."

She choked on a laugh. "Anal? I mean, sometimes. I can't say for sure with Ayden, but not every guy likes that idea."

"Oh, gosh, I hope not. I barely got out of my comfort zone to give him oral." I sat back in my chair, grabbing the book from her. "Maybe that's why...this has been harder."

"What?"

I gestured to everything. "This. All of this. Losing my wings. Therapy. Creating that...maternal bond with my baby."

"What do you mean?" She furrowed her brows.

Missing a piece of my soul made it that much harder for me to just enjoy Heaven. Subconsciously, I must have always known it wasn't there. I wasn't whole. I'd been broken. "Maybe if I had been whole, I wouldn't need therapy. But missing a piece of my soul...it, in a way, brings me closer to humans than I thought."

She shook her head. "No. Maybe a small part of it is because of that, but you've still been through a lot. It isn't fair to ask you to just move on. You've had a lot of unsolved trauma in your childhood and it's understandable that your soul didn't fully make it intact."

She had a good point, but still, I felt like some of it was due to my brokenness. Maybe then I never would have asked Ayden to help me bring out the dark side.

I thanked Sunny and left the library. I wasn't sure where I was gonna go or what I'd do, but I had to try. My soul deserved to be intact. I couldn't guarantee I'd find it, and maybe not in time either. I had so much on my plate already, but it was worth a shot.

I hadn't told Ayden yet, and I was going to hold off for a little bit. I didn't want him to brag about being right. I also wasn't prepared to admit it to everyone. It made it feel that much more surreal.

I searched the campus, including the old dorm room Selene and I had lived in together. It brought back so many memories, and I would have done anything just to go back to those days and relive them over again. It used to be so simple. My only worry had been about graduating college.

Now, I had to save lives. Save souls. Save the world and stop whoever was behind this.

Was it possible that the culprit was in charge of everything? Had he or she influenced Liam to do what he did?

If that was true, it would only complicate everything that much further. I hoped it was simpler than that.

Whatever it was that I'd forgotten, nobody knew about it and unless I found that piece, I never would. That scared me—not knowing everything I had when I was alive. How could I allow myself to forget? How could I have been so moronic?

The question was, which specific trauma kept me from arriving in

Heaven whole? According to Sunny, there was more than one.

Why hadn't Ayden lost a piece of himself? He had more baggage than I did. Was it possible that Ayden had healed, and I hadn't?

I'd been so focused on thinking I was okay because my future wasn't falling apart, and yet I hadn't realized I had to deal with my trauma.

Ayden, however, had somehow healed. He dealt with everything he endured, and I didn't know how he did it. I was probably going to have to ask him about it. As much as I didn't want to, I needed his help since he knew me better than I did. Admitting that was difficult, but it was the first step to recovery. I'd been too focused on saving everyone else all these years that I never noticed I had to rescue myself.

Damsel

I'd always wondered why I had more symptoms than the average pregnant Virtue. I was the one who wasn't whole. I'd been the one soul still connected to the living world, because I hadn't arrived here intact.

"So, am I like a ghost or something?" Sunny asked from the living room. "I mean, I'm just a soul without a body."

"Ghost implies that you're dead, and unsure of where you're going. Also, people wouldn't be able to see you." I snickered. "Ghosts aren't real, Sunny. This is *very* real."

"Then what am I?"

I poked my head out of the kitchen. "What do you mean?"

She laid her head back on the couch arm, feet across the cushions. "What am I? Not a ghost, angel, demon, or anything of that sort. I'm not even human. I'm just...a soul. So, what am I?"

I walked out of the kitchen. "Well, there's something we call Frens, and Wisps. Frens are those who use too much of their brain. Think parents who always told their kids their feelings didn't matter. They'd be a Fren. Then Wisps are the opposite. They use their heart too much. They're people who always make decisions based on their feelings." I put the plate down, frowning at the food. I knew how to cook. I just never needed to do it anymore, yet here I was.

"What do Frens and Wisps have to do with me?"

A chill ran up my back. "I never said they had to be purely human, or alive. They just must...be." Gesturing to her, I said, "And you are certainly a Wisp."

"Damn, that hurt."

I grabbed her feet and moved them, sitting beside her. "It wasn't an insult, Sunny. It was supposed to be informative. You are a Wisp. You are very emotionally connected, and sometimes it can hurt you, but other times, it's good. Empathy is wonderful." I reached over, grabbing her hand. "You think about others. Had you not suggested to me that I focus on my own mental health, I wouldn't be here."

She squeezed my hand. "I'm glad you decided to get help. I know it was a lot for you to bear, being pregnant and having to save everyone. Having to save me..." Sunny let go.

Did she think saving her was this huge task? She'd been my charge for a short while, and even if she was Ayden's ex, she was my friend, too. "I'm choosing to save you, and I wouldn't have it any other way." I glanced at my stomach.

Sunny put her hand on my bump. "Do you know how far along you are? I didn't think...well... I didn't think angels could get pregnant."

"Well, he's not technically ours *yet.* Only Virtues can get pregnant, and normally they don't have this many symptoms." I placed my hand on hers, closing my eyes. "He's the soul of a human baby."

"Oh..."

Oh wasn't even the half of it. There was so much I wanted to say, to tell Sunny. I knew she'd understand because she was the go-to for feelings. She understood them more than anyone, and she certainly empathized with people conflicted with their own thoughts.

She was a Wisp in the purest of forms.

I went to the bathroom to wash my hands before I ate my food. As I flicked the water into the sink, I reached for the towel, looking into the mirror. Widening my eyes, I gasped and faced the toilet, gripping my chest. I knew I had seen blood on it. Was I losing my mind?

I faced the mirror again, gripping the counter. No, that brought back horrid memories. *"Socially awkward—I like that."*

Why did he have to take something that I struggled with and turn it into a nightmare? Everything I did... Everything I was... It was *me*, and he twisted it into poison.

Walking through the never-ending halls of the university, I kept my head down. I ran into someone, dropping my bag. "I'm so sorry." I reached down and picked it up.

I glanced back at the guy, but he raised both eyebrows in surprise. I lowered my head and quickly walked away from him. It wouldn't have turned into one of those despicable romance books. That wasn't me. That wasn't my life.

After I made it to the girl's bathroom, I looked into the mirror. I reapplied my red lipstick, making sure it was as bold as red could be. My mascara and eyeliner had always stayed on no problem but finding a lipstick that didn't fade over the course of hours had been a challenge all in itself.

The door opened and I stepped back, looking at the boy who had just run into me. "This is the girl's b-bathroom," I stuttered.

He shut the door behind him, facing me. "This is college, Eliana. I came to talk to you." How did he know my name? He closed the gap between us. "You don't have many friends, do you? Socially awkward—I like that."

That was an understatement.

"Why are you in here?" I scanned the bathroom for any kind of escape. Who was I kidding? He was blocking the door.

"To see you, remember?" He reached out, gripping my wrist and pulling me against him. My heels echoed an odd pattern as I stumbled forward. Before I could protest, he leaned down to kiss me.

This was not how I pictured it. In a girl's bathroom? With a stranger?

I placed my hands flat against his chest, forcing him away from me. "Please, don't kiss me. I don't want you to kiss me. I don't know you." I didn't consent to this, nor did I ever imply I wanted this in any shape or form.

His eyes darkened. "I'm certain you do. I know you." He tried to kiss me again, but I was firmer this time, pushing against him. "Oh, Eliana, don't you want to kiss a boy before you die? Do you not wonder what it's like to be touched?" He grabbed my hips, digging his nails into the fabric of my skirt. "You can't stay a virgin forever."

As my eyes went big, he lunged for me.

I screamed, trying to get out of his grip. Once I managed to get his filthy hands off me, I tripped. He landed on top of me, and I pushed my strength to the max to get him off. The rest of him smelled just as putrid as his breath.

Finally managing to push him off, I scrambled for the door. He grabbed hold of my ankle and dragged me across the floor. I kicked at him, plunging my heel in his eye. He yelled out and covered it with his hand.

I grabbed the door handle, yanking on it until I realized it was locked. It wouldn't budge. He threw himself against me, knocking me into the wall beside the door. I fell to the floor, blinking a few times as my vision blurred.

Everything seemed to slow down as if I was walking through a strobe-lit room. His face came closer, and that awful odor got stronger.

I had remembered seeing him somewhere before this, and then it clicked. Liam. This guy was friends with Liam, but Liam would never condone this.

What was his name? Spencer? Simon?

"Sam, please..." I struggled to move my limbs, but they were too heavy for me to fight back.

His fingers touched my cold skin as he unbuttoned my shirt. I couldn't let this happen to me. This couldn't happen to anyone after me. "Stop," I pleaded. I knew better. He wouldn't listen to a girl. He wanted one thing and I couldn't beg away his sick desires.

He pulled down my underwear while lifting my skirt. He began to undo his belt, the buckle ringing in my ears. I wasn't going to let him win.

I brought my knee up into his junk, catching him crumbling in pain. "Bitch!"

I crawled away from him, standing up and fixing my underwear before I tripped. I grabbed onto the sink for support, feeling the right side of my head. Looking at my fingers, blood coated the tips.

Sam pushed me against the counter, trapping me against it. He attempted to remove my underwear once again, but I pushed back with everything I had left, knocking him into the stall door. It flew open, and he fell backwards. A loud cracking sound bounced off the walls.

I turned around, inhaling every ounce of oxygen left in this room as my body shook from fear. Sam lay on the white tile floor as a pool of blood formed around his head, and more of it ran down the bowl of the toilet.

I'd killed him. I'd killed a man.

"Angel?" Sunny knocked. "You okay in there? You've been in there a long time."

I blinked away the terror, opening the door. "I'm fine."

I knew I wasn't. Somehow, someway, I needed to find the missing piece of my soul. I couldn't be sure if I'd need to find it before or after I saved all these other souls. If I found it, would they let me keep my baby? Was that why I wasn't winning?

A thumb wiped away the tear on my cheek, and lips pressed against my forehead. "You seem like something is bothering you," Ayden whispered. He wrapped his fingers around mine, warming them up if I hadn't been dead.

Peering up at him through wet lashes, I sniffled. "You were right. I'm missing a piece of myself. I'm broken."

"Oh, Love..." He wiped away more tears. "You are not loved any less, nor worth any less. I promise." He planted a soft kiss on my nose.

It certainly didn't feel that way. I felt worthless. Less valuable. Like I didn't matter because I wasn't a whole soul. How could I call myself a real angel, or Virtue, if I was torn apart?

Was it Sam? Had he been the reason I never made it to Heaven in one piece?

"Ayden," I choked.

"Yes?"

"Thank you."

"For what?" His forehead creased.

I kissed his knuckles just as some of the loneliness fled my thoughts. "For never kissing me without me expecting it. Without me wanting it."

Ayden chuckled. "Did I not surprise you when I kissed you?"

Sure, it had been a surprise, but he never kissed me without hinting that he wanted to first. I'd known him for a long while before he stole my breath away.

"When you came to me that day, long after you broke up with Sunny, you begged to kiss me. You wanted our deal to be back on. But that's it, Ayden. You came to me first and foremost, asking for my consent. You didn't just steal a kiss from me out of the blue. I mean you did, but you also didn't. Not completely."

"As much as I wanted to, I didn't want my first kiss with you to be one you fought against. I had to make sure you wanted it as much as I did, and when I studied your eyes, I knew. You had already confessed your love. You wanted to be kissed, but you were afraid to admit it."

He wasn't wrong. I had wanted to kiss Ayden for a while before that moment. I wanted to know what it was like to be in his arms, to cuddle, and to know he was mine. Now I knew.

I rested my forehead against his. "But thank you."

"Of course. I'd never want to hurt you or do anything to completely jeopardize a relationship. I only did things that I could redeem myself from and forcing myself onto a woman—kiss or otherwise—is not something I could come back from. Not with that woman."

I furrowed my brows. "Really? You're justifying running a red light because I'd still fall for you after?"

He laughed. "Not what I meant, but sure. I'm just happy to know that you fell for me at all. I wasn't the best guy, Angel, and for that, I'm sorry."

I shook my head, parting my lips. "Don't be sorry, Ayden. You know what you want, and you go for it. I admire that kind of confidence. Maybe someday I can do the same."

Maybe someday.

Envy

Ayden watched me pace back and forth, but this was something I had wanted. If we could make this work, maybe I could find the piece to my soul, and save the others. "Is it okay if we meet her? Is it against the court?" I asked.

He shrugged. "Nothing says we aren't allowed to meet her or interact. Whether she's involved with us or not, she's involved in this court no matter what. It shouldn't affect anything."

I stopped in my tracks and looked at him. "Are we really doing this?"

"We are. We are really doing this, Angel."

"Let's meet Lucía Álvarez." I grabbed his hand, intertwining our fingers.

He and I wore regular clothes to blend in, but I didn't need it all that much. Not without wings. He couldn't risk exposure after Liam's damage.

My husband knocked on her apartment door and waited for her to open it. When she did, neither of us were expecting the woman we saw. "Lucía Álvarez?" I asked.

"Who wants to know?" She eyed us both.

Auburn hair fell down her back in thick, soft waves. Her brown eyes searched ours endlessly for answers, but her skin had been as light as mine.

She'd been on the shorter side, and her body type had been that of a rectangle, and even as she stood here, I envied her figure. I'd have given anything to get that reduction surgery. Anything at all, really.

"May we come in?" When she didn't budge, he cleared his throat. "We knew Liam," he told her.

Lucía stiffened at the mention of his name. "That bastard ruined my life."

Ayden chuckled and glanced at me. "Ours, too."

She opened the door more and let us inside. I took a moment to look at her stomach. She was carrying the body of our baby. It was bizarre to comprehend.

Lucía sat down on the couch and looked at me. "When are you due?"

I lowered my gaze to my stomach and fixed my shirt. "Soon. Very soon..." If I gave a specific date now, she would be freaked out. My due date was hers.

"Did Liam do that to you, too?" She pointed to my bump. "Cause you can be assured he did this to me. That bastard won't know what hit him."

I shivered. "No, gosh, no. I wouldn't be this happy if it had been his." And yet even with the baby being Ayden's, I still wasn't as happy as I should have been.

He turned to Lucía and gave her a comforting smile. "I'm Ayden and this is my wife, Eliana."

"Eliana... Where have I heard that name? You said you knew Liam?" Lucía asked.

How did we explain this to her in the easiest way possible?

"We knew Liam very well." I sat on the couch, pulling my legs up to a crisscross position. "Liam was...a friend before he became an enemy."

"They always started out that way. The worst ones are those who deceive you." She rolled her eyes and sat back.

I bit my lip. "Did he ever talk about Selene?"

She sat up and grabbed a pillow, holding it against her stomach. "No. Is she important?"

"More than you would know. Selene was his girlfriend. They were in love. I was Selene's roommate at the time." I smiled a bit.

"He loved her? And how the hell did he screw it up?" She gave me a look.

Ayden looked at us both, saying, "Let me get you both something to eat." He went to her kitchen, whipping up something wonderful. He came back with vanilla wafers sandwiching ice cream.

She was surprised by the treat and started to stuff each sandwich in her mouth. She didn't care to share with me which was not a problem since I didn't need the food.

She finished up her cookies and shook her head. "That was amazing."

"He's a wonderful baker." I sent him a soft smile. "If he can do that, he can whip up some quick treats as well."

He leaned down and gave me a quick kiss on the lips.

I faced Lucía and worked out a plan in my head on how to explain to her the truth about Liam. "Selene and Liam were together for a few years. They were very much in love. Unfortunately, Selene kissed another man one night and Liam was there to witness it. He couldn't forget no matter how hard he tried."

I had to wonder why she never told me. I was her friend, wasn't I? I wouldn't have hated her. I would've helped her make things right.

"One night, he went on a winter picnic with her." I exhaled. "He came back to my dorm and told me she was dead." I could never forget that scene. "He took me to the field and showed me her body. I grieved for days, and I thought it was over. Liam came back to help me find her killer and together, we started an investigation," I said.

Lucía lifted her eyebrow. "What does this have to do with any of this?"

"Liam made up lies about the suspect and once the details of the suspect were released, Liam wanted to make sure I never turned him in."

She covered her mouth. "Oh shit. He killed Selene."

I slowly nodded, fiddling my fingers. "He killed Selene. He killed me to keep me quiet."

"What... He..." She was puzzled by my words at this point.

"I'm an angel, Lucía. Ayden and I are angels. Liam killed Selene. He killed me. He killed Ayden." I swallowed.

"You're shitting me." She stood up. "This is some kind of joke."

Ayden wasn't ready to let her leave. "It's not. Every human being has a soul, including your child. My wife is carrying the soul of your baby. That is why we are here."

She shook her head. "Get out."

"We—" I started but got cut off.

"Get. Out." She pointed to the door. "I don't know who the fuck you think you are, but I want nothing to do with you and nothing to do with Liam. He's dead and I'm glad that asshole is burning in Hell."

Ayden grabbed my hand. "Come on. We have to go." He led me towards the door.

I looked at her. "If it helps, Liam really *is* burning in Hell." After those words, I left her apartment. "Where do we go now? She hates us. She thinks we're playing a sick joke."

He sighed and shook his head. "I don't know. I guess I can understand her frustration. Being told that the woman in front of you is carrying the other half of your child is not exactly the ideal conversation you want to have. Unless you're the father." He chuckled. "When you told me you were carrying the other half of me, I was very excited."

Was our baby half of us put together? If he was the soul of Liam and Lucía's baby, wouldn't our baby look like theirs, making him half of their DNA?

"She looks so different from Selene. I thought Liam would have picked a woman who looked like her, too." I peered up at her apartment as we walked down the stairs.

"Well, it would be a little creepy if she looked like Selene." He shrugged and scanned the shops throughout the city.

"Do you ever miss being human?" I asked.

"Sometimes. I wonder what it would be like if we were alive. We would be married and having a real child we wouldn't have to fight for. Humans let you keep your kid unless you're harming them." He shot me a look.

I sighed, sitting on the curb as he helped me. "I miss it all the time. It's nice never having to eat or sleep and use the bathroom. It is wonderful not having a period. I just miss the familiarity of it all."

Ayden sat next to me and put his arm around me. "When this is over, our baby will be the only child we ever have."

"What do you mean?" I laid my head against his shoulder.

"When we win this case, we won't have a chance to have another child. They won't let us keep anymore. Our baby will be an only child." He rubbed my shoulder.

I looked towards the buildings. "I hated being an only child but...if it means we get to have one baby, I'll accept that. We will love our baby regardless of what happens." Did Ayden want this baby more than I did? "Why did we come here? What were we expecting out of this? Were we expecting Lucía to agree to have her baby without its soul so we could win our case?" I glanced at him.

"I'm not sure. I thought it would help us figure it out if we met the woman ourselves. I'm not sure what we were going to do from here." He kissed my head.

"She hates us. She *hates* us." I started to cry. It was the hormones talking again.

"No, don't cry. Fuck. I have to fix this." Ayden stood up and walked back to her building. I quickly followed behind, not sure what he was planning to do. She didn't want to see us.

We walked up the stairs to her building and he knocked on her door. "I'm not going away. She's not going to make us out as the bad guys. We're the ones fighting for our child."

Lucía opened the door. "I'll call the cops if you don't leave me alone."

He shrugged as he walked inside her apartment. "Go ahead. We're dead and they can't contain us. Also, we can make ourselves disappear to the human eye so they will just think you're a crazy woman and put you in a loony bin."

"What the hell do you want from me?" She looked at me, then back at Ayden.

He grabbed my hand, pulling me closer to him. "Yes, we sound crazy. That doesn't make us the bad guys. My wife died at twenty years old. She was murdered by Liam and her dreams were taken from her. Her dream is to have children of her own and we just found out a few months ago we could get pregnant. We have to fight in the Heavenly Court to keep our own baby. This is hard on us, so don't you dare push us away."

She swallowed. "What does it mean for me if you keep your baby?"

"It means your child would be without a soul."

"I would have a demon child? An empty vessel is an open invitation to demons. Have you seen *The Omen*? I don't wanna end up with that kind of child." She pointed out the window as if she was pointing to a monster child she knew.

My husband rubbed his eyes. "Do you not understand? We don't want to take away your child and leave you with a demon child. We also don't want to lose our baby. We are trying to figure this out. We want to make this work, Lucía. We are here, telling you because we are searching for a solution that may not even exist."

"How do we find such a solution?" She plopped down on her couch.

He looked at me. "We are looking. We don't want to take away your child. We are not here for that. We just want your help so we can both have loving children." She had to understand that we couldn't just give up our baby. It wasn't that easy. We wanted this child.

"So, when you said you wouldn't be this happy if it was Liam's does it still apply if my baby is your baby which is Liam's baby?"

Ayden's face fell. "What? Why would you put that thought into my head?"

A small laugh escaped my lips. "It's technically not. I didn't magically get pregnant because you did. I got pregnant because...we were having sex at the same time." The realization smacked me in the head. "Which...makes this baby Liam's baby." I wanted to tear something apart. Throw stuff. Go crazy on breaking a car. How could I not see this before?

Lucía cleared her throat. "Let's change the subject."

I chewed on my lip. "Have you seen the gender yet?" I asked her.

She turned towards me. "Have you?"

"We don't know until you know. Baby ultrasounds in Heaven aren't exactly very common since most angels don't keep the baby. We aren't supposed to know." I sighed.

"Do you want to know?"

"I'm not even sure at this point. I want to know because I want to call our child by their name, but I also am scared that if we do, we will get attached, more than we have, and it'll be so much harder if we lose the case." I looked at my stomach.

"Would you like to know or not?" She lifted her eyebrows.

I couldn't believe it. Lucía *knew* the gender. I could ask her, and she could tell me and I would know what we were having just like that. Did I want to know? Did I want to wait? Whether I waited or not, it didn't change the outcome of the case. If we waited for the gender but lost the case, we would know once we gave birth, before our baby went to another.

I took a deep breath, looking Lucía in the eye. "Am I having a Skylar or a Connor?"

She put her hand on her stomach, which was far bigger than my own. "You're having a Connor, assuming that's the boy. In other words, you're having a boy."

Ayden Edward Dyer.

August 28th, 1997 – May 20th, 2021.

I stood at his grave, angry at the world for not burying him beside me. No, Eliana Bree Wilson was buried all alone at her grave. I needed to fix that.

I began digging with the shovel. My husband needed to be next to me. Maybe if I could bury us together, we might be more inclined to want to be together forever. He'd always want me, and only me.

The fresh dirt started to build a mountain beside the hole. Fortunately for me, it didn't affect my clothes.

Losing track of time was easy. I got so caught up in digging up a grave that I was just as surprised when I hit a coffin. *His* coffin.

I leaned down and pulled open the top half, staring right into the face of his corpse. He was also my husband. The same man I kissed. The man I watched bleed to death. He had given me a new purpose. Now, he was just rotting away inside of a box.

"Is he a better kisser?" Ayden asked from above.

When I met his eyes, he displayed a small smirk. This was a joke to him, just like everything else.

"He had a heartbeat. He once had a heartbeat," I said in a quiet voice.

He jumped into the hole, lifting me to my feet. "Why are you trying to dig up my body? Why are you trying to disturb my resting place?"

I swallowed, pushing against his chest. "I want you to be buried next to me."

"Why?"

"I just do." I turned to his corpse again, trying to pull him from the padded coffin. His eyes had sunken in, his skin gray and decomposing. Maggots popped out to say hello every now and then, and I almost said hello back. They wanted the old Ayden as much as I did.

"Angel, stop," he demanded, grabbing my wrist and pulling me away from the body. He flew us out of the grave. I attempted to rip my wrist from his grasp, stumbling over flowers. I face planted into the grass with my palms flat beside my head. The waterworks started.

He attempted to help me up, but I yelled, "Don't touch me! I don't want you anywhere near me!"

He ignored my words anyway, flipping me onto my back and sitting on top of me. "Please, Love, tell me what's wrong." He leaned closer, not giving me any space to breathe. As if I needed it.

"I miss the sound of your heart beating fast for me. I miss the way you used to love me, as if you couldn't fathom the idea of anyone else having me." I choked on a sob before slamming my fist against his chest. "And now you can't stand to look at me!"

He wrapped his fingers around my hand, softly kissing my knuckles. "Who says I can't stand to look at you?"

"She does. The voice in my head. She is begging you to come back."

"You never lost me," he whispered. "Never."

"There is so much I want to do, Ayden. So much I missed out on. The feeling of sex when I had a body. The longing for you. The need for you. And what about rebelling? I never stepped out of line. I never lived before I died. I regret who I was before I met you." I slipped my hand from his, hands against his chest.

He rested his forehead against mine. "I know you asked me to bring out your dark side, but do you understand the cost of what you'll lose? It's tempting to give into what you want, but it's not as pleasurable as it seems. That's why I chose you over anyone else. I love you as you are."

"Prove it."

"How?"

"Prove to me that even if I'm just the good girl, I'm the only one you want. I'm conflicted by my feelings, and I so badly wish to be the woman who makes you go wild. I want you to ravish me like you've never been able to fulfill your desires before. I want to be yours."

His hands slipped up my thighs and his fingernails dug deep. "You think I don't want you?"

It was selfish, and possibly wrong—but I yearned for my husband to take me by surprise. If only he understood how I wanted to feel sexually attractive. "Always."

Maybe if I felt pain, I could feel his nails digging into my skin. Maybe I could have begged him to take me there. Maybe I already had.

Ayden smashed his lips onto mine, devouring the taste of me. I returned the hunger, ripping his shirt open with just a finger. Every last inch of me screamed for his touch. I ached, and he was the only cure.

We both fought to get his pants off and I aided him in pushing down his briefs. Slipping my arms under his, I buried my hands under his shirt and pressed my nails into his back.

The feeling of him turned that ache into a blazing skeleton inside me, growing with every second that flew by.

He wasn't fazed for even a minute, placing his lips against my ear as he stirred the thoughts in my head with the way he moved. His warm breath fanned my lobe as he whispered, "You will always be mine, Angel, and *mine* alone."

I paced around the room. "Are we even capable of doing this? Look at me, Ayden. Between both of us and the shit we've been through, are we able to win?"

"What are you talking about?" He stood from the couch, taking long strides as he approached me.

"I'm talking about us! I'm talking about our child. We've been through so much and how are we going to pull this off? How can we keep our baby and let Lucía keep hers? It's not possible. We are going to take away her child and that isn't fair to her." I lowered my head, admiring the wood flooring. It was dark in color, almost black.

"It's not. It's not fair. But it's not fair to us, either. We died. We lost our chance to have a real child. This is the closest we can get. Connor is our sliver of hope. Lucía is still alive, and she has the chance to have another baby in the future. She has the chance to find love. Think about it, Angel. She hates Liam and she's having his baby. She didn't want to, but she is. We deserve our baby more because we are in love, and this is our one chance." He closed the gap between us.

I pulled away from him, nearly tripping. "How dare you? You

don't get to decide who's more deserving of their baby. Lucía hates Liam but she wants her child. We have no right to take this away from her. We have not a single right." I rushed from the cabin before he could catch me. I knew where I was going, and I was going to see if our court case was the right decision. Were we on the wrong side of the jury?

I cloaked myself so she couldn't see me as I watched her. It was hard for me not to see what Lucía did when no one was around, being that she was getting Connor's soul.

I stood in the corner, leaning into the connecting walls. Lucía was on her couch, stuffing her face as she watched TV. It wasn't anything too out of the ordinary. She was going to be a single mom. She was hungry and trying to entertain herself.

She gasped a bit as she put her hand against her stomach. I knew what she was surprised about. Connor kicked.

Our babies were almost the same. For that, we felt the same movements.

I put my hand on my belly, rubbing my hand against it. He was already kicking. I knew Ayden would want to feel this.

It didn't make any sense. How could other angels accept the fate of their baby? How could they go through the whole pregnancy like a human and have that maternal bond, and let them go when they gave birth? Was there not another angel who fought for her baby? Thousands and even millions had died before they had kids of their own. I couldn't be the first to take it to court. If I wasn't the first, did any of those other women win? I had to know.

I couldn't just feel Connor kick and allow him to go so easily. I had come here to watch her and see if I was making the right choice by fighting for Connor and now, I was barely questioning my decisions. I had to be on the right side of this case. I was a mother fighting for her baby. That wasn't a bad thing to do.

I didn't deserve to feel guilty for wanting to keep my child. I had been through so much crap, and I knew this was the one good thing to come from the bad. I was worthy of having a baby and being his mom. I couldn't lose Connor. I was putting up a fight so he would know I loved him. I couldn't let him go.

Lucía yelled out in pain, falling off her couch. She held her stomach and tried to make it stop. I felt the same pain she felt. It was sharp and constant.

She reached for the phone, immediately calling herself an ambulance. We both feared what was happening to our child. We couldn't lose Connor now. Not after everything we endured just to keep him safe despite the unwanted circumstances.

The paramedics arrived quickly and got Lucía onto a gurney. I followed them as they carried her to the ambulance and drove to the hospital. They asked her if she knew what could be going on, and I was surprised that she did.

"I have O negative blood. My baby is A positive."

I didn't really understand what it meant. I barely knew anything about pregnancy. How fitting, right? To want a baby so bad?

They got her to the hospital in an orderly fashion and her doctor was already on call. "Did you skip a shot, Miss Álvarez?"

Lucía gave her a look. "Yes, I forgot my shot a few days ago and now my system is attacking him."

She nodded. "We are getting your shot ready now. I can understand you're in pain but it's best to try and relax for the baby."

I sat in the chair, feeling dizzy. These were her symptoms projecting onto me.

The nurse brought the doctor the shot and she injected it into her. "There, it should calm down your auto-immune system."

Nodding, she tried to stand, but the doctor stopped her.

Within a minute, I was feeling better. I still needed answers. What was all of this? What just happened to Lucía and how did she know?

"Just remember to come in for your next appointment and he should be okay. We're gonna just check on some things and we'll let you discharge here soon." She left the room.

Could you even call it a discharge if she'd only been here for an hour or two?

Lucía eyed the white walls and window that led to a view of the outside. The city was busy as it always was. I wanted to ask her what happened to Connor, but I couldn't let her know I had been watching her.

She really wanted to have this baby even if it was Liam's DNA. She had come here to save his life. I really didn't want to take this away from her. I feared her love for Connor was greater than my own.

She got off the bed to go to the bathroom. That was the only connection we didn't share. Lack of bladder control.

The doctor came in just as Lucía came out of the bathroom. "You're free to go."

Lucía nodded and grabbed her stuff. She went to the lobby, and I followed close behind. She checked out with the doctors and walked outside. A car pulled up and she got inside of it. I sat in the back seat, watching her lean her head against the window.

The man in the driver's seat was just a bit older than her. Neither of them said a word the whole way home and as much as I wanted to ask who he was, I didn't say anything.

He dropped her off at her apartment. She sat on her couch and ran her fingers through her hair. She was stressed over something, and I wish I could make it better. I wanted to help her and support her. She had nobody else.

She didn't have a family. Liam had screwed her over for his sick game and I'd be the one picking up the pieces yet again.

She walked to her room, and I followed behind.

There was a crib in the corner. She was sacrificing a lot for this baby. The things mothers did for their kids amazed me, seeing as my own mother had never done things for me.

I hadn't done this much for Connor, ever.

Lucía grabbed some things from the dresser and sat on the bed, admiring a little blanket just for him.

I looked up, silently begging for a solution to be made. It was a longshot, but I could wish for nothing more than a happy ending to this. Lucía deserved this. I just wasn't ready to give up Connor either.

The room itself was small with two windows the size of thirty-two-inch TVs. Her bed was against the wall that was between the one with the bedroom door and the other wall that had the windows on it. The crib was in the corner farther from the door.

There was a dresser beside the crib, across from the bed that I assumed had her clothes and Connor's. On top of the dresser was a padded changing station. It was all she could fit here. She was ready for this baby, and she was trying her best. It was sweet to see how much she cared, and it hurt me more, knowing that one of us was gonna lose him.

If I had the chance, I would say she could have him, but now that was far too late. Ayden was excited to be a father and I didn't want to take that away.

Daze blanketed my face as Lucía began to cry. Why was she so sad? How could I help her?

"I'm so sorry. I'm so sorry," she whispered.

I wasn't sure who she was talking to, but she was in pain. I couldn't feel it, so I knew it wasn't physical pain. This was *emotional* pain.

She put the blanket back on her dresser and reached for something inside her drawer. She pulled out a bottle of pills and dread replaced the sadness. No. She couldn't be serious.

She set the bottle down on the top of the furniture before sitting back on her bed. Her arms were wrapped around her stomach as she looked up to the sky. "So, You're really up there and You refuse to help me. I've been fighting this battle and You never answered my prayers."

I wanted to tell her that I was here. I wanted to help her. There was only one way I could truly help Lucía. She was breaking on the inside and I could see it in her eyes. I cared about her. I always wanted to see people do better.

I was going to request from God that He send her a guardian angel to watch over her. It was the least I could do.

She got up from the bed and put on some slip-on shoes. "You never helped me when I needed help. You better not take away my child, too." She rushed out of her apartment. I quickly followed behind her, making sure she was always in my sight.

The pills she had gotten out earlier were antidepressants. Lucía had gone through a rough patch, and she attempted to deal with it. Knowing this much about her, I felt even worse about being on the side I was on. I couldn't take Connor from her. I would never be able to forgive myself.

I was determined to find a solution so both of us could have our children with us. I would need to go to Selene soon and ask for her help. She was always the best when I needed it.

Continuing to follow Lucía down to the cafe, I sat in a corner as she stood at the counter. "I'll get the bagel please, and that lemon cake. You know what, throw in a cookie, and I mean the big cookie." She pointed to a large chocolate cookie behind the glass in their display case.

The girl put in her order and took her money. She handed Lucía her receipt and Lucía walked off to the side while she waited for her food.

"Lucía, you're back. I haven't seen you in a while," a boy said from behind the counter.

She turned to face him and shrugged. "I've been extra busy. I have to learn to be a mom now." She put her hand on her stomach.

His eyes darted to her stomach, but he smiled regardless. "That's always a surprise but I'm sure you'll do a wonderful job."

"I'm pregnant, Thomas." She kept a straight face.

"I know. I thought that was what you meant when you said you were going to be a mom and you proceeded to put her hands on your belly." He pointed to her stomach and laughed a little.

She scoffed. "You wouldn't want to handle everything I'm carrying with me."

"Did you ask me?" He leaned against the counter. "I think it's nice to ask people. Every man is different. The father may be gone but that doesn't mean I'll be."

She hid a small smile behind a wall of her hair.

Oh my gosh. This guy was flirting with Lucía, and I think she liked it.

Commandment

She gave us a look. "Why did you call me over?" Selene crossed her arms.

"There's something you should know. You already know we are pregnant. You know that this is how souls are made and we are trying to win our case to keep Connor. What you don't know is who the woman is, the one who is carrying our baby's body." I laid my hands on my stomach.

She sat down on the couch, leaning back into the cushion. "Why do I care about who she is? I just know I want you guys to win this case and get your happy ending."

I sighed. "Her name is Lucía."

Selene sat forward and lifted her eyebrow. "Is that supposed to ring a bell?"

Ayden shook his head. "Not at all. Take a wild guess at who the father is."

Selene's expression dropped. "No. Don't tell me he's the father. This can't be true."

"It is. It's true, Selene."

She rubbed her face and regret filled her eyes. "I'm so sorry. I'm sorry I wasn't there to stop it."

"This isn't your fault." I sat beside her, rubbing her back. "It was never your fault. Liam just takes revenge to a whole new level. He wanted to ruin our lives and now he's going to pay for it. He's burning in Hell—suffering. I can promise you that much." I laid my head against her shoulder.

She rested hers against my hair. "I'm just sorry for everything. I wish I could take back what I said about you being poisoned. I hurt you and I shouldn't have done that."

I laughed and pulled away. "No. Don't say that. You were poisoned. You couldn't control yourself. You were sick and I can't blame you. I already forgave you so let's move past that. We can let you testify on our side if you're willing. I just want to let you know now that Lucía is nice, and she deserves her child. We are also asking for help to find another way for us both to have kids."

Selene put her hands together, resting the tips of her fingers against her lips and chin. "What if we replace your baby with another angel baby? How can we do that? We can give her baby a soul and you can keep yours." She stood up. "Yes! We can find another woman who is pregnant and at the same stage as Lucía. There are so many people on this earth that she's bound to be at the same stage as many others. We can take that baby's soul and give it to Lucía, but we should only take from a mother who doesn't deserve a child. Like one who is truly wicked."

Ayden's eyes darted to her. "You're a genius. This is why we came to you for help."

Her laugh echoed. "Yes, exactly. Let's go on a search for a terrible mother. We aren't supposed to be doing this but too many mothers have babies they don't deserve, and others don't have any when they deserve some."

We followed her outside and flew into the sky. Ayden held onto me, considering I was at light as a feather.

Selene scanned the city, shaking her head as we passed by. "There're none here. Let's check elsewhere."

"Are we killing a baby?" I pulled against Ayden. I wouldn't go further until I confirmed exactly what her plan was.

She looked back at me. "No. We are just giving a terrible mother a soulless human to deal with. It's like a punishment."

"How do we know if she'll be a bad mother? We are not God." I glanced at the land beneath us. We saw humans walking around but we couldn't see into their heads or pasts. We couldn't predict their futures.

Selene sighed. "Bad mothers don't give two craps about their babies. They don't put their babies' interests before their own. Look for a woman who is checking off all the bad qualities of a mother. We don't want a perfectly good soul to end up in Hell down the road because his mother abused him and told him he was worthless."

Ayden leaned towards me. "She's right, Angel. We really can't do anything else. This is our best option."

I chewed on my lip before giving into their plan. "Okay. Okay. But if we do this, how do we expect to put that baby's soul into Lucía's baby? We must match up the babies. We must connect the women. We must also find the angel who is pregnant with the soul of the baby who will be mistreated by his mother and then convince her that she should switch baby bodies. It's a lot of work."

She pushed my hair back, holding my cheeks. "It is. It is a lot of work but it's going to be worth it when you get to keep your child and Lucía has hers. If you are right about her, she deserves a baby, and this bad mother does not. Let's give the loving child to Lucía first."

"We'll figure it out as we go. The first step is finding a terrible mother." Ayden tightened his grip on me, pulling me with him.

I hope this worked. I really hoped that this worked for us because I couldn't live with the idea of Lucía hating me for taking away her chance to have one good thing left.

Selene swooped down and landed on the ground, masking her visibility. We followed behind her. "Let's go somewhere where a woman might be if she were a terrible mother."

She waved us to some apartments, checking them out. We came up empty.

"What if she already has a child?" Ayden asked us.

I looked at him. "A child? What do you mean?"

Selene faced him as he said, "What if she's already had a child? She's pregnant with another. Using her interactions with her first child, we can determine if she deserves a second child."

I lifted my eyebrows. There was a sense of pride as I realized my husband intelligence had no end.

Selene gave a small nod. "You make a great point. Let's go find a woman who has a kid."

We all decided to split up to cover more tracks.

I came across a few who had no kids and a few more with happy children.

The search was a lot harder than I expected. We had decided to try Vegas, which was also known as Sin City. We had to at least attempt to see if any pregnant women here didn't deserve a baby.

The streets were packed, and the air was clogged with noises of city life.

I left the city area and retreated to a more suburban area of Vegas, an area where I could get some space to walk around in peace.

I found a pregnant woman in her front yard. There were already some toys, so I guessed she had another child somewhere. I got my hopes up as a man pulled up to her house, but he got out and kissed the woman before kissing her belly. She gave him a smile before a little boy ran outside and hugged his father. They were happy. There was no bad mother in this household.

I turned around to meet a pregnant woman across the street. She was walking down the sidewalk. I followed her to her own home and took a deep breath as I took a step inside her home.

"I'm back, Allison." She walked into the kitchen and looked at the little girl who was covered in milk and cereal. "I told you not to get into things." She grabbed her and told her to get a broom.

The little girl couldn't be more than five years old.

"Mama, I was hungwy." She pouted.

"You don't need to be making messes in this house." The mother grabbed the broom and started sweeping up the cereal. She sent her daughter to her room, and I decided to take a peek.

She shared a room with her mother.

I watched as she went to play with some toys before she fell asleep on the floor. The little girl looked peaceful as she dreamt of unicorns and ponies—most likely anyway. She'd been the cutest child I'd seen in a while, too.

The mother came in and moved her daughter into her little bed before calling someone else. "She's asleep at this time if you want to come over. Great." She hung up the phone with a smile.

The woman left into the bathroom with some clothing in her hand and she came out dressed in lingerie.

I widened my eyes, covering them with my hands. She had to have been married or dating, right? Is that what this was?

The front door opened, and a man called her name. She told him where she was and he came into the room, giving her a quick once over. "I like what I see."

"I'm sure you do. Now come take it off me," she said.

I had been there when Ayden decided to touch himself and now I was going to do it again for the sake of this court case. What had I really gotten myself into?

Keeping my eyes covered, sounds of moans and kisses reverberated throughout the room.

I couldn't even believe she was doing this with her sleeping daughter right next to them. She was a *child.*

Using my hands to cover my ears, I kept my eyes squeezed shut as gasps grew louder.

"Mama!" her daughter shouted.

I opened my eyes, turning to see the little girl watching her mom go at it with some man. I glanced at her mother who looked at her partner. "We're just bouncing. See?" She continued to ride the man and I nearly lost my balance. These kinds of people existed?

There was no doubt I had to get this little girl a new home and we were going to leave this woman with a soulless child. I had made up my mind. Her sexual needs came before her daughter's innocence and that didn't sit well with me.

Nausea pooled inside my stomach as I stumbled from the doorway.

The mother got off him and looked over at her little girl. "I don't know if it's too late now, but I just don't know if I can do this."

The man sat up and rubbed her back. "Do what?"

"Be a mother again. I don't want to be a mother to another child." She gestured to her stomach.

My heart broke for her daughter, realizing her mother didn't love her. She didn't want her.

I had to leave before I lost my head.

I rushed out of the house and pushed against the ground to propel myself forward, running faster. I found Selene and Ayden, both of whom had yet to find a woman. Good, because my candidate was perfect for the job. She'd been working at destroying an innocent girl's soul. Soon, her new baby could destroy hers.

I wasn't too sure how I was supposed to explain this woman to them. She had a child and would sleep with men in front of her. Who did that?

"Angel, what is it?" Ayden's hand rested on my shoulder.

"I found a woman. She doesn't deserve to have a child. We can't let her ruin another good soul. We can't." I shook my head vigorously, failing to wrap my mind around this.

That little girl would grow up to realize what she saw, and she was going to be traumatized. Ayden was already dealing with his own trauma of watching porn before he was even capable of knowing what it was.

"She had sex with her daughter right there and then said she didn't want to be a mom again. That little girl was in the room, and she is going to know her mom chose sex over her. She's got another baby on the way, too." I bit my lip. For a second, part of me felt guilty for taking away a baby's soul. But I couldn't feel guilty about this. That child's soul would go to a loving mother named Lucía. That demon child would be left over for that selfish woman to deal with all on her own.

"Hey, we're about to go and search some more for those bodies. You ready?" Selene asked from the doorway.

Shaking my head, I barely looked at her. "I don't know anymore."

"What do you mean you don't know?"

"I mean I don't know if I want to continue this." I grabbed a pillow, holding it against me. "I know Ayden wants to keep going with the trial, but I see no point. Not like this, Selene. Not while I'm broken."

"What do you mean? You can't be serious about this, about quitting and leaving everyone out to dry."

"No, I'm not talking about that. I just don't want to keep fighting in court. That's all I'm saying."

She closed the door behind her and released a sigh. "Why? What about Connor? You're going to give that up because of your soul?"

I was. I wanted to. Why did I think I could do this when I couldn't even remember the biggest part of why I hated Liam more than anyone else?

Yeah, he had killed the only two people I loved, and that could have been the cause.

Being abandoned as a child, watching my parents leaving... It was easy for me to get over that eventually. I had plenty of time to move on. After killing Sam, I had a short time to deal with it, but eventually I had felt better. I reminded myself over and over that he would have raped me, and that wasn't something I wanted to happen. It was self-defense, and I couldn't feel remorse for trying to defend myself.

However, losing Selene was a whole other ballpark. I never did heal, even if I pretended I did. She had been my whole world after I had nobody for almost ten years. "Selene, I have to confess something."

"What is it?" She sat, sensing it was more serious than I ever let on.

"I..." I choked on a sob. "Living without you for a week before my death was the hardest thing I ever endured."

She reached out, wrapping her fingers around mine. "Elli... I'm here now. I'm here for you."

I threw myself against her, hugging her neck. "You were the first person in a really long time who made me feel like I mattered. You took me under your wing, and you didn't even have to." I tightened my grip, holding back the tears.

She kissed my head, petting it. "Hey, you don't have to feel ashamed. Grief is difficult and nobody expects you to get over that kind of thing in just a week. You can't really time grief, and it's impossible to tell when you truly accept the loss."

Closing my eyes, a few tears escaped and safety coddled me like a baby. With Selene here and now, it was finally beginning to register with me that she was here to stay. The only best friend I truly needed, aside from Ayden, was her.

Selene lifted my head, kissing my temple. "I think because of you, I felt ready. I was truly ready, Elli, to have my own baby. When I went to the clinic, part of me wanted to just go back to normal and pretend I never got pregnant. But when I thought of you, I thought of how supportive you would be. How much you had taught me, to be a great mother. I wanted to have that baby because I wanted her to meet you." She pushed the hair away from my face. "That's why you deserve to win this. You deserve to have a baby more than anyone I know. You would be the best mother."

I pulled away, wiping my tears. "I'm sorry. I don't mean to burden you with my problems."

"Is that not what best friends are for?" She gave me a playful smile, nudging my side. How did I tell her that maybe I had been wrong about everything? I wasn't so sure of what I wanted anymore.

"Tell me about being a Throne. I never thought regular angels could take such positions, but you proved me wrong," I said.

A smile spread across her face. "I think it's better if I were to show you. But you can't tell anyone I did this for you." She stood and grabbed my hand, pulling me off the bed.

I agreed to keep my lips zipped as she took me up to Heaven. She led me to the court, but it was not anything new to me. "I've seen the court before. Not very exciting."

Selene shushed me. She led me back behind the bench, towards a door. "Only Thrones are allowed back here, but I'll make the exception for you." She opened the door and let me go in first. She closed it behind us while I admired the room.

"Selene, this is fantastic." Papers and books littered every shelf. "What is this?"

"It's where they store every single case." She found a shelf, following the books with her finger. She pulled one out and flipped it open. "And there's yours. It shows...the future of the case."

"The future?" I glanced up at her, grabbing the book. "As in, the outcome?"

"Every detail."

Everything inside me screamed to read on. I needed to know what happened. I just had to know.

Alex lies through her teeth, telling the couple they will get to keep their baby, and everyone will get a happy ending. Lucía won't lose her baby, but that's a fat lie.

The couple discusses possibly taking a soul for Lucía's baby, despite believing what Alex had said. Deep down, something tells them something is wrong about this case. They're suspecting everyone.

Eliana and Ayden Dyer eventually come to the decision to take a soul, and the soul they rip away is that of a pregnant woman who's neglected her first daughter.

With the soul in hand, they get the news that their case has been made and won.

The decision of the court had been made under the impression that Lucía Álvarez's baby will be stillborn. However, due to the nature of what they did to steal a soul, they shove it into Lucía's stillborn child, bringing him back to life.

I closed the book, and my head began to metaphorically ache from the knowledge. "That can't be right. They promise us a happy ending and plan to kill her baby in the process. That can't be *right.* Selene, we must change this. I must change the course of things. How do I find out what happens before that so I can find the piece that sets us down this path?"

She pulled the book from my arms. "You can't. It only shows you the outcome of the court."

Sure, I could let this go on because we stole a soul, but what use was it to allow her baby to be stillborn? I had to do anything to persuade the court to let us keep our babies.

I thanked Selene and left the room. I wasn't sure where I was going, but I had to somehow get closer to Lucía. I needed to prove to Heaven that she was a good mother, too. So, whatever I was going to do, it was for everyone's happiness, and this time that included my own.

While sitting on the couch, my eyes shut as I ran through different scenarios in my head. The silence, and the last of visuals, allowed me to freely sift through ideas.

A pair of hands landed on my shoulders, massaging them as if that was what I'd been sitting here for. By the feel, I knew they belonged to Ayden. I didn't say anything yet at least. I let him scare away the stress and worry.

"Sometimes I want to punch someone," I said. "And I know it's wrong but… I still *feel* that way. It isn't fair to us, or to Lucía. Liam always ends up getting what he wants, and he wants us to lose Connor."

"What are you going to do about it?" he asked.

I opened my eyes, clenching my jaw. "I'm going to break him out of Hell and demand he helps me find my missing piece."

"Angel, whoa." Ayden came around the couch, gaze fixed on me. "You can't be seriously considering that."

"Who is in control here? Me, or Liam? I need to establish my power. It's my turn to win the battle. He keeps getting ahead of us, and even in Hell, he's two steps ahead." I stood up, squeezing my hands into fists. "He's the baby we're losing. He's the one who's caused everything. I'm missing part of myself because he killed me too quickly, because *he* murdered my best friend. And now, I can't even remember the full extent of why I despise him so much."

He snaked his arm around my waist, pulling me against him. "Let me help. That's what I'm here for."

"No. Only Liam can play the part now."

"Then what part do I play?" He scowled at the sound of our killer's name.

I wrapped one arm around his back while I used the other hand to grab the back of his head. "You know exactly what part you play." I placed a few kisses along his neck, but before he could get into the mood, I pulled away from him. "If I don't do this, everything could go very wrong." *No, everything will go very wrong.*

He stayed glued to the same spot as I started towards the door.

Was I going to break Liam out? Was it the right decision? Maybe. *Maybe not.*

Fingers grasped my wrist, spinning me around. Ayden caught my waist with one hand and my cheek with the other. His lips found mine in a matter of milliseconds. The taste of him always sent me into a frenzy.

He tightened his grip on me, moving the hand on my cheek into my hair. "Don't go," he whispered against my lips.

It would have been so effortless to tell him okay—to stay—but that wasn't the plan.

"I must, Ayden. If I don't do this, something terrible is going to happen. I must fix our problems." I slipped from his embrace, turning and walking out the front door.

Finding my way to Hell was easy by now. It was second nature. So was Liam's cell.

"You're coming with me," I said, unlocking the door.

Liam swallowed, standing up almost immediately. "Why?"

I tilted my head. "Why? Because you've managed to destroy everything in my life *and* my afterlife. And now you're going to help me find my missing piece. You're my bitch now, Liam. I won't let you forget it." I swung open the door. "Let's go."

He watched my every move as he stepped out of the cell. "How can you trust me not to pull anything?"

"I can't. But that's where the fun comes in." I gave him a cunning smile. "If you do, I happen to be in contact with a group of people who will chop your penis off the second they get the chance. Are we clear?"

"Crystal," Liam replied.

I closed the door and grabbed his hand. "Let's go, mutt." I dragged him behind me, leaving Hell. Whatever I had become, it terrified Liam. He didn't dare move a muscle, nor try to escape on any occasion.

Deep down, it scared me a bit, too. Whoever I was becoming, she was not the same Eliana who had been given the green light to become a guardian angel. She was not the same Eliana who fell in love with Ayden. Could I save her? Of course I could. Saving her was easy. I'd been the same Eliana my entire life and this kind of behavior made me uncomfortable on a normal basis.

However, that wasn't really the issue.

Eliana was still there, begging for me to make different choices. I could save her if I wanted to. But I supposed that was the real concern, wasn't it? I didn't *want* to save her.

Ayden's knock echoed throughout her apartment as he walked in with a vanilla cake that was topped with strawberry frosting. "Hello? Is anyone home?"

Lucía came out of her room and tilted her head at us standing in her living room. "What are you guys doing here?"

"We came to get to know Miss Álvarez." I smiled and clasped my hands together. I wanted more answers from her, but I couldn't give away that I stalked her. She was wary of us just on her own.

As for Liam, I kept him locked up somewhere safe for now.

Ayden lifted his cake in a box. "I brought you a treat."

This seemed to get Lucía going. Of course, why wouldn't it? Everyone wanted a taste of Ayden's sweets.

She walked over to him, taking the box out of his hand. She set it on the counter and cut herself a slice before taking a bite. "Fuck, this is fantastic." She took more bites. "What did you put in this?"

He chuckled. "I don't like giving away my recipes."

"I'm carrying your baby's body. Don't I deserve to know? Do you want him to be fed well?" She pointed to her stomach.

I smiled at him and decided not to tell Lucía about our plan just yet. I would tell her when we had more of this figured out. She deserved to be excited about it and I wanted to make sure she had a reason to be, and that this would certainly work.

Sitting on her couch, I pushed hair behind my ear. "We're here to learn about Lucía today. Tell us about yourself."

She took another slice of cake and shrugged. "All right, where do I begin?"

"Wherever you feel comfortable." I gestured to her using both of my hands.

She swallowed her food. "When I was younger, I used to have a sister. She was a bit older than me, and she was my best friend. Ma always said that she would beg to hold me when I was a baby. There are plenty of pictures of those. We were always together after that. When I was entering high school, Marie made it to a party with her friends. She didn't invite me because who would invite a little freshman?" She laughed without an ounce of humor.

I glanced at Ayden, not sure of what to say.

"I was so mad at her for being embarrassed by me. She got so drunk with her friends that night and they made the stupid decision to drive themselves home." Lucía's eyes lowered to the floor.

I swallowed the lump in my throat, knowing where this was going.

"My parents got the call that Marie had been in an accident. We rushed to the hospital to see her, and she was in a coma for the time being. My parents weren't even mad at her for what she did. They just begged her to come back to us. I wish I hadn't been mad at her because I don't want her to remember me as the little sister who hates her."

"I'm sure she doesn't remember you that way." I gave her a sorrowful smile.

Lucía took a deep breath. "During the night, her monitor flatlined.

The doctors couldn't bring her back. We lost Marie and I never got to tell her I loved her."

"What was she like?" I asked, testing the waters. I had to ask about her because I had once gotten therapy from an angel named Marie—my second and last therapist.

"She was studying to be a licensed psychologist. She worked hard on her grades. Ma and Pa were very proud of her. People would question if we even were sisters because we looked so different. I got the looks of our mother, but Marie looked like our father." Lucía smiled a bit.

It made sense to me now. Lucía had Latin heritage, but she did not so much look like she did.

Lucía was a pale woman with plenty of freckles and auburn hair to match. I remembered Marie from that first session. Marie had the skin tone that had been exposed to the sun daily. Her hair was dark as were her eyes. The two looked nothing alike and yet, they were sisters all this time.

"I met her," I said in a quiet voice.

Her eyes lit up. "You met Marie?"

I nodded with a smile. "I did. I've been dealing with trauma and she was the second therapist I had. She was sweet. She's happy where she is. I can promise you that much."

Tears began to roll down her cheeks and she wiped them away with the back of her hands. "Thank you so much. Thank you."

"Is there anything else you wish to tell us? I'm enjoying getting to know you." I couldn't lie. It was amazing to know who she really was and what her family life was like. It made me smile when I could tell her that her dead sister was happy and helping others in Heaven. This was what I needed. Helping people was my forte.

Lucía sat with more cake in her hand. "Well, I could tell you what it was like to grow up in my shoes. So many kids would tell me I was adopted. They said there was no way that I could be a Álvarez when I was so white. My parents always reassured me that I was never adopted. I just happened to look like our ma, and she was white. When you get a white woman and a Mexican to make babies, those babies generally come out looking like one or the other.

"Kids made fun of me. It did get to me. I won't lie about that. It got to me because I started believing I was adopted and something was wrong with me. Marie showed them up. She punched a boy in the nose for calling me names. Don't mess with older sisters." Lucía pointed, replaying the memory in her head. "After Marie punched a kid, they never bothered me again. The teacher did give Marie lunch detention, but that kid got into big trouble, too, for bullying me the way he did. I don't think it was justified because she was just defending me, and she didn't deserve punishment for sticking up for her sister. Unfortunately, the school sees defense against bullying as a bad thing and yet they don't do anything to stop it until another student has to take matters into their own hands."

My eyes narrowed as I kept my focus on her stories. "What happened after Marie died? What was it like going back to school?"

She took a deep breath. "It wasn't too bad, but I won't say it was peachy. Nobody really said anything mean. Marie was loved and people gave their condolences. After a while, I got sick of people telling me to think happy thoughts. It was impossible to grieve when people were practically telling me not to grieve, as if grieving was a bad thing to do."

"I'm so sorry..." I couldn't say the same. Nobody spoke to me aside from Liam after Selene was killed.

She sniffled and wiped more tears. "I just hate it. I lost my sister and my best friend. It was impossible to think happy thoughts. That wasn't going to make it go away. It doesn't work like that. That is not how the grief process goes. Happy thoughts don't make me feel better. It was frustrating to hear those words over and over and over. I wanted to punch someone in the face. I was dealing with enough already."

"I can understand how annoying that can become after some time." I let out a little sigh.

"People would also tell me that going to school would distract me. It didn't. It just reminded me that she wasn't there. When I was doing something I loved, I could forget. I could learn to smile. But when I was at school where people had once made fun of me, and where I didn't have other friends, it was hard to be able to distract myself." She stuffed more cake in her mouth. I was ready to stuff some in mine, too.

"Everyone grieves differently and not all distractions work the same on people. I get that. People need to screw off with their stupid words. It doesn't make you feel better." I reached out, rubbing her hand.

She sighed after she swallowed her cake. "It doesn't. It just feels like more weight on my shoulders."

"Have you ever been in love?" I changed the subject to something happier. Reading her, I could conclude she was having a hard time revisiting her sister's death.

"Have I ever been in love?" Lucía let out a pitiful laugh. "Yes, but he never loved me back. His name was Derek. With my sister's death and unrequited love, I went into a downward spiral. I got so depressed. I barely finished high school. Being rejected is not a nice feeling." She shook her head.

I laughed. "Oh, trust me, I know what that feels like." My eyes landed on Ayden for a second before pulling away. His cheeks reddened as the guilt weighed on him for what he said that fateful night.

She placed her hands against her stomach. "I got on antidepressants at the time. They were the only thing helping me. I refused therapy.

I just... It was hard to believe in a therapist when my own sister was gone. She was gonna be a therapist. Seeing a therapist would just make it worse... Right?"

She didn't grieve the way she was supposed to. She ran from her problems.

"I met Liam. He made me feel special. I let him in, and I regret it so much. Here I am, stuck with his baby and I can't even take my pills to make it better." She gestured to her belly.

I looked at my lap, not sure of how to respond. This was normal. Pregnant women did love their babies but that didn't mean they never had bad moments. Today was one of her bad days. As valid as any other bad day even before pregnancy.

Ayden stood behind her, not sure how he was supposed to comfort her. "Is there anyone else who could possibly care about you?"

"No, why?" Lucía looked at him.

He shrugged. "Well, because if I were pregnant, I would appreciate a support system. You have Angel and I, but I also want to know if anyone else is around."

She bit her lip and looked in different directions in just a minute. "Well... There's this one guy at the cafe. He always looks happy when I come in. I hadn't gone there since before I met Liam. So, I went there last week. He didn't seem to mind that I was carrying another man's baby."

This was exactly what I wanted to hear.

"What is his name?" I asked.

"Thomas. But why does this matter? He's probably going to bail when things get hard. They always do. Liam bailed." She threw her arms up.

My husband chuckled. "Liam also killed a bunch of people. I don't think Thomas deserves to be compared to Liam like that. "

Her cheeks burned and she looked towards the ground. "Fine...

What do you want me to do?"

I grinned, forming a thought. "Why don't you take him on a date, or whatever it is people do now? Give him a chance and see where it goes. If he hurts you, you can let us know. I'm a guardian angel. It's *my* job to protect people."

Sacrifice

There was one set of seats facing the back of the room, away from the double doors. The seats were stark white with gold trim made of the purest metal even man could never get a hold of. The double doors were rustic brown, golden knobs to embellish them.

In the back of the room stood the bench where the judge sat and a seat off to the side. This was the same color as the seats to match the theme of the Heavenly Court.

The judge spoke, "Have we weighed in the options of both sides and what the result would be either way?"

I had never been inside a courtroom before I lost my life. I had no first-hand experience with how the system played out. I knew for sure everything in Heaven ran differently since the justice system here was on the side of good and we could not sin. On earth, the judges and lawyers were still humans who made mistakes. They sent innocent people to jail and let bad people get off too easily.

Alex walked from one side of the room to the other side. "If Ayden and Eliana keep their child, there are only two different outcomes. The first would conclude that Lucía Álvarez's child would be without a soul and a soulless human being is the last thing we need on earth.

The second would conclude that Lucía's child must die in order for these two to raise Connor."

From this alone, I would never have guessed she was on our side.

Ayden squeezed my hand and I had to avert my eyes. I could never fathom the idea that she had to lose her child for us to keep ours. It was not fair or just. Was Heaven not about justice? Could God not just create a new soul just like that for Lucía's baby so we could have ours?

He could. He could very well make it easy on everyone, but life was never about being easy. If this situation had been between Heaven and Hell, God would always pick our side. Hell was a place of punishment and hatred. Nothing good happened there so He was always on our side.

However, this wasn't between good and evil. This was between *us* and *them*.

Humans were involved and that was a whole other ballgame. Humans were God's creation. They could be good or evil, and because there was the chance that they could make Heaven, God was on their side just as much as He was on ours. That was why we were in this court and fighting for our child. He couldn't make it easier on us because humans did not get to have the easy route. They had to go through the hardships and choices just as we had when we were once alive.

The judge glanced at her paper as Alex's words appeared in writing. The way of notetaking above the clouds.

She asked Alex, "What are some of the reasons these two should keep a human soul to raise?"

I kept my eyes fixed on the judge to watch her reactions to the reasoning. Alex could be very convincing, and the judge could be emotionless for all we knew.

"Eliana Dyer, previously known as Eliana Wilson, died on

December 25th, 2019. She was murdered by a man named Liam Brown. Imagine being murdered by someone you trusted on the day humans celebrate Jesus' birth. Eliana had no family at the time and no friends. Her only friend had been killed while her other so-called-friend was deceiving her." Alex made gestures towards me as she spoke.

Judges didn't normally know about our previous lives. They had a duty to fulfill, and our pasts became relevant if it involved a case.

"September 16th, 2020, Eliana was assigned to Ayden Dyer to become his guardian angel. He was in a car crash at 11:34 on September 17th, 2020. She knew in advance that she was going to fall in love with Ayden when Matthew told her that was why God said Ayden would be her toughest job yet," she said.

I swallowed, feeling Ayden's grip loosen. It didn't make a difference but I'm sure he was shocked to hear that I knew I would always fall for him.

"God gave her Ayden for His reasons. On the night of February 6th, 2021, Eliana confessed that love to Ayden. He proceeded to reject her, and she ran off into the woods since she had never loved and been turned away. The fallen angels got to her. This led to days of endless torture on her and Ayden as Ayden was eventually caught for Lucifer's personal gain. He was pleased in watching these two suffer by watching the one they loved was beaten as each of them was helpless."

The judge had tried hard to keep herself composed and neutral, but I could see the glint of pain in her eyes. She sympathized with what we went through.

"Skip forward to May 20th, 2021, Eliana and Ayden decided to go to Liam's apartment and search for evidence of her murder. They wanted to get justice and stop him from further damaging more lives. Liam knew their plan and murdered Ayden, the man she loved bleeding out in front of her. She couldn't stop it. She had no idea where his soul would end up." She turned to face us, giving us a look that told us she would fight to give us the child we deserved.

The judge seemed to sympathize with us with the more information she knew. This was working in our favor. The pro of being in Heaven where everyone was good meant the judge gave a crap about you and your case even if she had to judge both decisions equally. She wasn't human anymore so she could never be heartless. If she had ever been human at all that was...

Alex continued, "Fast forward to the war, Ayden and Eliana fought hard. They chose to fight against the creatures of Hell to save humanity. They didn't have to do that because they are not Archangels, yet they did. Liam was behind it. The man who murdered them both had caused this war to happen, and during the battle with the demons, Eliana was taken back to Hell. She was tortured for a second time, far worse than the first time. She knew she was pregnant, and they threatened Connor. She had to be his mother and protect him.

"Everything she has done has been in Connor's best interest. She has gone through counseling to get better because she wants Connor to not feel the emotions she feels. She wants him to be happy because his soul is the permanent part of him. She has wanted kids for so long. This was taken when Liam killed her. She went through hell to do good for humanity and for Ayden as her duty of being a guardian angel. I can't make the decision, but I am here to help you understand why these two deserve the chance to have one child. Thank you for your time," Alex finished.

Court ended and we left the room, letting the judge process our side of the case. I followed Ayden back to our cabin, feeling guilty.

We had been attempting to find the soul of the baby who was inside the vile woman I saw last week. There had been no luck with that, and we couldn't present a third option until this fell through.

Ayden stopped and turned around, meeting my eyes. "You knew?"

I was about to ask him what he meant until I remembered what Alex had said. I gave a slow nod and chewed my lip. "I did. Matthew told me before I met you."

He was stuck on his words as he tried to come up with a coherent sentence.

"I never told you because I just forgot about it. Knowing didn't make a difference. I couldn't stop it. I couldn't change what was meant to happen. I fell in love with you and I don't regret it. But back then, I tried hard to stop it. I vowed to never reveal my identity because I was afraid it would bring us closer and make it worse. As you can see, that didn't matter. You can't help who you love." I put my hand against his cheek, rubbing my thumb along it.

He smiled a little as he closed his eyes and replayed his memories. "You told me that guardian angels were never supposed to tell us their past lives because it didn't matter anymore. I should've known that was a lie when people here kept calling you by your human name." He pressed his forehead against mine.

I sighed as I used my other hand to grab his shirt. "You are so cruel to just leave your wife hanging." I pushed my lips on his. Even after I pulled away, his touch lingered. "We should talk about the second result of what happens if we win."

"What are you referring to?" His eyebrows moved down, pointing towards the bridge of his nose.

"If we win, Lucía loses her baby. She has already lost too much. We cannot let that happen. What do you think she will do if she loses her child? She lost her sister. She's been on medication because of her inability to deal with her grief. We are terrible people if we do this to her. We can't take away the one good thing left in her life. We owe her that." I lowered my gaze.

"We have been trying to do everything we can to make sure she doesn't end up down that road. She will be okay. We are going to do this. We will make sure she has her happy ending, and we do, too." He used his index finger to lift my chin.

Words slipped my mind, and I couldn't respond. What could I say?

"We will get through this. We always do. We aren't quitters." He planted a soft kiss on my forehead. "Do you remember when we first met? You were determined. You wouldn't give up on me. You refused to fail, and I love that about you. You are strong-willed. You are a fighter. Patience and determination are a virtue you should keep. That is why I fell in love with you. If you fought this much to change me, you would fight this much for our child and our marriage," he whispered.

I knew my husband was right. I had to continue to fight and find a way to make this work. We had to do this for Connor and Lucía.

I worried about Lucía and her breaking point but I was going to make sure she didn't hit rock bottom. I would be her guardian angel until she was assigned another one for good. After these past few weeks and getting to know her, I knew without a doubt in my mind that she was the victim in her and Liam's relationship. He conned her into being with him. She never knew who he truly was.

She had been working hard to fix the mess he left behind and do better for this baby and even after this case was over, we wouldn't stop visiting her. I was going to visit her until the end of eternity. She needed the support and some friends to stick around and help her out. Ayden and I would be exactly what she wanted.

"We have less than three months to get this figured out. Is that enough time? Lucía needs this win. Can both sides of the court come out on top?" I wasn't sure if it was possible, but we were willing to make it.

Ayden rubbed the bump. He bent down to level his face with

Connor's. "Your mum and I promise to make sure everything goes well. No matter what happens, we promise to be there for you. We want you to know we will always be your parents."

This broke my heart, hearing him making a promise to our baby that could very well mean we'd lose this case. Lucía would have Connor and Ayden would have *nothing.*

SIN

Stars shined bright and the crickets chirped loudly. Tonight was just any typical night in nature, but for the beings that inhabited this planet, it was not. Every day was a new day, and we couldn't predict where our lives would end up.

I could never have imagined I would be an angel by the year 2022.

Lucía didn't think this year would have been the year she ended up pregnant. With winter now approaching, she was beginning to contemplate her choices throughout life, Liam being the biggest mistake she made.

Ayden and I had visited Lucía this morning to get to know her some more. She was one interesting human being. Today, she had replayed the events of what it had been like to meet Liam and date him. She had no idea what was happening during the time they were together.

They met in 2021, right around the holiday season.

With no family, she had nobody else to turn to. *He* was there. Liam was attractive and charming. That man could deceive any woman he wished. This was before the official war between good and evil on earth. This was when Ayden and I weren't even engaged yet.

They met in a shop, one that was small and local. It was an antique Christmas shop that Lucía visited every year to keep up her spirits and hope for a happier year ahead.

Liam happened to walk in at the time she was browsing the objects. It took one smile at her to put her under his spell. Lucía was hooked.

Liam began chatting up a small conversation about her, questioning simple things like where she grew up and her interests. Eventually, she gave him her number and left with a new tree topper.

He called her a day later and asked her out on a date, to which she accepted. She had been so excited to go on a date with a nice guy.

Friday rolled around and the two of them headed to a Christmas light show. I had never been to one myself, but she mentioned it was very beautiful. It made it feel a lot more like Christmas.

She said between the holiday cheer and winter festivities, it was a far more romantic date than a picnic in the spring. She wore her warm clothes, and it began to snow as they were leaving the place. She was wrapped around his finger as soon as he leaned down and kissed her. Kissing in the snow was the equivalent of kissing in the rain, if you were me anyway.

He took her home and they continued to go on more dates throughout the months. May rolled around and this was where things got dark.

Lucía and Liam had been having sex for a few months throughout their relationship. She had no clue that when he wasn't with her, he was with Lucifer, destroying the world. He was helping Hell go free and other cities were being attacked by demons, fallen angels, and shadows. He was fighting to get rid of Ayden and me.

She got pregnant about this time, but she had no idea that she was. Connor was still in the early stages of development so even I didn't know he existed.

As a month passed by, she realized she was late. She began to worry about why this was, and she bought a few tests to confirm her theory. She wasn't sure how to tell Liam yet.

This was the part of her story where Ayden and I told her that Liam planned for her to get pregnant. His condom probably had a hole in it. He did something on purpose, without her consent. He put his child inside of her.

She hid it from him for a few more weeks, trying to decide on what she would do. She was a young woman with no future. She wasn't sure if she was ready to have a child.

She came to the conclusion to tell him the truth because she wanted him to know. She had to hear if he was going to stay.

Spoiler: he didn't.

Lucía wasn't super fancy with the revealing news. She told him that she was pregnant, and she was going to keep the baby. He turned on her, his true colors beginning to show.

Liam no longer treated Lucía like a queen. He didn't offer to help. He didn't promise to stick around. He broke up with her and left.

Lucía was scared. She was angry. Depressed. She was questioning her decisions and wondering if she should abort at that point. She wanted to take her meds, but she couldn't.

Following many sleepless nights and headaches, she decided to keep going with the pregnancy.

With Liam gone and nobody to support her, she struggled to push through. She did it for herself and for the new child that would rely on her to keep them both alive.

He ruined a part of her that she'd been working hard to repair since. She had trusted someone, and he screwed her over. As much as I wanted to see her with Thomas, I could understand why she was so skeptical to be with someone else. She had a hard time trusting people and a harder time learning to let them in.

Everyone had been deceived by him. I had. Selene had. Lucía had. Ayden was the one who had never trusted him, yet he still became his victim.

With Liam dead and being guarded by me, Lucía was not at any risk for being murdered. That was one less worry on our shoulders. Between finding and switching a soul with Connor's, we needed all the relief we could get. Knowing Liam was unable to hurt anyone else, we were breathing clean air.

Ayden walked into the room and neither of us said anything. What could we say to make everything okay? Lucía may not have been killed but she had been deeply wounded by Liam's touch.

My eyes glanced at the clock as I watched the hand spin around. What was there to do on a night like this? I was out of imagination.

It had been a while since we had seen Ayden's family and I wanted to see them again so we could really connect. They had been the only people who loved me for who I was and took me in as their own, aside from Selene.

I could never forget how Esme knew what I was before I had a chance to tell her. It was a bit hard to hide from someone after I'd been tortured to the point I couldn't put clothes on well.

The pain haunted me much like a ghost amongst the shore on a foggy winter night. Slow to appear, moaning in echoes that one could not quite shut out. Always coming back for more.

I always wondered how Esme and Arabella were doing. They had been like sisters, and I loved getting to know about Ayden's stupid moments when he was a kid. I heard about the time he left the neighborhood with a friend and he took a dump under a bridge. Kids were the craziest of all.

Ayden brought me back to reality as he got on his knees and rested his hands on my thighs. "Are you all right?"

I smiled a little and gave him a nod to reassure him. The silence had been something I relished. A soothing piano melody. My mental stability was becoming more prominent these days.

"Would you want to go baby shopping?" he asked.

"Is that a good idea? We aren't sure if we are winning the case," I whispered. I wasn't even sure if I wanted to go into public. I was enjoying the tranquility, and clearly far more than he was.

"We've almost finished his room. I think it would be nice to get baby booties." He chuckled at the word *booties*.

I bit my lip, picturing baby-sized shoes. "It would be cute."

"Then we shall." He pulled me up and we changed into regular clothes to hide.

We walked to the store which was not an issue since the cold temperatures couldn't nip at our skin.

Ayden searched the aisles with stuffed animals, but I was too busy looking at the baby shoes. I began to cry, holding them close to my heart. They were just so small and so adorable. I still couldn't fathom that I was pregnant in the first place.

The shoes were blue and white in color, and they looked like mini converse. Looking at baby things brought out the mom inside of me and I was beginning to see why we opened this case. I was still determined to be a mother. I desired more than ever to hold my baby.

I mentally promised Connor that I was going to be his mother and nobody else would be. As much as I loved Lucía, I loved Connor more and I had to have him in my arms. Ayden was right when he said that she had a chance to have another child, and with someone she truly wanted to be with. This was it for Ayden and me. This was our last option.

I grabbed a onesie from the shelf and held it up to my stomach. It was the smallest size they had for a newborn. I could picture it on Connor already.

It was no surprise that I had wondered what he would look like.

Which pair of eyes would he get? What would his hair look like? These were the things that kept me guessing. He could be a mixture of us both or look like Ayden. I would be happy either way. I only wished he was a mini-Ayden.

Connor Dyer. It had a nice ring to it. The feeling was surreal as we would become the Dyers. I had never thought of it that way. It sounded like a cheesy American family, despite Dyer being an English name.

A white picket fence with a home behind it. In front of the fence stood a husband, his wife, and their son. Maybe there was a dog named Dog.

We didn't have the white picket fence or the pet, but we had a cabin and our son. It wasn't the American dream, but it was *ours*. This was what mattered most to us.

The more I thought about it, I realized I hadn't picked a godmother. I knew without a doubt who was going to be my pick. Would she accept? Of course. She was the one person who cared about me when nobody else gave a damn.

This led me to think about a godfather, but we didn't know any males who would fit the bill. Ayden had no male friends. He needed male friends.

I frowned at the fact that Ayden had no guy friend to relate with. If we were going to be parents, he would need a guy to watch the game or play poker night with. I had found him a friend once but that didn't work out so well. He dated the guy's sister and then dumped her, so it was no question. Mason pretended he was fine, but I knew he didn't really like Ayden that much.

I jumped when two hands wrapped around my stomach. "You scared me."

He kissed my ear. "I'm sorry. Did you find anything you like?"

"I've found a few things. Have you found anything for Connor with stuffed animals? Does he need more?" I laughed to myself.

He faked a gasp. "You can never have too many stuffed animals."

I put the onesie back on the shelf, folding it up beforehand. "Whatever you say."

He whispered, "What were you thinking about? Me, perhaps?"

"Us. Connor. I was picturing our future and what we were going to do with him. What about friends? An education? Would we raise him like a human or an angel? These are important questions. We *are* having a baby." I turned around in his arms, peering into his emerald eyes. "It's no longer just about us."

The sun rose high in the sky today, shining on a green forest floor as if winter wasn't coming. I knew better. The weather was unpredictable and could change at any given moment.

"I think I may have a solution," Selene said from behind me.

"What would that be?" I didn't turn to face her as she spoke to me.

She started, "What if you meet your parents?"

My head snapped back so fast to look at her. "Excuse me?"

She put her hands up in defense while Ayden stood a few feet away, not saying a word. "Hear me out. I know that you don't have a good relationship with your family. That is to be expected and they don't know you're an angel. Don't you ever wonder what happened after you died?"

"No. I know what happened. They didn't care because if they really cared about me, they would've been there before they lost me. They took me for granted and assumed I would always be around. I wasn't. My life ended just like that." I chewed on my lip, trying to remember my parents crying over my dead body. It'd been fake. I *knew* so.

"What if you're wrong?" Ayden asked. Wonderful—now he was on her side.

I pressed my lips together before I spoke, "Why do you think I am? I know my parents. You guys never met them. Do you think I would lie about who they were? They were workaholics. Their careers came before me. I was alone all the time. I never had friends or siblings. I didn't even have parents to confide in. How the hell would they help us with our case?"

She wasn't giving up so easily. "Because it would look good to the Heavenly Court if you reunited with your family. You would put your child first. You are giving them grandparents and trying to do the right thing. Think about it, Elli. If you told your parents you were pregnant and they were excited, it would be mean for the court to take away Connor from everyone expecting him, and they couldn't do it without feeling guilty since you made up with your parents for Connor."

I wrapped my arms around my stomach. "You don't get it, do you? It doesn't matter to my parents. They never cared about me. They weren't there when I was alive. Why would they be when I'm dead?"

"Were you there when I died? Of course. I was watching you." She let out a sigh. "I was watching you and my parents. I know that you had good intentions when you wanted to investigate my murder. I wanted to tell you it was Liam, but I couldn't. I wasn't allowed. I was just an angel. I was not able to show myself to humans at the time. I was fresh out of the grave."

"So what." I shrugged while looking at the floor.

"So, I know you. When Liam took your life, I was so angry with myself. I know that you probably don't know this, and I kept it from you because I was scared. I was so mad and then I thought about your parents. My parents knew about me. They knew. But did yours know? Would they care? I went on a search to find them," she said.

I sat down in the chair beside the couch. "And let me guess, you couldn't?"

She sat on the floor in front of me. "I searched everywhere. I wanted to see how they were doing, just like you had done with my parents. By the time I arrived at their hotel, they were gone. It was like a wild goose chase. I finally caught up with them months later. They were at your home. Not our dorm, but *your* home, where you grew up. The guilt was overbearing. I could feel it radiating off them. They believed it was their fault."

"Good. It was. They never loved me, and I had to die knowing I had nobody on earth to give a shit about me at my funeral. Did I even get a funeral? Did I get a memorial? Hardly." I put my hand against my mouth, trying to silence the sobs that wanted to escape my throat.

Walking through the hall, I glanced at the picture on the wall. Nobody knew my name. They never remembered me, and they still pretended they were my best friend. They had no right to mourn over a stranger.

There were lots of flowers surrounding my image. My picture was next to Selene's, who also had an abundance of flowers near hers.

People continued to pass by me as if I wasn't there. I wasn't. I was dead. They had no idea I was right next to them. Everything I had ever wanted was ripped away from me. Love and the future. I couldn't do the things I wanted in life. I was no longer living.

I left the building and walked down to a chapel nearby. I went inside, grinding my teeth together as people spoke by the altar. How dare they speak as if they knew me?

My parents were in the front row, pretending to love the daughter they lost. Their cries echoed throughout the room.

It was fake. I knew it was.

I made my way to the front, peering into my own casket. They dressed me up as if my body mattered. I was dead. Why did it matter? It was a waste of money to spend on dressing me up when I didn't have a heartbeat.

I wanted to scream at them. These people didn't care. They didn't know me. They never cared about me in my life. It was painful to listen to them lie through their teeth, in a church of all places.

My father held my mom in his lap as her body shook. My mother took her chance to go up to the stand and she was already a mess. It wasn't because she was grieving for me. It was because she was lying.

"Eliana was always fine being by herself. We thought that was what she wanted. We would go to our jobs in other places and leave her home for weeks. It became routine. We never thought we would see the day when—" She took a moment to herself as she sniffled through the tears. "We lost our daughter. We deeply regret all the time we didn't spend with her. Please do not make the same mistake we did."

I rushed up to the altar, yelling, "You didn't care! I wanted a family! I just wanted to wake up on Christmas morning like all of the other children while you told me that I was a good girl and that Santa brought me presents!" She couldn't hear me. She didn't know what I wanted. She had no idea that I was here, and I saw through this façade.

The tears were streaming down my face at this point. This was the end of my life. I had to begin anew and forget about the life I'd once lived on earth.

"She wasn't there when she needed to be. She deserves to feel guilty for what she put me through," I whispered, wiping away a tear.

Ayden stood on the side of the chair, leaning down to plant a kiss on my head. "I had no idea you went to your funeral."

"It was made up of lies. It was the worst part of being dead. My parents could tell lies and I couldn't stop them. I just wanted them to spend time with me." I took a deep breath, suppressing my tears.

Selene grabbed my hands, holding them inside hers. "Elli, I know that you've been hurt. I was there for you and I wanted to make your life better when I became your friend. Okay, so that may have sounded a little conceited. I just mean that I wanted to give you someone who would care about you. I have always loved you. I just want you to think about this. Connor is your priority now. Everything you do should be for him. I want to see you win this case and I never would have suggested this if I was not putting Connor first. I am not here to hurt you this time around."

I closed my eyes, picturing the life my parents could have now. I hadn't seen them since the funeral. I had no interest in that. "How can I do this? This isn't a simple as ripping a band aid off." No, it'd been much more like getting fresh stitches only to do something so stupid that they'd rip open and you couldn't mend the wound the same way.

"Yes, it is. But Ayden and I will have your back. We support you every step of the way." She squeezed my hands.

Ayden said, "You were there for me and you helped me reunite with my family. Let me do the same for you. I want to be your husband and help you. I know things have been tough lately. You've been through a lot. Life is throwing lemons at us. We must return the favor. We will make sure Connor is our son."

"We're throwing lemons back by doing things we don't want to do just to keep our baby?" I asked him.

He nodded and smiled at me. "Yes. I'm willing to do whatever you are doing if it helps us win this case."

"Okay. Okay... I'll agree to go see my parents." I wasn't sure if I believed my own words but there was no turning back. I was nervous—unsure about this. I didn't want to see them after so long. Did I have much of a choice? It had almost been three years since my death. That was how long it's been since I'd seen the people who raised me.

I imagined where they could be now, at this moment. They were probably in the Bahamas. Maybe they had a new baby or maybe they knew they were free from being parents.

"Elli?" I knew whose voice it was.

I looked at Selene.

"Are you ready for this?"

"As ready as I'll ever be. You're right. I must do this for Connor. If it'll help us keep him, I must put my feelings aside. I made Ayden reconnect with his family. It's my turn to reconnect with mine. I'm not saying it's going to go well. I just want this to be for Connor and if it works out for me, that's a bonus." I put my hands on my stomach, feeling him kick. It was wonderful to know I got to experience this at least once.

My husband placed a small kiss on my cheek and rubbed my belly. "We got this. I know we do."

I looked at the window, watching the sun attempt to burn the earth. It was too far away to do so, and it wasn't hot enough but that never stopped the giant star from trying. Brown leaves rotted into the damp earth, everything freshly watered due to the rain from the night before.

Barren trees stood loud and proud as their leaves had left them long ago. The only trees that were still full were the pine trees that were made to last year-round. They were the perfect trees for the winter. The snow would fall and coat their needles, fitting into the theme of a winter wonderland. It all tied into the Christmas season, the only season I truly despised for multiple reasons.

If we won, I would make sure to reinvent Christmas for us. We would start new traditions and be with our families as we raised Connor with love. All I had ever wished for was a family on Christmas so I could experience the joy everyone else had. I was going to get that chance even if it meant I had to see the very people who never even gave me the time of day when I was supposed to be their daughter.

Fret

I'd been the only person in the waiting room. I had no need to wait, since I'd been one of the few angels who needed therapy. Yet, I was afraid to go in.

"You got this. It's okay," Sunny said. "It's good for you. Remember that."

"I was supposed to be done with therapy and now I'm back again. It's a never-ending loop." I shook my head.

She laid her head against my shoulder. "It feels that way. I promise. But the best way to get through this? Spill everything. Get it all out now. If she knows everything, you'll never have to worry about something else resurfacing and hurting you."

Inhaling, I nodded. Then I exhaled. "I got this."

I left Sunny alone in the waiting room as I entered Marie's space again. It felt too familiar. It both comforted and saddened me. Marie seemed happy to see me, but it wasn't in the sense that she liked having the company. She just liked to listen to someone talk.

And boy, did I have so much to say...

"Welcome back, Eliana." Not something I wanted to hear from my therapist.

I sat on the couch, leaning back. "Start wherever I want. I got it. You're here for me. I know that, too." I knew all the things she would tell me.

Yet, when the words started to spill out, the rest came with so much ease.

Selene and Ayden had suggested I reunite with my parents, but that wasn't something I wanted. I agreed, but I was trying out this therapy first to convince them I didn't need my parents. I never needed them. I raised myself just fine.

How could they suggest such a thing?

My parents had never once been there. They were present for the birth, but they never came to any school programs. I was in choir as a kid, then I made it to the spelling bee. They never came to anything. Even in second grade when I had a parent picnic at school, I had to sit with a girl and her parents because mine never showed.

It sounded more depressing when I continued to talk about it.

And then they had the audacity to pretend they cared at my funeral. It was so insulting.

"I don't want to see them, but everyone keeps saying I should reunite." I shook my head. That wasn't why I was also here, though.

So I continued. I told Marie about all the things I could. The lonely lunches at school. The senior prom I never had a date to. Deep down, it bugged me. It made me feel like I had never been good enough because nobody wanted to do anything with me.

But then Selene stepped into my life. She came into my life and made me feel loved. She accepted me for who I was, and I had never met someone so kind before. Kids were cruel, but that was an understatement. It wasn't until college that I realized just how vile kids could be. They didn't want to befriend the weird girl.

Selene did. She took me under her wing because in the adult world, reputations were not as heavy anymore.

Then Liam came into our world. She began dating Liam, and he seemed so sweet—so *perfect.* I'd been a tiny bit jealous, but it was never enough to hate him. No. And after she died, he took advantage of me with my grief. He acted like the innocent best friend. And... I liked that.

Maybe a little too much...

"Do you think it's possible I could have fallen for Liam?" It wasn't the question I wanted to ask, and I was afraid of her answer. But it didn't change the importance of this topic.

Marie seemed to be wary of saying anything, but that didn't stop her from responding. "I think if you find this missing piece of yours, you'll find out the truth. I can't say yes or no, and that's because I don't know you or Liam. But whatever it is, I think it's important for you to remember. Maybe it'll finally be the key to severing the grip he has on you for good."

I could make guesses all night, but none of them felt more right than that last. I wouldn't know until I was whole.

I told her about how it felt to be a guardian angel for so long, just to have my hard work go to waste. Liam came in and released the creatures, then these innocent souls got ripped from their bodies in the process. Every corner I turned was a new battle to fight.

I told her about how conflicting my emotions had been lately. One minute I was happy to be pregnant, but the next I didn't want kids. It never made much sense to me, but I kept ignoring it. Marie suggested that I not ignore them, and eventually they would sort themselves out.

Every single nook and cranny had been exposed. I pushed it all out there this time.

Marie glanced at the plant to her right for a moment before looking at me again. "You've dealt with a lot, and that's normal. Humans go through so much, even as children. It's a lot to bear. However, your life was cut short. You were murdered, Eliana, and you feel as if you never got to fully accept your death. Even now, you can't accept it. I apologize if this comes off as rude, but your court case proves that. You can't accept the reality that this is your life now." She leaned forward. "I want to suggest something that might seem crazy at first, but it could help you make sense of everything. You should try to get as close to your human life as you can. Dress like you used to. Act like you used to. Talk to the same people if you can. Visit those old places. Connect to that life until you can come to terms with being here."

Her words made sense, and I knew I never would have come up with it myself. So I was going to take her advice.

As I walked to the door, I paused. "Lucía is doing okay."

Silence hung in the air, and I reached for the knob, ready to tug the door open. "You've talked to her?" Marie's tone changed. It wasn't calm and comforting. Now it sounded melancholic with a hint of hope.

"She's having my baby, Marie." I looked over my shoulder. "Ayden and I are making sure she's taken care of. I just thought you deserved to know." I pulled the door open and stepped out. Before I could close it, I heard a sob.

Maybe I was a terrible person for dragging her into this. She didn't deserve to know that my Liam—the villain—was the same one who got her sister pregnant. But now she knew. It all came full circle.

Sunny asked me how it went, and I simply told her I needed to do something. She tagged along, but I went to Esme for help. She was the only female in my life who had a beating heart at the moment.

"You want me to let you borrow my clothes?" she asked.

I nodded.

She gave Sunny a look. "I mean, just one outfit, right?"

"That's all I need."

"All right. I suppose you are my sister now." Her smile brightened the room. "I have another sister. That's awesome. Ayden is surrounded by so many women, and that's what he gets for being straight," she joked.

Esme led me to her room and searched her closet. "I have this black skirt." She gave it to me. "And a plaid red and black long sleeve. Oh! This gray cardigan, too." She gave it to me.

I looked at the outfit. It would fit the bill. "And heels?"

Esme smirked as she took me further into her closet. One side was filled with just heels alone. Damn. She stocked well. "I might have an obsession with shoes."

I'd never really taken much time to get to know Esme, but I wanted to. She considered me her sister. I never really had one before Selene, and the more I had, the merrier I would be.

I picked out some red heels. "Thank you." I went into her bathroom and changed into the outfit, tucking the shirt into the black skirt. I grabbed a hair tie and flipped my head downward, gathering all my blonde hair. I whipped my head back up, twisting and wrapping it up into a ball.

Before using her makeup, I asked her if it was okay. She didn't mind. I used some to create winged liner and enhance my lashes. I applied that bold red lipstick to bring it together.

Something was still missing.

"I need glasses. I wore glasses." Ah, yes, the curse of terrible eyesight.

Sunny squeaked. "Let me find some!" She ran out of the house and left me with Esme. I left the bathroom.

Esme scanned my outfit. "This is what you looked like?"

"Minus the glasses. I was...a big nerd. Introvert. Quiet girl. Book lover. Crime enthusiast. I was...this." I fixed the cardigan.

"Your style is so cute." She sent me a soft smile. "I think Ayden would have loved you had you met back then."

Her words somehow stung yet brought me peace. I missed that life, but Marie told me to get as close as I could. I wanted to do that. As conceited as it sounded, I had loved who I was even if everyone else didn't. It hurt because people didn't like that version of me, but I never wanted to change for them. So, I never did.

She grabbed my hand and pulled me to the living room. "While she's looking, we can get you back into that vibe. Crime enthusiast you say?"

We sat on the couch while she found a crime show for us to watch. One of the shows looked interesting to watch, based on true stories of cold cases that finally got solved later. It was so sad to think about all these innocent people who had their loves taken so early.

Ironically, it turned out to be me.

She reached over and squeezed my fingers. "Should we stop?"

What?

As I looked at her, the air against my cheek warmed. I'd been crying.

"It's okay. We don't have to watch this show. I know it's hard."

Hard. Was that the word I was looking for? No. Anxious was closer to it. Here I was, sitting on a couch and watching stories very similar to my own death. And yet I had my killer hiding under the floorboards at our cabin.

But didn't Marie tell me to talk to the people I used to?

Liam was part of that. I needed his help to find who I was.

"No, it's okay. Keep watching. I must face the reality that I'm no longer alive. The truth is painful, Esme, but it's still the truth. The sooner I believe it, the better off I'll be." I squeezed her hand and faced the TV.

"I found them!" Sunny yelled as she came running in. "Well, I found *a* pair." She laughed as she plopped down beside me. "Look at me."

I did as she said, and she pushed a loose strand of hair from my eyes and slipped the glasses on. I blinked a few times, but my vision didn't change. My eyes couldn't be affected by prescription lenses anymore.

"Let me see," Esme said.

I faced her. "So, how do I look?"

Sunny tilted her head into my view. "Doesn't she look great?"

Esme laughed. "I think she always looks great. But I will admit I see you differently now, knowing the real Eliana." She gestured to my outfit. What did that mean?

Sunny nodded in response. "Seeing a literal angel who looks like a model? Makes sense as to why Ayden couldn't get rid of you even if he tried. But this? This is the real girl behind that feathery curtain. And I think that this real girl is going to make Ayden go crazier than he already has."

This had never been for Ayden, but rather more for me. However, it would have given me security if he got to know the real me. If he fell in love with me all over again—just maybe, we could be saved.

IMPOTENT

The second I stepped through the front door, my anxiety rose. What would Ayden think? It was for my own mental health, but I wanted him to look at me and still feel the attraction. I didn't want to learn that my husband had no desire for me when I dressed like this. Unfortunately, nobody else had, so why could I expect him to?

"Ayden?" I called out.

He came out of the bedroom, wiping his hands and looking at the floor. "I'm making little progress with the nursery."

I cleared my throat. "That's great. I mean, any progress at all is great." *Yes, butter him up.*

He chuckled and lifted his head. His eyes went down my body, and for some reason it made me blush. Even years after, he could make me weak. "How was therapy?" He didn't even hide the lingering look on my legs.

"My therapist suggested I actually get as close to my previous life as possible." I swallowed the anxiety. "I can't accept that I'm dead and this is supposed to help me."

He came closer, grabbing my chin and lifting it towards him. "This is Angel before the angel."

Was he disappointed? Repulsed? *Bored?*

He pulled me against his chest and rubbed his thumb across my bottom lip. "I like it. It suits you more."

My heart almost thumped.

Before I could even ask him if he really meant that, and confirm that he wasn't turned off by my appearance, he leaned in. I prepared for a kiss, but Ayden tilted my head and planted them along my neck.

"I was...afraid that you wouldn't like it," I said as I exhaled.

His lips explored until they found mine. "Why wouldn't I like it?"

It was nearly impossible to concentrate on my thoughts. "Why wouldn't you like what?" Locking his lips with mine kept us both from responding.

Ayden began unbuttoning my shirt, pushing the sleeves down my shoulders. Had I known this would be his reaction, I would have gone back to my roots so much sooner.

He reached under my skirt and pulled my underwear down and went straight to undoing his belt. He forced his pants down without wasting any time. He grabbed my thighs and lifted me, pulling them around his waist. I leaned my head against the wall.

Then the front door swung open, and Sunny walked in, looking at us. "Oh my, no." She covered her eyes. "Um, I'll leave you." She ran back out the door, but the mood had been ruined. The damage was done.

Ayden rested his forehead against mine as he lowered my legs. "Well, that wasn't so much fun," he grumbled. I pulled my sleeves back up, but Ayden pushed them down anyway. "Keep it like this."

"The mood is ruined. What's the point?"

Instead of answering me, he traced his finger down the center of my chest, reaching a button. He unbuttoned it the rest of the way, pushing my sleeves down some more.

"Ayden, look at me." I cleared my throat and grabbed his hand. "I want to know why you like this."

He looked into my eyes. "Where do I begin?" He slipped a hand under the shirt, slipping it around to my back. "It's dark. Sexy. It screams to me that you're a smart woman and you know your worth. You won't settle for less." He pulled me back against his chest, using his free hand to remove my hair tie. My hair fell everywhere, and Ayden pushed it away from my face. "Do you know how easy it is to seduce you when you're wearing a button-down with a little skirt?"

"That's it? That's what's on your mind?"

"You asked for my reasons," he murmured, backing us up until I fell onto the couch. "Do you not like them?" He leaned down, rubbing the small piece of fabric connecting the cups of my bra.

He ran his hand up my back, undoing the clasp. Using the same index finger on the middle, he hooked it, tugging. It didn't move far with the sleeves in the way of the straps.

"It's not so much that I don't like the reasons." I released a sigh. "I just didn't... I was afraid. I was afraid you wouldn't like me this way because nobody else did. It's one thing to appear to you in a flowy white dress with white wings, but to appear to you as...this? This is the real me. This is Eliana in her purest form."

Ayden gazed at me with a frown. "Did you really think I wouldn't love the real you? Angel, you make me go crazy. And I'm not just saying that. Yes, you showed up looking like this stunning model with your perfect body, but that wasn't enough for me. I mean, it was, but... I didn't ask you to come back because of your body. I didn't kiss you because of your body.

"I kissed you because of how wonderful you are. You are like a mix between fire and ice, as cliche as that sounds," he said with a chuckle. "I asked you to come back because I wanted to experience more with you. You frustrate me at times but you're always so calm. You're so collected. I want that. You somehow fell in love with me, knowing all my sins. I want to learn to love like you love me."

"Are you saying you don't love me?"

"I'm saying that all of this," he paused, "is a test for me. Your therapy. Your dark side. I've always been the kind of guy who runs when things get hard. And things have been very hard, and I'm sorry. I'm doing everything to be supportive and help you get through this. I swear I'm trying."

Now that I had thought about it, I'd realized he wasn't used to this. He knew what it was like when it was happening to him, but then he'd chase it away with sex and alcohol. Now, he was using sex as his means to cope with my problems.

I wasn't sure how I was supposed to feel, nor did I know how I *actually* felt.

However, I knew how I wanted to handle the situation. "Ayden, something bad happened down there. When I went to Hell the second time...everything I'd ever been was completely ripped away, so when I came out of that dark place, I didn't know who I was. I've been struggling so much to find myself again."

He sat beside me, grabbing hold of my hand. "Tell me about it. I'm listening."

So I did.

When I died, I was no longer Eliana Wilson. I'd been floating away from my body, staring into those lifeless eyes. Blood covered almost every inch under my body, and I knew that I couldn't jump right back into it. Liam took his time to clean up the mess, and then...

"He...took my glasses." I furrowed my brows. "I watched him take my glasses."

Once I was dead and my soul couldn't return to my body, my feet hit the ground. I had stopped floating away. Liam cleaned up everything, and nobody ever suspected a thing. The police questioned him, but they never had enough evidence to convict him of anything. And eventually, the killing ended.

The case went *cold*.

I decided to try out for a guardian angel position. I passed the test, and I was already out on jobs, helping people. It made me feel whole. It filled the cracks in my heart for a long while, and I was happy that way. Liam couldn't hurt me anymore. He couldn't take that away.

But Ayden was assigned to me.

From there, I tried not to revisit my old life as he worked hard to pull it out of me. Because I was dead, he couldn't get rid of me, and I got the chance to fall in love with him.

Being tortured in Hell was a hiccup, but it never really strained my love for this. It pushed me to try harder, and I did. Then, Ayden called to me, and my world started to make so much more sense.

When he died and pulled me from the car, I knew I had finally found what I'd been looking for. A purpose.

Everything seemed to be okay for the most part, even when Liam started the war on earth.

However, I ended up in Hell a second time, and I had nobody there to say it would get better. I filled my own head with nightmares, lies, and empty promises. Something had completely snapped when he chopped off my wings.

I lost everything, including myself.

Maybe it sounded ludicrous that I had put that much into having wings, but the fun part about being murdered was being able to fly. Liam took that, too.

He stripped me of all my hard work, and the life I built here. When my wings were taken, I didn't recognize myself anymore. I didn't feel like I belonged anywhere, and that included being married to Ayden.

He pushed some hair behind my ear. "I'm sorry, Love. I had no idea."

"That's because nobody ever asks."

Peeling the floorboards up from the kitchen, I grabbed Liam by the collar and pulled him out. He looked at my outfit and tried to reach out and touch me, but I backed away. "It's been a long time..."

"No, that's not how this works. You killed me." But Liam's eyes weren't on my face, and when I lowered my eyes to follow his, I fixed the button that had popped open. Perks of big boobs. "Any idea where we should look? I've already checked all the places I used to go when I was alive."

Liam cleared his throat. "You don't like to be quiet, do you?"

"Excuse me?"

He started to moan loudly. "Oh, Ayden. Yes, Ayden."

My eyes went wide, and my cheeks burned from the memory of embarrassment. "That is our business!"

"Then don't have sex when I'm right below you!" He pointed to the floor, wrists cuffed together.

I fixed my skirt. "You should have tuned it out."

"Yeah, cause that's easy to do." He rolled his eyes. "Ayden is not that good, Eliana."

"And who are you to say that?" I crossed my arms.

Liam shrugged. "I saw everything. The little crack? Yeah, that gave me front row seats to the show. He can do better."

I reached out and slapped him, and it hurt only him. "You are disgusting."

He smirked a bit, showing me his handcuffs. "And you like it extra dirty. What does that make you?"

Ignoring his comments, I dragged him out of the cabin. Wherever we were going, I wasn't sure, but it had to be somewhere where he would learn to cooperate rather than make crude comments.

There was nothing wrong with me and Ayden, right? I mean, we were married. I was allowed to like sex as dirty as I wanted it. No, I wasn't going to allow Liam to get into my head like that. He was just trying to fill me up with false ideas so he could escape. I wasn't going to fall for it.

"What would you have done if Lucía had an abortion?" I asked.

Liam glanced at me. "Wouldn't matter to me. You still wouldn't get your child."

"And what if I had never even figured it out? She could have easily terminated before I knew, and the baby would disappear from my belly. No harm, no foul."

His laugh made me recoil. "I'm not stupid, Eliana. I purposely got with a woman who I knew wouldn't make the best decision for her baby."

"Are you saying her keeping him isn't the best decision for Connor?"

He stopped walking. "I'm saying there are many things Lucía won't tell you, and depression is only the *tip* of the iceberg."

Sure, that much was true. But I was not going to leave a woman to suffer from her own sorrowful thoughts. I was better than that, wasn't I? Or had I become the villain of this story, too?

"I'm sorry, Eliana."

"Sorry? For killing me? Killing Ayden? Killing Selene?"

With a shake of his head, Liam met my eyes. "I'm sorry that Sam did what he did. It's not your fault he was such a douchebag, and he got what he deserved. Just know that what you did to him was justified. Nobody truly blames you or pins you as a killer. And I'm sorry I didn't stop him sooner."

I'm sorry I didn't stop him sooner.

Was Liam taking blame for Sam's actions? Possibly. Maybe deep down, Liam wasn't all bad. It was tragic that it was too late for him to change now. If only he had turned his life around earlier...

Firstling

"Any luck?" I asked as I pushed the brush out of my face, returning to the clearing.

He shook his head. "None."

I faced him, blocking his path. "This is serious, Liam. I need to know what memory I lost. I need that piece." I also needed to find the bodies, but I wasn't going to ask for his help on that.

He lifted both eyebrows in amusement. "Yeah, I know this is serious. But I can't help it if I don't know what to look for specifically or where. I don't do this stuff."

I groaned as I kicked a tree, feeling a whole lot better about it. I sat on the ground and placed my hands against my stomach. "Why were you ever friends with Sam?"

Liam shrugged. "Because he was a good guy."

"Good guys don't corner women in the bathroom."

He did something I didn't expect. He sat beside me. "That's why I said he *was* a good guy. Believe it or not, when Sam and I went to a party one night, we got drunk. What else do guys our age do? There was one girl who wasn't very social, so she didn't have any friends there. She looked lost. Sam made a comment that she had been looking for him and she didn't know it. I thought nothing of it. I went to get more beer and find someone to hang out with outside by the pool, and Sam disappeared." He twisted his wrists in the cuffs, wincing at the cuts. "I found him in one of the bedrooms with that same girl, forcing her to blow him. It pissed me off, so I pulled her away from him and told her to leave. Sam and I got into a really bad fight that night, but we made up the next day."

"What a dick."

"He never apologized to her. He never made any effort to at least try to be a better guy. I guess I should have assumed that he would end up hurting you, too. He was too sick to see how force was the wrong way to do things."

I fixed my skirt, pulling the hem down and flattening it against my thighs. "If I'm being honest, what happened in the bathroom with Sam was more terrifying than being murdered by you. With you, it happened too fast. I barely had time to process anything and then it was over. With Sam, I had time to fear everything. He didn't see me as a person. He saw me as a worthless sex object. And I'm not sorry that I killed him." I looked at Liam. "It was either me or him, and I had to choose me."

He didn't respond to that. Maybe he didn't want to. It was hard to get a reading on him, but as far as I knew, he didn't support what Sam did. At least I hoped not. However, it was too late for him to change now. When this was over, he was going right back to Hell. He'd had plenty of chances to change.

I guess what they said about rock bottom was true. People had to hit it to turn around. Hell was Liam's rock bottom, but if you hit it after death, it became moot. The decision needed to have been made before the heart stopped.

If I had known about the girl at the party, I could have been there. I could have listened, or been a shoulder, or just a friend. Wherever she was now, I hoped she was okay. I couldn't imagine what she was feeling the moment Sam did that to her.

I stood and pulled Liam up. The walk back to the cabin was silent, and once I got him back under the floorboards, a hint of guilt ate at me. Was I supposed to feel shame for putting him under there? No, he killed me and my friends. I didn't have any reason to feel sorry for him.

"Elli, hey," Selene said from the living room. "I came to ask you something."

I looked back at her, the front door wide open. *Well, if you leave it open, everyone thinks they're welcome.* "Ask me what?"

"If you wanted to go see the ultrasound."

"What? I can do that?" I glanced at my stomach.

Sunny ran out of the bedroom. "I wanna go! Let me go!"

Selene rubbed her temple, flashing a fake smile. "You can if you're going to see it with Lucía."

"Oh, right." I should have guessed. Heaven didn't willingly want to show women ultrasounds of the baby they were giving to a human.

The three of us decided to go see the ultrasound with Lucía. I kept thinking back on Liam and how Selene might have reacted had she seen him. What would she have said to him?

Selene and I both turned invisible, but Sunny couldn't quite do that. So instead, she told the doctors she was Lucía's ex-girlfriend, Angel. Lucía recognized the name and let her come in but narrowed her eyes. "You're not Angel."

Sunny laughed nervously and stood beside the bed. "Nope, but she is here. You just can't see her. I don't get to turn invisible."

As true as that was...

A woman came in and lifted Lucía's shirt, put the jelly on her belly, and then moved the wand around until she got different angles of Connor.

He moved around, kind of like he was pushing himself off the walls of the womb and rolling. Lucía smiled and looked at Sunny. "Is Angel seeing this?"

Sunny nodded. "She can also hear you. You just can't hear or see her. I..." Her eyes roamed the walls and landed on me. "I can, because I'm kind of in between. It's complicated." Complicated indeed.

I started to cry, looking at Selene. I knew she'd be angry at me, so I looked away before she saw me. It didn't make much of a difference because Selene grabbed my shoulder and made me face her anyway. "Elli, what's wrong?"

I shook my head, trying to lose the thought as quickly as it came.

"Elli, tell me."

Sunny watched us but she tried to keep a poker face for Lucía.

My chest would have ached if I'd been alive. It was not something I wanted to admit, and yet I had to. "Do you ever feel like you're in something too deep that you can't turn around and take a different path?"

"What do you mean? Did you have other ideas?" Selene tilted her head out of sympathy.

I lifted my skirt, showing her my baby bump. "I'm supposed to be happy. I'm supposed to be overjoyed seeing this ultrasound and I'm not. What's wrong with me?"

Sunny slipped in a few words when Selene didn't know what to say. If only Lucía hadn't heard. "You don't want to keep him anymore, do you?"

Lucía's head moved back a bit as she furrowed her brows. "What? Wait, what?" She looked in my direction, unable to pinpoint me.

The woman looked at Sunny and Lucía, clearing her throat. "Did you want me to talk to another doctor? I can see what I can do, but you are far along."

Lucía's head jolted some more as she looked at the nurse. "What?

No, no. Can you give us a moment?"

She left the room.

Selene and I removed the veil. Lucía looked at me, moving back at the sight of my tears.

"I can't tell Ayden. None of you can tell him." I smoothed my skirt back over my bump. "I don't want to hurt him. He's excited to be a father. He's almost done with the nursery."

Selene sat me down in the chair beside the window. "How long have you known?"

I wiped my tears while shrugging. "I can't pinpoint an exact moment, but I've been questioning myself for a while now. I keep thinking about everything. I was so excited at first, and I care about Connor, but... I don't want to keep fighting and putting all my energy into this case. I'm okay if I don't get to keep him."

"Do you want kids?" Selene asked.

When I pondered that question, I released a sigh. "No. I don't want kids." I don't think I ever had, either.

It was too late to change my mind now.

Lucía pushed herself into and upright position. "Sometimes you just know." She smiled down at her stomach. "I know I want him. Whether I do this alone or not, I want to raise him. I was terrified at first, and I still am, but that's what makes it okay. Life is scary, right? I think. I just think about what it would be like to hold him in my arms."

Sunny sent a smile to Lucía. "You'll be a great mother."

Selene rubbed my back, but it didn't make me feel any better. I was taking this away from Ayden. What would he think of me if he knew?

Lucía went her way, and we went ours after the appointment. Selene offered to stay with me, but Sunny said she could handle it. So Selene left, and Sunny kept me company.

She laid her head against the back of the couch. "It's been quite the day."

I rubbed my chest. "Yes, quite."

She turned her head, frowning. "I'm sorry. I didn't mean it like that."

"Hey, no, it's fine. I'm fine." Was I?

Someone—Liam—banged against the floorboards in the kitchen.

"What was that?" Sunny asked as she lifted her head, twisting her body that direction.

"Nothing."

Thump.

"That was definitely something." Sunny stood, following the sound. "You can't convince me otherwise! And now you're making me suspicious. I watch a lot of movies and trust me when I say that I can spot a liar."

Thump-thump.

Sunny looked down at the floor between the island and the sink. "Oh my, you've got someone hiding under here." She ripped the floorboards up, gasping. "There's a man!" She knitted her brows together. "Who is he?"

"Name's Liam." He sat up, planting his elbows on the wood as he rolled and climbed out. "And I don't suppose your name is Ayden?" He chuckled. "Unless Eliana decided that she liked girls. It would make so much sense."

I scowled. "Shut your mouth if you know it's good for you." Shifting my eyes to Sunny, I gripped the back cushion. "Ignore him."

"Liam..." Her eyes narrowed into slits. "As in the one who killed you, Ayden, and Selene? What is he doing here?"

She remembered too much. It was both a blessing and a curse. "He's just hanging out."

Liam chuckled. "Eliana calls me her bitch."

Sunny burst out laughing. "Holy shit, you made him your pet?

That's golden!"

What was so funny about that? Liam was the killer and he deserved to be someone's toy. If anything, he would have ended up mine because he hurt me the most. Selene didn't love him that much.

Well, *I* didn't either. But he had still killed those I loved. Selene never lost anyone before she died. At least not to Liam. Same with Ayden.

Liam walked into the living room and dropped down. "I came to join the party. Word on the street is you had quite the day."

Sunny leaned over the back of the couch, elbowing Liam in the head and pretending not to notice. "She did. If the bitch must know, Eliana here doesn't want her baby anymore. She's decided she doesn't want kids."

A smirk rose on his face. "No? That makes this so much sweeter."

"Whose side are you on?" I gritted my teeth.

He put his hands up in surrender. "Nobody's. But I can't lie and say it doesn't get me a little happy that you're unhappy. Come on, we both know I don't like you."

"Or, or," Sunny interrupted, "maybe you do. And that's why you're so angry! Wait, no that doesn't make any sense."

However, I decided to take the route of higher power. "That's not what my missing piece says." I cleared my throat. "I happened to find it, which is partly why I realized I don't want kids. But I also remember what I forgot about you, Liam, and I remember every little detail."

Terror swiftly slithered into his eyes, swirling as he scooted away. I'd caught him in the act. This entire time he pretended to not know what I forgot, but he knew exactly which memory of mine had been ripped away. Somehow, I was going to get it out of him. Even if I had to do things I'd never done, I would figure out the truth.

Sloth

Passing by the bathroom, I stopped by the door as I heard someone singing. I opened the door, walking in and cocked both of my eyebrows at the sight before me.

"Shit, Angel, you weren't supposed to see this." Ayden pulled the curtain closed.

I couldn't contain the laughter that erupted from me. There were candles and bubbles, and Ayden wore a light green face mask. It was the best thing I'd ever witnessed.

His voice carried through the curtain, "This is not what it looks like."

"It looks like you're having a spa bath." I continued to laugh until the point of crying.

"Hey, sometimes a man needs it." He opened the curtain and his face mask was gone.

I leaned against the counter and crossed my arms. "What could you need it for?"

"You're pregnant. That is terrifying sometimes. Pregnant women are—" He stopped speaking as he saw my face.

"What? Pregnant women are what? Say it." I leaned closer.

“They’re great.” His laugh had been more anxiety than comfortable.

I rolled my eyes and shook my head. “Finish up your spa bath. We’re going to meet my parents.” It wasn’t ideal, but I had no option at this point. Ayden kept nagging and the therapy wasn’t doing any good. I had to fight for Connor so I could show my husband how much I loved him. Even if he was taking more spa baths that he made for me… I left the bathroom but smiled to myself, acknowledging that I married this man. He was *my* loser.

The trees rushed by us as Ayden flew us through the forest. Every second closer caused my head to go whack. It was worsening at the thought of seeing my parents after so long.

Our feet landed on the ground. I was frozen at the sight of my childhood home. It brought too many memories, and not even one was good.

His hand squeezed mine as we walked up to the door. He knocked to take off some of the stress. I couldn’t do it myself. Being here was terrifying enough.

The door opened and revealed a man—my father—who had aged greatly over the years. He saw me and his eyes lit up. “Eliana?”

Mom rushed to the door when she heard my father call out my name. She gasped as she covered her mouth and stumbled over her own feet. “Eliana…”

I didn’t say a word. I wasn’t sure what I could say.

They let us inside and I sat on the couch. I didn’t have to ask. I was pregnant, and these were my parents. “So, I see you’ve come back now." Dad looked at me.

"Come back? I was dead. How the hell was I supposed to just come back here before? You didn't exactly care about my existence." I scoffed. The insults were already beginning, as I expected.

"How can you say that?" Mom asked me as she sat down.

"Because it's true! You left me alone all the time. I needed my parents and you put work before me. You didn't realize what you had until I was gone. You took me for granted. I wasn't always going to be around. Death proved that. I was murdered too young, and it just goes to show why family should be so important. Life is short." I was trying hard to keep my temper. It was challenging when Connor was messing with my moods.

She shook her head as if I was wrong. "We love you so much, Eliana. You must know that," she argued.

How dare they? They couldn't even admit their mistakes. "I don't. You never showed it. Actions speak louder than words and your actions did not match your words." I gripped a pillow.

"Let me go make some snacks," Dad said as he headed for the kitchen.

The silence was beginning to suffocate me. I knew my mom was pissed, but it wasn't her right to be. She was the one who screwed up.

I focused my attention elsewhere for my own mental health. The smell of fresh paint hung in the air, and dust still covered the windowsills and new flooring. Most of the furniture still had tarps over it.

All the appliances were now stainless steel while the furniture looked brand new. My parents still worked as much as usual. Only workaholics with a dead daughter could afford to renovate.

Mom's eyes lingered on my stomach. I didn't have to explain to her how making babies worked. She knew. She knew I had sex and she could guess it was with the very man standing in the same room as us.

We were saved from having yet another talk about how we were angels. My parents were the ones who had taught me about God and angels and Lucifer. As much as my parents irked me, they were right about this. The supernatural world was a very real place.

"Eliana, please, look at me," Mom said.

I kept my eyes glued to the front door as if I were planning to make a run for it. "I don't want to."

"Please, I'm so sorry for the mother I was to you." She gave me those sad eyes, the ones I despised. She used those same eyes on me when she would ask me to let her go off to work in the Bahamas. Yeah, right. *Work.*

I shook my head. "Sorry doesn't fix it. It doesn't bring back my childhood. It doesn't erase the pain. It doesn't let me recreate a better memory of you. I remember watching Christmas movies by myself. Kids would be too excited to be able to sleep. They would wake up early for presents. I didn't even have parents to be there on Christmas. Do you understand the pain that I felt? No, you don't."

"We tried our best, Eliana." Her attempts to justify her bad parenting were piss-poor.

I bit on my tongue, thankful I couldn't feel the pain. "Your best? Your best would be spoiling me because you were afraid to let me down. You don't have to be Einstein to know that you should never put your job before your only child. You are so mistaken if you think this is your best work."

Dad came back with snacks. "All right, let's just take some deep breaths. Eliana came back; let's not scare her away so fast." He set the tray on the coffee table.

Ayden stuck his hand out for them to shake, but neither of them did. "I'm Ayden Dyer, your daughter's husband. It's nice to meet you."

I sighed, shaking my head. "I get it. I just have a lot of bottled emotions and now they're coming out."

"Why did you decide to come here?" Dad asked as he sat in his chair.

I gave Ayden a look, letting him know I wanted him to tell them. I was far too stressed to make another sound without losing my head.

"You can see that Angel is pregnant. We are here to hopefully make things right again because Connor needs it, and we need it. We've been fighting the Heavenly Court to keep our baby and it's been rough. If she fixes her relationship with you, it may lean the judge in our favor."

Mom's eyes narrowed. "And, why do you have to fight?"

"Because our baby is just the soul of a human child." I gritted my teeth, using the pillow as a punching bag.

"And what's wrong with God's plan? Why do you need a child?" She crossed her arms.

Ayden knew this wasn't a good direction for her questions.

"You don't know what the hell I've been through." I stood from the couch. "Don't you dare judge me. You have no right to judge my parenting skills when you were the shittiest parents ever. You couldn't even be there for me. A real parent fights for their child. They make their kids their priority. I've been through Hell twice. They scorched my soul; they burned me and cut me. I deserve this. I deserve one win for everything I've done for Heaven and humanity. I was murdered because I had to rush to leave home as soon as I was eighteen. I wanted to get away from you and I ended up being a victim of your mistake." I got in her face. My mother was the same height as me, and she sure as hell didn't scare me.

Dad got between us, trying to prevent a fight. "Eliana, Diana, please."

"You could never understand a mother's love for her child because you never had any for me. Don't you dare tell me what to do with my kid until you get your shit together." I stormed out of the house and Ayden followed behind. I didn't care where I was going but it sure as hell was anywhere but here.

He didn't say a word until I stopped and he ran into me. "Whoa, that was some nasty argument."

I turned to face him. "How could she? Who the hell does she think she is, telling me to not fight for my baby? She makes me want to rip my hair out."

He placed his hands on my cheeks, planting a sweet kiss against my head. "I know, Angel. I can see how angry she makes you. Your family problems go back farther than mine ever did." He chuckled.

Closing my fingers around his wrists, I shut my eyes. "I hate her. I truly hate the woman who birthed me. How could she not love me? What about her own grandchild? Am I that bad?" A whimper escaped my lips before turning into sobs.

He pulled me into his chest and stroked my hair. "No, no. You're not bad at all. You're a wonderful person and you deserve love just as much as others. You've always put others before yourself and I love that. You're just thinking about Connor and what he needs. Your mother has her own issues."

I cried into his chest, wrapping my arms around his torso and hugging him. Tightness raided my chest. It constricted me as if someone was trying to suffocate me. My head ached and that feeling only grew stronger. Warm tears flowed from my eyes to top it all off.

Ayden leaned down and wiped my cheeks dry. "I will always love and support you. You've taught me that I can be myself and enjoy what I love to do. I am so happy that I married you. We will be fighting for Connor until the end. I promise you that."

I nodded and pressed my lips against his. "Thank you," I whispered.

He brushed his knuckle across my cheek. "I will always be your husband first."

I put my head against his chest and coughed a bit. I had to regather myself after that fight. My mom managed to ruin everything once again. It seemed to be her specialty.

He wrapped his wings around us, keeping me safe. I didn't need it, but the gesture was always welcomed. If I had a heartbeat, it would be racing a million miles a minute. Ayden was able to keep me under control when I lost my temper. His love was enough for both of us.

Deep down, I was hurting. I had many unsolved issues from my broken mind. It was a long journey, but Ayden was here to guide me to a better place. He would be there the whole way and I needed his support to keep me sane. I couldn't do this alone and that was why I married him. I chose to do everything with him by my side.

I wasn't sure where we would go from here, knowing that my parents couldn't help us anymore. I refused to go back there after the way my mother talked to me. I didn't need to be judged. I did nothing wrong. I just wanted to have something good in my life. Who didn't want that? What kind of parent didn't want their child to have good things happen to them?

My parents were those parents. If they had witnessed me get murdered, they wouldn't have stopped Liam. I knew them. They did not love me the way they claimed to. I was never going to be enough to them, and that was something that broke my every being.

Why did others get to be loved but I didn't? What had I done to deserve this? Had I not done everything right from the start?

No, not according to God.

Hell may have tortured me endlessly, but my parents had refused to love me since I was conceived. No feeling could ever top that kind of pain.

Reds, grays, black, and white colored the room. The bed was perfectly made from the day I left it. Two pillows wrapped in red pillowcases sat at the headboard with a gray decorative pillow in front, and the comforter was a lighter shade of gray to combat the darker shade of the pillow.

White walls complemented the washed-out charcoal hardwood floor. All the furniture came in black with a big TV hanging on the wall, facing the bed.

This room hadn't been touched in over five years now. It'd been just as I left it.

"This is where Eliana Wilson grew up," Dad said from behind me.

I swallowed, not willing to face him quite yet. "Before she left for college and got killed."

"And that didn't stop you." He chuckled, stepping inside. He circled around the front side of me, meeting my eyes. "Look at you. You're dead and you've been through more than when you were alive. That is the woman we raised."

I rubbed my stomach. "I raised myself, Dad. You weren't there. I know it seems crazy that a child like me could end up as good as I did but that's just... That's how it works. Sometimes we do a better job than our parents."

He didn't say anything else on that note.

I heard a knock, knowing who it was. "What do you want? Are you here to tell me to let Connor go so I can lose my only chance at having a child?" I looked back at my mom.

Her eyes darted away from me. "No. I'm sorry, Eliana. I didn't mean it. I had no place to tell you what to do."

Shaking my head, I dropped onto the black leather ottoman in front of my bed. "You did mean it. It didn't just slip out. You meant it, Mom. You meant it just as I meant what I said. Let's not lie to each other."

Mom pressed her lips together. "Fine. I meant it. I meant what I said and I'm sorry that I was rude. It was uncalled for, and I should have appreciated the fact that you were giving us another chance to be in your life again. We were terrible parents."

I wasn't sure how to respond to that. I didn't want to make this harder than it was, though. I knew it was time to patch things up. They screwed up and that was certain, but I had no energy to hold grudges.

She closed the gap between us, kneeling in front of me. "I want you to come by more often. I want to make up for lost time. We abused our time with you, and we regret it. Please let us try and fix our mistakes."

I nodded slightly. "Only if you can accept mine."

"What do you mean?" Mom looked at Dad, but I didn't respond. Instead, I led them downstairs. Ayden gave me a look, asking how it went. I didn't exactly respond.

I took a seat on the couch, pushing my hair behind my ear. "There's something I did in my past life that I'm afraid is going to ruin our chance of keeping Connor. Liam knows what I did, and it's bad..."

Ayden sat back, spreading his arms over the couch. "You've never told me about anything bad. What did you do?"

"His name was Sam." I swallowed the fear in my throat. "I killed him."

Mom gasped and looked at my dad. Ayden wasn't sure how to respond.

I spilled all the details of what I did that night. Sam came into the bathroom and tried to kiss me, but things took a wrong turn. Before I could really process it, he had cracked his head on the toilet and his blood would forever stain those bathroom tiles.

"I felt bad, but I knew I would never tell a single soul what I'd done. It wasn't on purpose. I just wanted to get him off me. I had to..." I took a deep breath to calm my nerves.

My husband hurried to my side, pulling me into his chest. "You did it to defend yourself. You are not a bad person. God knows everything we do, and He still let you into Heaven. He knows that what you did was an accident and out of self-defense."

"It's not what he did to me that angers me. He didn't do anything. He couldn't. What gets me is the fact that I killed him..." I turned to face Ayden.

Mom said, "Your husband is right. God knows. It can't affect the court decision because it was part of your past life and that was wiped clean when you died. If you got into Heaven, it's nothing to be ashamed about."

Dad leaned down to my level. "You did great. You defended yourself and put that prick in his place. You taught him not to assume a woman like you is defenseless. He had it coming with his intentions."

I wrapped my fingers around my wrist, rubbing my thumb against it. "That's what gets to me every now and then. I had to tell you guys before someone else did. I didn't want you to find out that dark secret."

Ayden whispered in my ear, "It's not dark. You had to protect yourself. You were just being human." He kissed my temple.

I still worried about that being thrown in my face. Would this take Connor away? Would they find me unfit to parent?

As if reading my mind, Mom said, "They would be terrible if they took your child over this. You were protecting yourself and this proves you are capable of protecting those you love. I don't know what you've been through, but Heaven is lucky to have you. It sounds like you've protected so many lives and that is what God truly sees. He sees how you put yourself last to protect those around you. He may see that you killed Sam, but He knows exactly why. In the Bible, He still sent His people to kill in defense. It is always okay to fight back if someone is attacking you." She wrapped her arms around my neck.

I was surprised by the gesture, but I returned the hug. My emotions poured onto my mom's shirt. It had been too long since I'd had my parents like this. I missed this growing up, and now I finally had what I asked for all along. The timing could've been better, but it was better late than never, right? They were trying and I had to give them credit for that.

Right?

My mom and I stayed in this hug for a while. It was comforting and I needed all the reassurance I could get at a time like this. It was only a few more months until Connor would come. I was already halfway through month seven. My belly was beginning to show at this point. It was still not the same size as Lucía's but that was because I had the soul, and she had the body.

And even if we were carrying the same person, our structures were different. No uterus stretched the same way. Or in my case, stomach.

However, there was a part of me that craved something else.

Something more familiar than the rest of my soul. My missing piece was part of it, but aside from that, it was the part of me that wanted to take on a position I had when I was saving Ayden.

Guardian angel.

Virtue.

A dead therapist.

These titles meant something to me, and maybe a little more than Connor. I loved him so much, and I did want him, but I didn't want to think that my entire eternity would be spent with just Connor. I wanted a chance to do what I loved.

And being able to help these souls was part of that. It gave me that feeling I'd greatly missed when I decided to give up being a guardian angel for Connor. At the time, it was exactly what I wanted.

Now, I wasn't so sure.

I wanted more. I wanted the opportunity to do exactly what I wanted with my afterlife. Marie had told me to return to my roots, and when I first died, this was who I was. She was the piece of Eliana Wilson I held onto—the piece I had clung to like someone drowning and grabbing onto a lifesaving tube.

She had been the part of me that I loved the most, and everyone else appreciated her just as much.

Could I ever find her again? Could I make it back to that part of me and hope that everything would stay the same? Ayden and I had already begun having a few troubles. I didn't want to add fuel to the fire.

Maybe it was a lost cause. There was a large part of me that worried that I wouldn't be able to find my way back to that version of Elli.

I missed the days when I followed Ayden to the library at night and he got pissed off with me. I proceeded to walk away and get into some trouble with the fallen angels, and Ayden was unintentionally by my side even then.

There had been the time I watched him masturbate, and that was certainly the most awkward moment of my life. It wasn't a sight I was happy with, but maybe a small piece of me wondered who he was thinking about to get off.

During another moment, he compared me to a rose. He struggled, and I stepped in to try and help him, but as soon as I had, he realized I was worse than he was. And somehow, he came up with the perfect comparison. He'd been drunk a few times, and one of those times he admitted I was prettier than Sunny. That was probably one of the highlights of my memories.

However, there was one single memory that stuck out the most. One single memory that tugged at my heartstrings with barely a thought. Ayden had prayed when I left, and I heard him calling me back. He'd never done something like that before, and after how much he wanted me gone, he proved to me that he never actually enjoyed my lack of company. He loved me the same way I did him, and that alone brought an inner serenity that no man or woman could ever replace between us.

Mom eventually pulled away from our hug and I stood from the couch. "Ayden and I should head back to the cabin. We have work to do. But with this relationship mended, I'm sure the court will realize we are here to make sure Connor has a good structure to grow up into."

My parents nodded and said their goodbyes. Ayden and I returned to our cabin, and I fell onto the couch, exhausted. "My head is aching. I can tell Lucía is going through headaches. They're intense." I rubbed my head with my hand and stared at the ceiling.

"I'm sorry, Angel." He kissed my forehead from behind me and the couch. "Aches are never fun."

"No. You know what would ease this?" I gave Ayden a small smirk.

He lifted his eyebrows. "Oh, bloody hell. I am always down for that."

"No, no, silly. I mean a spa bath. Make your famous spa bath and we can soak together." I got off the couch, walking to the bathroom.

He followed me and stared into our tub. "The whole point of a spa bath is to relax. It's hard for me to relax if you're squished with me."

I gave him a stern look. "Excuse me?"

He gestured to the tub. "Look at the size! It's barely enough to fit one of us! Tubs are not made for adults now unless they're hot tub-size."

"Ayden Dyer, the man of the hour, is trying to complain now that he can't control himself, despite waiting until marriage with me? Is that correct?" I tilted my head in question.

He lowered his head. "I can control myself. Unless you change your mind..."

I smiled with triumph. "I might, if you get lucky. But I'd like a spa bath regardless, please and thank you. Don't forget a face mask, too."

PREDESTINATION

With fear etched on his face, eyes wide in horror, Ayden yelled, "No!" He fell to his knees, and I almost felt sorry for him. The poor guy was traumatized.

"Ayden, it's okay." I rubbed his back. "Just make another cake."

His masterpiece laid on the floor, smushed in a pile of smeared frosting and crumbs. He had been up all night working on it.

"I can't make another cake. I don't have time. Bloody hell," he grumbled. He got off the floor and looked at me. "Can you clean it up while I bake something else?"

I looked at the cake and laughed. "You want me to clean up a cake off the floor with Connor in the way? Not going to happen."

"You dropped the cake!" He threw his arms up in frustration.

I put my hands on my hips. "You trusted me with your masterpiece and I'm a clumsy pregnant woman. That's your fault." I walked over to the stool and sat, eyes fixed on him. "I'll be here, watching the professional bake his sweets. What will you make?"

He sighed, grabbing random ingredients. "I guess we'll make Rice Krispie squares. I know how to make them extra moist. This method makes them sweeter." He grabbed his bowl and started pouring ingredients. "You want to use sweet cream butter, marshmallows, and vanilla extract. This gives extra flavor and makes them taste just right." He melted it all into a pan, stirring it around. He poured it into the bowl with the Rice Krispie cereal, mixing it all together.

I was mesmerized by his work. His brows furrowed in concentration as he tugged on his bottom lip with his top teeth.

He put saran wrap over the pan after he evened it out, then stuck it in the fridge. "All right, let's get there. I want to let this cool in the fridge for after dinner."

We flew to my old home and knocked on the door. It was crazy to see all these Christmas lights out on the house. My parents must have put them up after knowing I was back, had forgiven them, and wished for one hopeful holiday.

Mom opened the door and greeted us with hugs before letting us in. Ayden put his treat in the fridge and looked over at me. I knew this was going to be the strangest Christmas we'd both ever had.

The tree sat right in front of the big window at the front of the house, next to the door. It was decorated in a perfect array of silver and red ornaments with white lights strung about, bringing together everything I'd ever dreamed of. Lots of presents were stuffed underneath the tree in all the different paper she'd collected over the years. Mom had favored pretty paper over everything else.

Why? Wrapping paper got trashed whereas the decorations would be reused every year.

More Christmas lights lined the doorways as a few garlands hung here and there, wrapped with some tinsel. It certainly felt like Christmas. Mom made sure of that.

"Angel, what's wrong?" My husband rushed over and wiped tears from my cheeks—tears I had no idea were falling.

"I can't believe after so many years, this is coming true. This is all I ever wanted, Ayden. This is my dream. If we can just win this case, we will finally be happy. I feel like everything is beginning to come together and I don't want it to be taken away." I glanced at him, stifling my sniffles.

He shook his head and pushed my hair back, placing a kiss on my nose. "It won't be. We're angels now and Heaven is supposed to be a happy place. Everything will work out because it's supposed to. Come, let's go to the kitchen." He grabbed my hand and took us.

He had been watching our families converse and talk about whatever came to mind. Esme and Arabella were happy to see their brother in such a good place. Any sister would feel that way.

Our parents were having a conversation about what they were going to do for Connor when he came. It was as if they'd already expected us to win. I could only hope it would be true. For Ayden's sake.

I sat down at the table, not sure of what to say. It had been a long time since I'd seen his family and a long time since we'd celebrated holidays.

My love sat beside me and smiled, a smile so warm and inviting you'd have guessed he was Christmas itself.

His mom looked at us as she sat across. "I find it so hard to believe that our son settled for a woman. We're glad it's you."

"Ah, yes, he fell in love with his dead therapist." I let out a little laugh. "The correct term is guardian angel, but Ayden was never into using correct terms. He was always just making remarks and insults." I shot him a smirk.

His eyes moved between both of us. "What can I say? That was my favorite thing to do. It still very much is. It's just harder to make remarks when your wife is constantly battling trauma. I don't want to be *that* husband." He rubbed his neck.

I laid my arms on the table. "I'm aware. I miss that part of you, truly. It's part of the man who I'd fallen in love with."

All over again, the shame weighed in. *Shame*—something I was. I couldn't quite refer to it as guilt, for this wasn't just a fleeting thought that I'd done wrong and I'd learn from it. It had always embedded itself into my soul and now I'd become the wife who simply looked at her husband and wished he'd never changed at all.

"You want me to make jokes and insults like I used to?" he asked.

I shrugged a bit, my gaze slowly meeting his. "Some days I do. It grounds me in reality. Makes me feel safe, Ayden. You've always made me feel safe. Even when you weren't supposed to. Even if you despised my presence, you'd come to my aid because the thought of someone else threatening me was far worse than your silly insults. Your insults meant no harm, and you knew they would never penetrate my thick skin. But others? You couldn't trust they wouldn't hurt me, and so you stepped in to make me feel safe even when you never meant to. It was far too easy to fall for you, and damn you for being my ruination," I whispered the last sentence.

"I'll be right back." Ayden stood and left the room.

I looked at his sisters as they seated themselves on either side of me. "I can't believe our baby brother would get married and have a kid. He really loves you," Esme said.

"You were there when we were first tortured. I would hope he really loves me if he put up with that *because* of me." I rubbed my hands on my stomach.

"May I?" Arabella asked.

"Of course." I nodded as she put her hand on my belly.

She laughed a bit. "This is so weird. I know you guys are angels and all, and I know Connor is, too. It's just strange to think this is my nephew! Esme is taking forever to settle." She rolled her eyes.

Esme gasped. "Excuse me, I'm barely thirty. There is really no rush. What about you? You're twenty-seven. Where is your man?"

Arabella turned red. "I told you he's looking for me."

My laugh saturated the air. "So this is what it's like to have siblings, eh?"

Esme crossed her arms. "If you want a sister, Arabella is all yours."

A grin graced Arabella's features. "Great, I finally have a sister I like to be around!" She gave me a side hug.

After a few more minutes of sibling banter, I stood up and left the room to look for Ayden. I checked the bathroom and then headed upstairs. I stopped inside my old bedroom, in tune with the snowflakes falling outside my window.

I giggled as arms wrapped around my stomach and lips kissed my cheek. "I was wondering where you ran off to."

Ayden trailed kisses down my jaw and along my neck. "Why don't we try things on your old bed? It looks so cozy."

"Sounds like a wonderful idea, if we weren't in a house filled with our families. They're downstairs and I am not comfortable having sex with other people near." I turned to look back at him.

"They won't hear us… I promise. We can hide ourselves as we do all the time in public." He kissed behind my ear.

"What about Connor?" I asked.

"He doesn't mind. He won't even know or remember." He undid the first few buttons of my shirt.

I blew out a breath. "I love you… I really do."

He kissed me, slipping his hand inside my shirt. "That's great."

"You didn't let me finish." I took his hand out. "I love you but right now, we need to be spending time with our families. I want to experience a real Christmas. We have plenty of time to have sex later. We're dead."

"What about when Connor is born?" He bent down, kissing my stomach as I fixed my buttons.

"Well, considering I'll only feel the pain until he's born and Lucía and I are no longer connected, we can have sex whenever. I don't need six weeks to heal like humans. I won't be damaged. I won't have to breastfeed because angels don't eat. We don't sleep. Oh, shit. Connor doesn't sleep either. Okay, okay. New plan. We can have Selene babysit whenever so we can have a date night." I nodded too many times to count.

Ayden groaned but agreed anyway. "Okay. Okay. We'll have sex another day." He leaned in to give me a peck.

"Come on. Our families are waiting for us." I grabbed his hand and pulled him downstairs. Ayden was very attractive and there was no doubt about that. With my hormones going crazy, I very much desired to have sex. I just knew tonight wasn't a good time. We had our family gathering to focus on.

We sat at the table as both of our parents set out what looked to be the most delicious food. I could enjoy as much as I wanted without getting bloated, either.

"I call the turkey skin!" I yelled.

Ayden shot me a look.

I patted his shoulder. "Oops, you're too slow." I peeled off the skin as my excitement grew. "It's the best part. So crispy and full of flavor."

Our parents sat around the table and Mom nodded at us as everyone bowed their heads.

"I want to thank You for bringing my daughter to a better place and taking care of her. I am so thankful that I have a chance to be in her life and all I wish for is to be in my grandson's just as much. I couldn't be happier, knowing she found a good man and has made something of herself. She is the best daughter ever and I am so sorry for ever abusing my motherhood to neglect her. I am working to make things right again. Today our families come together on this special day, and I couldn't ask for a better Christmas. Amen," Mom finished.

We all repeated, "Amen." Everyone started to dish up their plates and I went for the skin before anything else. The sweet potato casserole, green bean casserole, and mashed potatoes looked the best.

The amount of food on my plate was too much but did it affect me? No. There was no gluttony where I lived. I didn't even have to care because I was pregnant, and I was craving food just from that alone.

"Connor, I get it. You like food. I can't eat everything. There are still seven others here, not including you and me. We must share. You're going to be taught about sharing and you're going to like it."

Esme sat on the other side of me, laughing at my lecture. "He's already having to learn the ways of being...alive? What would that word even be?"

"Probably alive, in a way. We are dead, but we are also alive."

"Like the undead?" Arabella asked.

"Sort of, although we prefer terms like angels. Zombies and the undead fall into another category so it's offensive to group angels with a different species, considering we don't eat brains, nor do we suck blood. We are the good guys." I took another bite of my food.

She snapped her fingers. "Noted." She looked over at Arabella, who then looked back at me.

With a smile, I cut a piece of my turkey. "It's the correct term for what we are, anyway. I became an angel the day I died, and so did Ayden. We've saved humanity and stopped Liam. We're the guardian angels of the earth. We are always going to be the *heroes*."

OBLATION

AYDEN

Standing in the doorway, I leaned against the frame as I crossed my arms. The nursery had almost been finished. Diana helped so much.

"Can I see?" a woman asked.

I glanced back at Angel's mom, Mrs. Wilson. Also known as Diana. Had I known she was Angel's mom all along, I never would have asked her for help. There was no turning back now. "It's almost done thanks to you." I moved out of the way, showing her the room. "You never mentioned you had a daughter."

She shrugged. "You never asked. I did not lie when I told you I have plenty of money and no child to spend it on. My daughter died years ago. I didn't know she was living here with you."

"Angel can't know that we've been building this together."

"The last thing I want is to give my daughter a reason to be mad at her husband. Your secret is safe with me." She zipped her lips.

Diana helped me get the last of the nursery together. Walls had been painted with new flooring installed, and the furniture was all there, too. She made it look like a real bedroom for a baby.

"Tell me, Ayden, what was your initial thought when you found out your wife was pregnant?" she asked.

I closed the drawer to the dresser. "I suppose a big part of me was scared. When I met Angel, I didn't want her around, and at some point it had changed. She told me she was in love with me, and I rejected her. I didn't want to build her up and hurt her later, so my best bet was to hurt her then and there. When I found out she was pregnant, part of me wanted to run and let the child have a good life. I didn't want to end up hurting our baby. But ultimately, I knew I needed to—to stay, not to hurt our baby. It was time for me to grow up, and with Angel by my side, it was easy to do. Or it will be. Not quite sure if I've fully matured."

Her mother, and my mother-in-law, smiled. "I'm happy that she found you."

Someone cleared their throat behind us, and I looked back at Angel in the doorway. How long had she been there?

"Dad made dinner," she said.

Diana nodded and went to the kitchen to help.

Angel looked around the room. "What were you two talking about?"

"She asked me what my thought was about you being pregnant."

"And?"

"And I was honest. I was scared and I wanted to leave but I didn't, and I'm glad I stayed for both of you."

I could almost hear her heart cracking. "You wanted to leave?" Her voice got so quiet, barely above a whisper.

Approaching, I brushed my knuckle across her cheek. "I was scared of being a horrible father. But when I saw you, I knew I could do it. I didn't want to leave you alone. I couldn't be happy without you."

"Ayden, do you want kids?"

I chuckled. "We're having one."

She shook her head. "No, I mean do you *want* kids. As in present tense. Do you want kids right now? Pretend I'm not pregnant."

I furrowed my brows. What game was she playing? I didn't want to answer the wrong way. So, I lied. "Of course I want kids. At one point along the way, I realized I wanted to be a father and after building this nursery, I'm more than excited." But what if Connor knew about my past and saw me as lesser?

A puzzling smile appeared before she left the room to go get food, and I followed closely behind.

The dinner with her parents wasn't bad, but it wasn't exactly the best. We'd had Christmas together, but my family had been there to help mellow things out. When it was just Angel and her parents, the tension thickened.

Relationships were not wholly mended.

Diana cleared her throat. "Well, I suppose we should be leaving. Don't want to overstay our welcome." She reached for a hug, but Angel stepped back. It was painful to watch this strained family dynamic struggle to get back into the boat.

Her dad waved and they both left the cabin before driving off into the night.

Angel sat on the couch and laid her head on the arm. "Lucía isn't feeling too good."

I grabbed a rag from the drawer and got it wet with hot water. I brought it to her, placing it on her head. I wasn't sure if it would help but I wanted to try. "Anything else I can do?"

She locked her ocean-blue eyes with mine. "Just be here."

"I can do that. I know how to be here."

However, the more I started to think about it, the more I started to wonder if Lucía was okay. She seemed to have a lot going on all the time, especially with the pregnancy.

"Ayden?"

"Yes?" I pushed some hair away from her face.

"Would you be mad at me if I told you a secret, something you don't like?"

What kind of question was that? "How can I know if I'll be mad if I don't know what it is?"

She shivered, and I reached over and pulled the blanket around her. "That won't help, but thanks," she mumbled. "I've been hiding Liam under the floorboards in the kitchen."

I chuckled. "Oh yeah?"

Frowning, she sat up. "Ayden, I'm telling you the truth." She looked over at the kitchen. "Liam," she called.

Someone banged on something. What in the bloody hell?

She stood and went over to the floor and pulled it right up. We had just redone the floors! How the fuck did she do that?

She pulled Liam out. "See? I wasn't lying."

I swallowed, not sure how I was supposed to react. She didn't want me to be mad, but how could I not be? She brought him into *our* house. She exposed him to our private lives. "Why would you do this?"

"He's helping me find my soul."

"I can help you! Did you forget I was your husband?"

"It's not the same! Don't you see? I have better luck with Liam. He's involved. He's part of the memory I lost. Believe it or not but I really need to be whole again. I feel so lost without this piece of me." She came towards me, grabbing my hands. "Please, don't be mad."

I pulled my hands away from her. "He's the cause of all your problems. You brought him into our lives to ruin us some more. You don't get to ask me not to be mad." Turning on my heel, I left the cabin. I wasn't sure where I was going, but where I went, I could never let Angel find me.

Somehow, the bar scene always comforted me. I'd been so angry so many times and this was the one place that took away my problems.

Granted, I used alcohol to do so, but it still felt familiar enough to provide the peace.

I popped a few pretzels in my mouth, but the salt didn't give me the same happiness it used to.

As I closed my eyes and took a few deep breaths, a pair of arms wrapped around my neck. Somehow, my muscles relaxed. She could always do that, even if I didn't want her to. Her lips landed behind my ear, and as soon as she began to nibble, my eyes shot open. This wasn't Angel.

I grabbed her hands and pulled her around. "I'm married."

The woman shrugged. "Not happily, or you wouldn't be here." She then again attempted to run her fingers through my hair, but I caught her wrist, and maybe a little too hard. She pulled away and rubbed it, scowling. "You're not worth it."

When she began to walk past me, I turned my head over my shoulder, saying, "No man is."

Maybe she was right, and I shouldn't have been here in the first place. On the other hand, it didn't give her the right to get handsy with a stranger—or me.

That didn't distract me from the real issue, though. My wife had lied to me. She brought trauma right into our house and didn't even consider how it'd make me feel.

How could Liam help her in ways I couldn't? Hadn't I always been there? That wasn't even the biggest question I had. I needed to know exactly *why* he was helping her. He had to have some sort of game plan. No man like him changed that quickly.

Laying my head on the table, I closed my eyes for just a few minutes...

Maybe a few more...

And a few more...

And more...

"I thought I'd find you here," a soft voice said.

I lifted my head and looked at the woman sitting across from me. She fixed her clothes, using her sky-blue eyes to apologize.

"I'm sorry," she whispered. When I didn't say anything, she continued, and louder. "I'm sorry for bringing him into our home."

"I thought we were meant to be a team now. I want you to at the very least act like my opinion means something," I said. When I glanced at the clock, I furrowed my brows. Had it already been three hours since I came in?

Angel got up and grabbed my wrist, pulling me into the bathroom. She locked the door behind us before pushing her underwear down and sitting on the counter. Was she serious?

"You once told me…that I should learn how to please myself when you aren't always around. Right now, you're not around." She slipped her hands down her thighs, pulling her legs open. She pulled her skirt up.

It didn't make a difference. Not this time.

"Ayden, look at me." She put her hand between them, trying to make me watch. As if she was trying to tease me…

Maybe I had been going soft. This would have worked on me long ago, but now I was far too hurt to even pay attention. "I've been around this entire time, but you wouldn't let me in," I said with a sigh.

Angel dropped her skirt and brought her knees together. "Oh…"

"You hurt me."

She slid off the counter. "What can I do to make it better?"

"Get rid of him."

"You know I can't do that. Not until I find that missing piece."

Why was she fighting me? "What's so wrong with me?"

"It's not about you!" She stepped away. "It's about me, Ayden. I need to do this for myself. For the past three years, I have been walking around without a piece of myself. You are the one who told me I might be broken, and you were right. Liam is the key to finding that last memory." She gulped. "And he's not that bad. He hasn't been terrible company."

Was she...catching feelings for him?

I crossed my arms. "What about everything he's done?"

"That's just it! You act like he killed your baby, but you're not the one who watched everyone die! I watched Selene die. I watched you die. I watched myself die. I have the biggest reason to hate him, and right now... I don't." Her eyes watered as they grew.

She was beginning to like him. What happened to *us*?

She had *no* idea. "He did."

"What?"

"He did kill my baby." I cleared my throat. "He killed you. He killed your spirit, and your passion for so much more. I hate to admit it, but I don't like this side of you. He tortured you in Hell for a second time and broke your spirit. I fell in love with this wonderful woman passionate about so much, including helping people. And now, it's like you don't want any of that. And yes, people say that we change, and we should still love the people we become, but—"

"But you don't love me anymore."

"But you are falling for someone else. You're falling for the very man who killed you, and you don't even realize it. I'm worried that maybe you didn't fall in love with me because you liked how real I was. I think you fell in love with me because I provided an escape, and a haven for you to express your selfish desires. Now, you're doing the same with *him*."

How could he? How could he suggest such an awful thing? Was he trying to tear me apart?

No, he loves me. He's just an honest man.

Yet, I felt like all my pieces had been picked apart and analyzed every time he was in a bad mood. There was no way in hell I could love Liam, or ever. Sure, he wasn't so terrible now that he'd seen the error of his ways but that did not mean I *loved* him. Nor would I ever.

And maybe I had put Liam before Ayden, and that was wrong. But it didn't make my love for Ayden less true. I craved him for many reasons, but it wasn't because he gave me a haven for my selfish desires.

As I stood from the bed, I made it to the bathroom to look in the mirror. Something felt off. The world around me began to spin, and my vision began to blur in and out.

Lucía...

Before I had a chance to scream for help, the edges grew fuzzier and then the world went dark.

Students piled into the halls as classes ended. As fun as it would have been to head back to my dorm, I needed to go to the store and grab some tampons.

It worked out anyway as Liam left with Selene. They were going to go on a picnic today, and it certainly seemed odd in the dead of winter, but I couldn't question their relationship now.

I drove to the store and went directly to the feminine aisle. I saw a new kind of tampon and I was tempted to try it out. I always wanted something more absorbent than what I'd been stuck buying.

"Have you ever thought about a finger?" a man asked with a thick English accent.

I turned back to see a man watching me. Every bit of clothing he wore was black as if he had a point to prove. "Excuse me?"

He chuckled. "It was meant to be...nevermind." He cleared his throat. "I wish this snow would stop."

I shrugged, grabbing a box. "This small talk doesn't interest me much." I shook my box. "Sorry." I turned to walk towards the cashier, but he cleared his throat and stopped me.

"Ayden."

"What?"

"You were wondering what my name is. It's Ayden." He caught up to me.

"I was not wondering what your name is."

"You're right, I got it mixed up. I was wondering about yours."

I made a face. "Does that really work with other women? That is so terrible."

Ayden laughed. "Well, I mean my accent usually helps me out. But you don't seem at all interested, even if I am English."

I purchased the tampons and took them out of the store. The boy followed me. "I've read enough mystery and crime thrillers to know how this ends. A man that looks like you doesn't take genuine interest in a girl looking at tampons. Not unless he has one thing on his mind." I faced him. "Which is gross by the way. Why do tampons of all things turn you on?"

Crossing his arms, he lifted an eyebrow. How the hell was he so expressive with his eyebrows? Americans certainly couldn't pull that off. "Who said it was the tampons? Had you come to the store for a pillow, I would have made another joke, too. Believe it or not, I might actually like you."

"Answer me this. When was the last time you had sex?"

His face fell. "I mean... I don't see how that's relevant..."

"When?"

He rubbed his neck. "Last night."

I threw the box in the car. "Those are my exact thoughts. But if it makes you happy, I'll break your little bubble for you. Sex with me would be awful. No experience. It would be painful. There'd probably be blood. I'd get clingy." I opened my door, looking at him. "And I'm waiting until marriage." I wasn't going to give it to this stranger because he thought he could charm me.

He stood there as I got in my car and drove back to the campus.

Night fell quickly and Selene returned with Liam, practically melting. "Eliana! Just the girl we are looking for. You should come with us to this party. Pleaseeeee. I would love to have my best friend to keep me company."

"Selene, you know I'm not the party girl. I'm not going to have any fun." And yet somehow, I knew that's why she wanted me there.

Her smile radiated like the sun, and I certainly needed it to keep me from my seasonal depression. "You *are* fun. You don't need to grind on some weirdo to have a good time. Please, come. Liam said he wants you to come."

I glanced at Liam, but nothing gave away his tell. "Fine. One condition. I get to wear what I want."

"Deal!"

"And I'm wearing this." I wasn't going to dress up for a party I didn't care about. Ultimately, I was going to keep an eye on Selene. That last thing I wanted was to hear she got drunk and drove home, killing someone else. I'd be her designated driver. Besides, I wasn't old enough to drink.

They dragged me along to their stupid party, and I put on my best smile for her. Everything I did was to make her happy. It was always for her. She'd been the best friend and sister I needed all along.

We parked on the street, a few houses down. I knew the neighbors would be upset, but it was better them than some poor family.

The music got louder the closer we got to the house, and as soon as we got to the lawn, I cursed under my breath. "You two go ahead. I'll meet up. I must find the walkway." I nodded. Selene and Liam started walking through the thick layer of snow, across the grass. I, however, had heels. I wasn't planning on a long fall to the center of the earth tonight.

I walked along the sidewalk, testing the snow every now and then. Eventually, I found the driveway and used that to find my way to the paved path to the front door. I wasn't so lucky though. When I got to the front door, the place was packed. I couldn't find them anywhere. I knew this was a terrible idea.

Over the next thirty minutes, I weaved through the crowd, searching. I ignored the advances some guys made, and some girls, too. I went to the kitchen and poured some juice into a cup. I pulled my phone out to text Selene, but she didn't reply.

I sipped. "Damn, that's good." I drank it in a few seconds and got more. I spent the next hour waiting for a reply while looking for my best friend. I even searched the bedrooms in case she was trying to get dirty, but thankfully I didn't find her there in any compromising positions.

Every now and then I would stop by the kitchen for my juice. I stopped drinking it when the world around me got fuzzy. I hadn't realized it had alcohol, but I should have assumed.

I stumbled into the table. "Oh, I'm sorry." I ran my hand along the wall to help me walk to the bathroom without tripping over my feet. I closed the door behind me and ran water over my face.

While gripping the counter, I looked into the mirror. "Eliana, you idiot... How can you be the designated driver now? You should only trust water from the faucet."

Someone came into the bathroom. "Fancy seeing you here." Ugh, this guy again. What was his name? Aaron?

"I was talked into it."

He leaned against the door. "I wouldn't peg you as the party girl."

"I'm not."

"Good, because I was confused when you said you're waiting until marriage, then I find you walking around a party with sex-crazed people, alcohol in your system, and just that little skirt."

"What the hell are you saying?"

"Nothing. I just don't trust anyone here."

I left him in the bathroom. I checked my phone again, blinking until my vision became clear. "Damnit, Selene, where are you?" I slipped into an empty room, plopping onto the bed. I released a sigh and ran a hand through my hair. I decided to call her this time, but her phone went straight to voice-mail.

I fell back onto the mattress. Even after I closed my eyes, the music was still too loud for me to think. Where could she have gone? Was she in trouble?

No, Liam would never hurt her. He loved her.

A pair of hands ran up my thighs, pushing my skirt up. I immediately shot up, eyes wide. "What the hell?" I yelled. I had expected to see that English guy, but no. This was...Sam. Liam's best friend. What was he doing? "Get off me!" I shoved him.

Sam pushed me back onto the sheets. I kneed right between his legs, sending him down to the floor. He groaned.

I jumped off the mattress and ran for the door, throwing it open and running into someone else.

"Whoa, you okay there?" Ayden asked.

One look into the room at Sam and he knew. Sam stood and faced us, glaring.

"I've been looking for you, *angel*," Ayden whispered, his eyes flickering to Sam's. He lifted my chin and placed his lips on mine. Maybe I'd been drunk just a bit, or maybe just so desperate for an escape from Sam, but his kiss intoxicated every inch of me.

It would have been so much easier to get drunk on his touch than it had been the juice.

He knew what he was doing every step of the way.

"Let's get out of here," he said. I barely agreed before he grabbed my wrist and pulled me through the crowd. When we were outside, I gasped for air. It was so much easier to breathe. "Who the bloody hell was that guy?"

"Liam's friend."

"And who is Liam?"

"Selene's boyfriend."

"And she is...?"

"My best friend."

Ayden drove me back to my dorm, the drive home left in silence. What was there to say? He'd kissed me. I wanted to be mad, but I wasn't. I couldn't be angry. A small part of me wanted him to kiss me again.

He walked me up to my dorm to make sure Sam didn't follow us back. "If he sees you leave, or knows I'm alone..." I didn't finish my thoughts.

He frowned. "He won't."

"But if he does," I paused, "I could..."

He reached out, fixing my glasses. "I'll stay here to make sure he knows you're not alone tonight."

Relief washed over me. I didn't want to ask him to, but if he offered, it wasn't weird for me. It was only for the night.

I let him in and closed the door. There wasn't much for us to do, so we sat on my bed, and I left a text for Selene telling her I made it back to the dorm safely.

Ayden, however, leaned back against my pillows with his arm behind his head. "Not bad for a dorm."

"It is a step down for me." I shrugged as I scanned the small space. I'd lived in such a big house before. As my eyes landed on him again, thoughts began to run amok inside my head. His shirt slid up his stomach a bit, revealing a V. I could see the defined muscle in his bicep, too, and all of this just had me lost for words. Why would someone like him want to help someone like me?

"What's on your mind?" he asked.

A voice screamed at me, and for some reason I listened to it.

Kiss him.

"Don't move," I said.

He furrowed his brows. I leaned forward and my heartbeat sped up each second. By the time I reached his lips, it had nearly burst from my chest.

I moved my lips against his, and he wasn't slow to return the favor. Why did kissing him feel so electrifying? Whatever the reason, it didn't matter to me. I knew what I wanted in life now, and what I wanted was Ayden.

Amiable

"She's coming to!" someone yelled. "Give her space."

My eyes fluttered open as I took in my surroundings. I was in our bedroom, and before me stood Ayden, Selene, and Sunny.

Before I could sit up, the dream came rushing back to me. It was hard to forget when you hadn't dreamt in over three years. Sure, I had fallen asleep once when I got pregnant, but I didn't like to count that. This—this was serious.

"I had the strangest dream," I whispered.

Ayden sat beside me, holding my hand like it was the most precious stuffed toy. "Tell me about it."

"You were there...and Selene...and Liam." I looked at Sunny. "You weren't there. Sorry." Shaking my head, I continued, "but it was odd. Liam and Selene went on a picnic date. He didn't kill her though. Then I ran into Ayden at the store when I was buying tampons." I rubbed my head.

Ayden chuckled. "That sounds nothing like me. Going to stores?"

"Liam and Selene invited me to a party but then I lost them inside, and I kept trying to find them. I found juice instead, but that had been spiked. So I went to the bathroom and Ayden was there, too, at the party. And minutes later, I found myself in a bedroom trying to sleep it off. But Sam..." I groaned at the thought. "Sam was trying to take advantage of me. I was a little tipsy, but it wasn't to the point where I couldn't comprehend my surroundings.

"I ran into Ayden outside the door, and I practically begged him to get me away from Sam. So, he did. He kissed me, pretending we were together or something. And he took me back to the dorm. But I was afraid Sam would come back for me, so he stayed with me. And before I knew it..." I relaxed my shoulders. "I kissed him."

Sunny smiled. "Sounds like you know what you want."

Selene sighed, fixing my hair and smoothing it over my shoulder. "We got worried. We figured it might involve Lucía and we got her to a hospital. It sounds like she must be feeling better."

Ayden nodded, kissing my knuckles. "And so are you."

But was he?

Sunny left to get some water for me, but Ayden kicked Selene out, too, locking the door before Sunny could return. "Angel, we should talk."

"We should." I sat up while he helped me. "But I'm not—"

"No. Let me speak, please."

So I nodded.

He released a sigh. "You don't see it. We do. You have this thing where you want to fix people, including Liam. And whatever memory you forgot, it's important to you. I get that. However, I want to say it. You're going to fall for him whether you like it or not. You said we can't control who we love, and that makes me angry. My blood is boiling at the thought. The more I think about it, the more I realize I can do something about it."

Oh no. He wanted to separate.

"You can't change what's going to happen. However, I can change my reaction. I'm upset. I'm hurt. I'm angry. But I love you so much." He scooted closer, leaning his forehead against mine. "I love you like I've never loved anyone before, and I'd be damned if I gave up on you this easily. I have changed, and I will show you that. Liam? He hasn't, and eventually he will show you that, too."

"Ayden, I—"

"Answer me this. Who do you love more?" He squeezed my hand.

Yet, I refused to believe he was right. I didn't love Liam. I never would. "I didn't love Liam in my dream, Ayden. I only saw you. You were the one who got me to go against what I wanted. You gave me the confidence to kiss you." I took a deep breath. "I have always and only ever loved you."

He closed the last of the gap and allowed me to savor the taste of him. I ached for more. Whatever I felt in my dream had carried over into this world, and I loved the feeling. I didn't have to hold back.

I begged for me, attempting to devour him, tugging at his shirt. My dream reminded me that in some way, even if I never died, Ayden still would have found me. We'd still fall in love.

He lay back and pulled me on top, and before I had time to register what was happening, it was happening. A part of me felt a little bad because Selene and Sunny were here, but they could leave. It was still *our* cabin.

It hadn't been on just me. No, he gave me the green light, digging his fingers into my hips as we proved that nothing could come between us no matter how hard they tried.

And I? I'd learned more of what I enjoyed. The noises he made told me he'd felt the same way, too.

When we finished letting our emotions take charge, I rubbed my face while pushing the hair away from it.

"That was so much fun," he said, rubbing his thumbs along my waist. "We need to do that more often."

"We need to find my soul first." I leaned onto my hands, splaying my fingers on his chest. "That is important to me. You admitted it."

"I know it's important. I just wish you would have at least included me." He let go and grabbed my wrists, pulling them out from under me. I slipped right onto his chest, and he took advantage of it by kissing me with as much white chocolate as he could promise. "I want to be included," he whispered.

"I didn't think you'd want to help. There's already so much going on..." I frowned.

"How could you think I didn't want to help? I wanted to. I suggested it to you because I wanted to help you find yourself and be the best version of you. I wanted to be there every step of the way. I care about you more than you tend to let me." His hand slid down, grabbing hold of my butt.

With a snicker, I grabbed his arm. "You care about my body."

He shrugged a little. "Partly true."

"So rude."

He smiled and pecked me. He flipped us, sliding off the bed and pulling his briefs on. Then he put his shirt on over his head. "Come on, let's go check on Lucía."

"Shouldn't we have done that before we had sex?" I hugged a pillow.

He kissed my forehead before unlocking the door. "Isn't there a saying that you can't pour from an empty cup? I thought so." He left.

After I got dressed, I walked into the kitchen where Ayden baked a cake for Lucía. Sunny watched him with a cup of water in her hands. "Remember when you made a cake for my birthday?" she asked. "Those memories feel so far away now."

Ayden smiled. "Well, I am dead now. And you're somewhere in between." He cleared his throat. "And speaking of which, any progress on your body? Someone has to have it somewhere. My best guess is it's somewhere cold, since it's cold temperatures that can preserve life for longer."

She shrugged, tracing her finger around the ring of the glass. "I don't think Angel has any interest in looking. But I'm not trying to say that to insult her or blame her. I get it. She's missing a piece of herself, too. She's spent so many years trying to help everyone else and she's tired of it. I would be, too. And I told her to do that. She needs to focus on her mental health."

He nodded, pouring the batter into a pan. "And what about you? Are you still looking at all?"

"Where do I begin? I barely know my way around this world. I don't have the power to fight whoever it is that stole my body."

Chuckling, he put the pan in the oven. "I think you are capable of more than you believe. That's what Angel taught me."

A small smile rose on my face. He really took things I taught to heart. Had I made that much of an impact in his life?

I ruined the moment by entering. "I'm really sorry." I sat beside Sunny, putting a hand on her shoulder. "I didn't realize I was neglecting all my other duties."

"Oh, no, it's okay. You have so much on your plate already." She was too nice to admit that she wanted *and* needed my help.

So, I admitted it for her. "I haven't been making any progress with my search. I've only been hurting everyone around me, and it hasn't been doing us any good. From here on out, I'm going to focus on helping all of you and Lucía. My soul is my last priority." And maybe it would never be one at all, knowing how many problems seemed to pop up since I had met Ayden.

He stared at me with this pitiful look. I knew they both wanted me to focus on myself, too, but it had caused nothing but rifts.

Once his cake was made, we took it over to Lucía's. She'd been released from the hospital, but she wasn't looking too well when we went in. Whatever had happened to her, it was taking its toll.

Lucía met me in the kitchen while we cut the cake. "I know you want to know what happened."

"Did you...forget your shot again?"

She stiffened. "No. I just... I think this has been too much on me. Thomas has been helping me a little, but I feel like it's all mine to take care of. I'm terrified." Her hands began to shake, and I grabbed the knife, taking it from her. I set it down and grasped her wrists, holding onto her. "I'm so sorry."

"You have no reason to be sorry," I said. "You were in a bad place and Liam took advantage of that. He was the one who purposely threw a baby into your mess. You're doing your best with what you have."

She nodded, but she didn't say another word. I wanted to climb inside her head and see what she was thinking, but I couldn't. Whatever it was, it wasn't supposed to be for me to see.

We all ate Ayden's cake in silence. It wasn't ideal for the night, but it would have to do. Lucía was under our care and Ayden was satisfied to have fulfilled his desire to bake again. I, however, was upset with myself to have let everyone else suffer because I wanted to please myself first. Looking for my next high. Desperate to find the next best thing.

It wasn't me, and if I was ever going to heal from my trauma and get closer to the real Eliana, I needed to act more like myself just as much.

When the night ended, Ayden brought Sunny and I home. Sunny lay on the couch while I went to the bathroom to face myself. If I did that, maybe it would remind me of what I was fighting for. I was Eliana Dyer and I had much more to worry about than just my soul.

Ayden appeared in the doorway, crossing his arms. "We should talk about Liam."

"Again?" I frowned. I didn't want to, but he wasn't going to let this go.

"Yes, again. What happens to him now? If you're so set on putting everyone else first, he can't just stay in our kitchen under the floor."

"Well, I suppose...he could help us?" I wasn't ready to sneak him back into Hell just yet.

His laugh sent a blow to my gut. "Help? Why would he do that?"

"Let me talk to him. Let me at least try to convince him to help us. I'm sure he'd rather help than go back there and get tortured. Any sane person would. Usually, they choose that option before they die—once they know the supernatural world exists that is."

After taking a long look at the ground, he agreed to give me a chance. "Under one condition." He said that if Liam was going to stay, he would have to be around every time Liam was there. He trusted me, or at least I hoped so. Liam, unfortunately, had not a single ounce of trust. Not from Ayden, Sunny, or Selene. I seemed to be the only person who had any *faith* in him.

"No, Liam, tell me this isn't true."

How foolish I had been...

"Tell me this is a sick joke. Please, tell me."

How blind I had been...

"Whoever did this is pure evil, someone who doesn't deserve to see the light of day again."

And yet, I had let him.

He ripped the one person away who had been my everything. Selene came into my life and refused to let me go. Yet, I had allowed just that too easily.

How could I let him do this to me? To her? How could I bring him to our home?

Was I truly sick? Mentally unstable?

Maybe both. Maybe neither. It was difficult to say.

As I closed my eyes, I replayed the scenes over and over. It was probably counterintuitive to Ayden, but for me, it was crucial to relive every moment. I watched them like movies, studying everything because my life depended on it.

A drawled-out breath left my lips and I bothered not to say another word about it. I was not about to argue with the only other person who understood what I was going through. Sliding my hand across my thigh and into his lap, I locked my fingers with his to bring some sense of comfort.

Wait, no. That was wrong. That memory had been tampered with, right? I never held his hand.

He sat next to me and pulled me in, letting me cry on his shoulder. I had nobody else to comfort me and share my hurt. And maybe I didn't want anybody else...

What the hell was that? Anybody else would have been better than Liam. Anybody but him. He was faking his emotions the entire time. He played me like a piano, with grace and without effort, but never truly appreciating me for who I was or what value I brought to the world. He'd run his fingers along the keys and note them perfectly. Then, when he finished the song, he'd get up and walk away and forget all about my existence.

Shaking off the horrid memories of death and decay, I dragged my feet along the forest floor. I'd been searching for any kind of indication about their bodies, but I came up with nothing. I'd even asked Matthew, as much as I hated that, and he told me there was no secret chamber to store soulless bodies for preservation. Which seemed fair...

It meant for me, however, that whoever did this had created their own freezer. It couldn't have been in Hell where it was too hot, and it couldn't have been in Heaven where they wouldn't have had access.

Somewhere on earth was a big meat locker for humans. And somehow, it had gone unnoticed.

I looked in all the butcher shops and abandoned warehouses where there might have been butcher shops once. I found nothing. I needed a lead, and I needed it *fast.*

"Come out, come out wherever you are," I said quietly.

The bodies didn't listen to me. I certainly wasn't a *necromancer* and I'd never want to be. This was as far as I'd ever wish to go to deal with the dead and bring them back to life.

My foot caught on something—a ring—pulling me to the ground. When I sat up and inspected it, I found a trap door. I scooted closer, making sure nobody was around before I pulled open the hatch and landed inside.

When I scanned the place, my food almost came back up. Bones hung in every corner, and the place smelled of rotting flesh. An odor only a serial killer could withstand.

This was in no way a meat locker, but I had to stop whatever it was. Innocent lives were at stake.

A grumble echoed from the door, and I immediately shed my clothes, turning invisible. A large man climbed down and noticed the pile of clothes I left. He searched the entire area before realizing I wasn't here and throwing them into the fire. Shit. I had nothing to wear now.

He went to the fridge and opened it, looking through some of the jars. He pulled one out, my scream piercing the air, but not enough to penetrate the barrier between him and I. There was an eyeball in that jar.

The man set it on the table and unscrewed the lid, pulling it out. I turned away before I saw him swallow it like a grape. "You saw nothing," I whispered with my hands on my belly. "You saw nothing."

Something had caught my eye, though—something hidden between his mattress and sheets.

When the man turned away, I reached in and pulled it out and found myself in a corner. "Oh my gosh." I covered my mouth, choking. "No...No..." In my hand was a small bracelet with the word *sunshine.* I knew a girl who'd been nicknamed that by her brother. Sunny.

After the man left the dingey bunker, I searched the place for more things. I found them stashed in odd places as trophies. Between the mattress, taped under the shelves, and stuffed into corners behind the fridge. One had been a locket with a picture of a little girl and her mother. Becky.

"No! This can't be right!" I clutched the items to my chest as I dropped to the floor and started to sob. This couldn't be true.

Every bone in my soup ached from the memory of pain. My chest replicated a heartbeat, and my hands shook from the rage inside me. I had promised to save these souls, but they had been long gone before I even had a chance.

How was Sunny going to react? Someone had ripped her soul from her body, then they gave her body to a killer to do what he wanted. He had cut her into pieces and there was no way I could reverse that.

After the crying had come to an end, I gathered as many items as I could, carrying them all out of the hole. I took them with me through the forest, towards the cabin. "How could You let this happen? You told me that they didn't have death certificates! You gave me false hope! How dare You?" I yelled up at the sky. But I supposed they couldn't have them if they were ripped from their souls. If the soul was detached from the body against its will, could they even keep track of the bodies? Sure. But would they?

Two halves of a whole were separated, making sure they were hard to track.

I stumbled over a root and the items flew out in front of me. Why was my life so full of demise?

I buried my head into Ayden's shoulder, allowing tears to pour out. "Come back to me, Ayden." I locked his fingers tightly in mine as the choking sounds slowed until silence filled the air.

Sure, Ayden did come back to me as an angel, but that never made sense to me. I mean, it did in a way, but in another direction, it didn't. Everything seemed to work out and I was the one who took the fall for that to happen.

I took the fall for everyone to get their happy ending, and sometimes, even I couldn't promise them that.

I gathered up the items and made it home at last. To regain some sense of security, I went straight for the closet in our bedroom, hiding in it. It felt so good to just retreat into a small piece of my mind.

Ayden used to bring me more comfort, and I feared he had a point. Did I only love him when it was wrong? Did I only love him because he helped me escape my selflessness?

He was everything to me, and yet, somewhere along the way, I didn't crave him like I used to. I was the worst wife in Heaven, and I ought to fix it. Unfortunately, I didn't know how to quite make it right again.

"Angel?" someone called into the bedroom.

This went on for some time, before the voice faded out and disappeared. He couldn't find me here. He'd never think to, either.

I spent hours inside the closet, reliving my life. Liam was there when Selene was murdered. Selene was there before that, to replace the love I lost from my parents. Ayden was there to give me some sense of belonging, and to remind me what it was like to be human again. But now, he wasn't human. I had no connection.

Sunny could have been my one connection left to the living, and now she'd been chopped into pieces. She was nothing. *I* was not a single thing.

The closet door slid open. "Angel?"

I looked up at him, wiping the tears away. "Where did everything go wrong?"

He squatted in front of me. "Tell me what happened."

More tears rolled down my cheeks. "I think you were right... I want to so badly return to what it was like before you died, but I can't. I love you, Ayden, but I'm scared it's not in the same way anymore."

He leaned forward onto his knees, pulling me into his arms. "Can I tell you something?"

I nodded a bit. "Anything."

"I knew all along that you liked the bad boy in me. You liked the danger, the thrill of doing something against the rules. It was never any secret. The more I pushed, you pulled me back. The way you loved that part of me, I loved the part of you that shoved." He lifted my chin. "And you've done it to me so much lately, that I fell in love all over again."

"Is our marriage built on lies?" I asked.

He wiped the tears away with his thumb. "I don't think so. I think we just need to fall in love with each other as we are now." He pressed his lips against mine, whispering, "I'm not giving up on us. *Ever.*"

I slowly began kissing him, but I was taken off guard when he returned with so much hunger. He scooped me into his arms and dropped me onto the bed.

Sunny came barging in. "Um, oh, shit, I didn't mean to interrupt. I just wanted to see if you found her."

Releasing a sigh, I sat up and pulled the sheets over my naked body. "It's fine. Come in."

Sunny hesitated at first, but she closed the door and sat. "Any luck?" She had this hopeful look in her eyes, and it hurt so much more that I was about to crush it.

I got off the bed and grabbed a bracelet from the pile of items. I brought it to her. "I found a trap door... He had every trophy from every body a soul was ripped from." I set what rightfully belonged to her in her palm. "I'm sorry. Not a single one of you was still intact."

Sunny stared at the bracelet. "No..." As I stepped back, she closed her fist around the jewelry with her name on it. "This isn't fair. This isn't..." The cries poured out.

I sat beside her, wrapping my arms around her shoulders. "I'm so sorry. I wish I had gotten there on time, but it was far too late. Whoever did this had given the body to this man, and he didn't waste time on doing what he did."

She sobbed into my shoulder as her chest heaved. I didn't dare let go of her, because I knew if I did, something would happen. "I got help!" Her wails grew louder. "I didn't kill myself and this is the price I pay."

It would kill Mason just as much.

Ayden sat on the other side of her. "How does this work? She's dead, so why hasn't she...gone to Heaven?" He didn't want to dare suggest she could go to Hell. I didn't blame him.

Resting my chin on her shoulder, I cleared my throat. "Heaven doesn't know she's dead. When her soul was torn from her body, it disrupted the balance of nature. When her body was killed with no soul, they couldn't tell that she was dead because her soul didn't automatically go where it was meant to. But now that we know the truth, we need to go to the Heavenly Court with a new case. We are going to find these souls a *permanent* home."

Artillery

Even after I returned home, my room didn't look more lively. Maybe it was because I wasn't alive, or just maybe it was because my afterlife was a chaotic disaster.

Someone knocked on the door. "Come in," I said. Mom walked in with something in her hand. "What is that?"

She brought it over and sat beside me, placing it in my hands. "This is something I should have shown you a long time ago."

I looked down as tears filled to the brim. "Why?"

"Because you need it the most now."

I stared at my own baby book. I never thought my parents had one, but when I skimmed the pages, I saw all the handwritten notes. She had filled every single space.

"Mom, I have something to tell you."

"What is it?"

"I don't...want kids."

Mom reached over and cupped hair behind my ear. "I know, baby. I know. I've seen it in your eyes. How you are with Connor is not how I was with you."

A cry slipped, but I held the rest back. "Am I a horrible mother?"

Shaking her head, she kissed my temple. "How? You have done everything to fight for this kid and make him feel wanted, even if you don't *really* desire him. I was the one who made my daughter feel so alone and unloved when I thought I'd given her everything. You are a far better mother in these past eight months than I ever was in twenty years." She placed her hand on my shoulder, to which I leaned into.

In a way, my mother was right. I was going to commit an entire eternity with a son that I didn't want to raise but would for his well-being.

But at the same time, I wanted to end this entire thing. "I'm going to go to the court and tell them I've made up my mind. I'm going to let Lucía have her baby."

Her smile couldn't be missed for miles. "You always put everyone else before yourself. I wished I had been a part of that."

"Don't focus on the past, Mom. Focus on the now." I grabbed her hand. "You're here now, to be a part of my life. Forever and always "

She stood. "Why don't you come downstairs? We made some dinner. It's your favorite."

"Really?" I stood, following her to the kitchen.

The smell hit me, and memories rushed back. Were they right? Was I wrong all along?

I looked over as a transparent version of me ran into the kitchen, the widest grin on her face. She jumped up onto the barstool. Her joy was directed at the woman who birthed us, and the ghost of my mom returned the smile as she set a plate of lasagna and salad in front of her.

I choked and a single tear left my eye. "Was I wrong? Had I been the one who remembered it all wrong this entire time?"

Mom set a plate in front of me. "What do you mean?"

Once I sat, more memories flooded. My nanny was let go, but I overheard the entire conversation. Mom told her that she couldn't afford to keep her, and she wanted to be in my life more than she had been.

Another memory was of my mom tucking me into bed and reading a book, a thriller. It hadn't been too dark, but it was enough to pave the addiction to thriller novels.

"I... You were right this whole time. You took the fall. You let me accuse you of not loving me enough. But you did... You *always* did."

She leaned forward, giving me a small smile. "I just wanted my daughter back. When you're a parent, you do anything to have them by your side, even if it means admitting to things you see differently."

"Why is my life such a mess?" I picked up my fork.

She kissed my head. "We're here to fix it."

"What about my husband? He says that both of us fell in love with the versions we once knew, and now we're different people. How did you and Dad stay married for so long? People change over time." I took a bite.

She shrugged. "People do. It's the reality of existing, and we can't reverse that. What we can control is how we react to things, and how we continue to love someone. Your father and I made a vow until death do us part. We take that vow seriously. It gets rough at times, but at the end of the day, he's exactly what I need. Emotional support. He is always the one I come home to. He's my best friend." She nudged me. "And the physical support isn't too bad either."

I was supposed to be repulsed by the thought of my parents having sex, but it gave me hope. I wasn't disgusted simply because they had kept to their promise.

I swallowed. "So, even if Ayden and I won't have a love like when we first started dating, we can still try?"

"The love won't be the same, because *you* aren't the same. But who's there when you need a shoulder? Who is there to fight beside you? Having a marriage partner isn't just about one aspect of love. It's about all. And sometimes, it becomes something else. It becomes more pure, and more intimate. To be able to stay married to someone after they've become someone different takes so much more than people give credit for, but it's raw. That is the beauty of eternal love."

Knowing my mother was right, my nonexistent heart swelled. Ayden loved me so much he was willing to fight for us even when everything had flipped.

"Will we ever get that kind of attraction back?" I looked at my mother.

She gave me her warmest smile. "Sometimes you do."

Deep down, I hoped and prayed that it would be us. Anything that brought us closer was a force to be reckoned with, and that was the force I wanted to hold inside me.

After the visit ended, I returned home to gather the items. I gave them to their respective souls, promising I was going to give them proper closure.

That was when I went to Matthew. "I need to talk to you."

He appeared a little irritated, but he did his best to hide it. "Yes?"

"Those souls I told you about, they're here."

"Pardon?"

"They're outside your office. I must ask a favor of you, and I need them to know the answer as soon as I walk out this door." I pointed to the door of his office. "Upon my journey, I discovered so much. What I found was devastating." I laid the folders on his desk. There were about twenty or so. "Each file is of a different soul. Each soul was ripped from their body. Someone had lured them into a dark fate, and when they were detached from their mortal vessel, the soul was locked up in a cell in Hell while their body was given to a sick man living underground. They never had a chance."

Matthew grabbed a file, sifting through its contents.

"From my perspective, it doesn't seem very fair that these people had a chance to change, and when they did, they were punished for doing what they were supposed to all along. I want to ask the court to drop my case with Connor, and instead replace it with these souls getting a final destination."

He closed it, looking up at me. "You realize what you're asking, right? The repercussions," he paused, "can be harsh."

I straightened my posture, folding my hands in front of my belly. "I'll take it. These souls matter to me, and this is what I had signed up to do when I became a Virtue. I keep my views, Matthew, and I'm going to keep this one."

Something on his face caught me off guard. A smile. Matthew was *smiling* at me. "Eliana, I am so proud of you."

I furrowed my brows. "Excuse me?"

He pushed himself out of his chair, fingers on his desk. "You are absolutely one of the most persistent guardian angels we've ever had. You saved Ayden Dyer, even after finding out you were falling in love with him. You saved Sunny from herself, after she dated the man you love. You saved the entire world from Hell, and just when we thought everything had come to an end, you stepped up and saved these souls. You manage to find your way back to the girl you're supposed to be. You're like a student of mine, one that asks many questions but still delivers her promises."

"What are you saying?"

"I'm saying we will take your offer. We will go to the court and tell them to switch out the cases." He nodded. "It shouldn't be too hard to do."

"Thank you." I bowed my head and walked back to the door.

"And Mrs. Dyer?"

"Yes?"

"Whenever you're ready to become a guardian angel again, the position is always yours." He sat back down.

I left the office with more weight on my chest than when I entered.

Everyone gathered around me, and I told them Matthew agreed to let them all go plead their cases in court. Without a body to go back to, they couldn't return to earth, but they would get a final decision from the judge so they could properly die and be given a memorial by their loved ones on earth.

After everyone celebrated and let me be, I found myself sitting at the edge of a cloud.

A guardian angel.

I had given up the title when I got pregnant, but now that I was letting Connor go, I could have the chance to do what I loved. Ayden would see me as the woman he fell in love with, and I would see him as the husband I always wanted.

Tears slipped down my cheeks, and the more I pondered the thought, the bigger my smile grew. Things were starting to fall back into place after all this time.

My parents had always loved me. Selene was by my side. Sunny would probably always be there, and now I had reassurance that Ayden would always fight for us. I knew I had married someone special—and made just for me.

How many women got to say their husband would fight for them even after they had died?

Liam could no longer hurt me, and I had hope that for once, things would return to the way they used to be. They wouldn't be exactly the same, and more like they'd become the same image with a different filter, but they would still bring some sort of peace to my soul.

I couldn't wait to tell Ayden the good news. I wasn't so sure he'd be super ecstatic, but I could only pretend he would be. It would make my soul feel complete in a way it never had, just to know that he supported my dreams.

And I'd help him find his. Maybe he could start a bakery in Heaven, and everyone would love to stop by and eat. Maybe he could start one on earth. It was all in his hands, and I'd be by his side every step of the way.

Maybe he could even teach me some of his tips. I'd certainly love to learn.

"I'm going to let you go now, Connor," I whispered. "Lucía will love you more than I ever could. You'll be so happy, and maybe someday we will reunite. I'll get to tell you all about it." And it would be quite the story to tell.

But it would be *ours.*

I took the elevator back down to earth and went to the city, watching the world pass us by. I couldn't keep the smile off my face no matter how hard I tried. Matthew had told me he wanted me back, and I wanted to be back. More than anything else I wished for in this world right now, I desired to return as a guardian angel. And I would.

Resurrection

I screamed out from the bathroom, "Ayden!" Every part of my soul filled with dread.

He rushed in, finding me gripping the counter as I kneeled to the floor. "What's wrong?" His eyes were plagued with fear, and he had a right to be terrified. I was just as afraid as he was.

"Something's wrong," I said as tears rolled down my cheeks. "Something's seriously wrong with Lucía. We need to get to her immediately."

"What is it?" He put his arm around me, helping me off the ground.

Selene came running in and helped him practically carry me. "Something—something very serious is wrong. I feel like I'm *dying*."

"Oh, shit," Ayden whispered.

They carried me as we flew to Lucía's apartment and went inside without bothering to knock. We rushed into the bathroom, and I covered my mouth. "Oh my gosh." I looked away and my tears broke into uncontrollable sobs.

Ayden rushed over to Lucía's unconscious body, lifting her head.

Selene grabbed the empty pill bottle, trying to hold herself together.

My husband didn't think twice before shoving his fingers down her throat to initiate her gag reflex. All the contents of her stomach came up and spilled onto the floor, along with whatever pills she took.

Sickly, and pale, with bags under her eyes. She grabbed onto him.

I wiped my tears and sat on the edge of the tub. "Lucía, let us help you. Please. Suicide is not the answer..."

My husband glanced at me before turning his attention back to her and helping her sit up. "We care about you, and not just because you have the body of Connor. We can't let you make this choice."

Lucía was unable to say any words between the waterfalls of sorrow streaming down her face.

I covered my mouth, breaking into another fit of cries. "How could you do this? I'm a guardian angel, and I can help you. I will help you if that's what you need. It's my job. I can't just let you do this to yourself." The cries intensified as my chest began to rapidly expand, hiccups oncoming. I couldn't control any of this. I felt helpless and wanted nothing more than to *save* her.

Selene bent down and wrapped her arms around me, kissing my temple.

Lucía finally spoke with words that tore my heart, "You're only sad because you would've lost Connor." I hadn't had a chance to tell her, or the court, that I wanted to let her keep him for herself.

Ayden wrapped his arm around her head, pulling it against his chest. "Don't say that. Don't you dare say that. Connor brought us together, but we have truly come to care about you. Angel loves people more than I ever could have, and I know her. She is devastated that she has to see you so hurt like this. She wants to help. We all do."

I slid down on the floor and grabbed her hands, squeezing them. "Please, let me help. I want to save a life if I can. I want to save *you* and see you smile. I want you to have a happy future."

Ayden stood, helping Lucía out of the bathroom and onto the couch. "You can tell us how you feel. We will listen. My wife is basically a dead therapist."

I hit him lightly before moving him out of the way. "I'm here for you. Let me try to help."

"You can't help me. I'm a lost cause," she said as she gazed at the wall in front of her.

I glanced at my husband. "Everyone says that. It's never true. I believe in miracles. I'll be here as long as it takes." I took a deep breath. "I wasn't going to say this until I knew it was certain, but we are giving up. I'm going to give you Connor."

She looked at me, brown eyes locked on mine.

"I don't want kids, Lucía, and I've realized that after all this time. I'm going to let you have him and I won't try to take him from you anymore. I never should have in the first place." Nodding, I rubbed her back.

She didn't exactly react, at least not outside of her shell.

"Does that sound like a plan?" I looked at Selene. "It seems fair for a woman who wants her baby to keep him and his soul. A woman like me can survive without kids. I'm happy as I am, and you don't need to worry about me." I sighed. "We don't want you to get stuck with this soulless monster because of me. You will love your son. You deserve to give a soul a loving home. The body is temporary. It rots after death. You deserve to raise the soul of Connor, the piece of him that lasts forever. Your child will get to experience love and compassion and a mother who deserves a child."

Lucía wiped her tears. "I didn't do what I did because of this. I've been in this state for a long time, long before Connor and Liam came along. Marie is gone." She swallowed another cry. "You said she's happy, and I want to be with her. If I go to Heaven, I will get to keep my baby and see my sister."

"I understand. You miss your sister. I promise she is content, and you will have your chance to partake in that. But you should try to fix your life before you die. Trust me, I wish I had saved myself from this pain before my demise. I don't enjoy it. If you die, your body and Connor's body rot in the earth. Your soul goes to Heaven but Connor's soul stops growing inside of me after his physical form is dead. They must remove him from me and he will forever be stuck at this age, just shy of being born." I grabbed her hands.

She ripped her hands away from mine. "So I'm screwed no matter what I do."

I shook my head. "No, no. You're not screwed. I will help you. All three of us are here to support you the whole way. We will make this work."

"How can you promise something you can't control? It's not up to you. It's up to God what happens in this case." She lay back, facing the ceiling.

I had no answer to that. It wasn't ultimately up to me. I was just on the other side of the case. I wasn't the judge, nor was I God.

"I wish I had an answer for you... I don't. But I can promise that I will be here no matter what happens. Even when you win and get Connor, I will be here no matter how hard it is," I said.

Her silence spoke volumes. She didn't believe this was going to turn out okay in her favor. I wanted to promise it would, but I couldn't make her drink the water. I could only bring her to it as an offer. How was I supposed to help her with her depression this way?

I stood up from the couch and walked to the bathroom. I lowered myself to the ground using the counter for support. I grabbed a cleaner and a rag from under the sink, beginning to clean up the puke on the tile. It was the only way for me to concentrate right now.

Ayden and Selene knew to leave me to my own vices. I was not sure how to truly help Lucía from this place. Without a guarantee that she was going to be happy, I couldn't pull her out of her rut.

She also mentioned she wanted to see Marie. How could I do that without letting her kill herself?

I had to bring Marie back here. I had to talk to her and let her know that her sister was in trouble. Being Lucía's sister, an angel, and a therapist, she would agree just like that.

I finished cleaning up and exited the bathroom. "I'll be back. Watch Lucía for me. I have an idea."

Leaving her apartment, I went for the elevator, and when I stepped in, it'd been like stepping into an ice box, as if nobody had used it in ages. My feet touched the clouds as I stepped out, and I walked to the same room I had been to the first night of my therapy. I knocked on the door, before hearing someone tell me to come in. I did.

"Marie Álvarez?" I asked.

She looked up at me and knitted her eyebrows together. "Who told you my last name?"

I put my hands on my stomach, taking a deep breath. "Lucía. Lucía Álvarez. How did you think I'd put the two together?"

With a gulp, she went silent. She'd forgotten that I knew her sister. Not quite sure how to respond. They'd once been bonded by flesh and blood, and so much more. But now, she'd been the one she hadn't seen in so long. Lucía had been a freshman when Marie died, which had to have been like seven years or so ago.

"Lucía needs you. I know you have a job here and I won't take that from you. But Lucía just needs you to talk to her. She has been in pain ever since your death. She was on antidepressants before she got pregnant. She..." My eyes began to water. My vision blurred. "She tried to kill herself today."

Marie gasped. "No, no. Why would she do that?"

"Because she feels alone. She misses you and she believes you still hate her. She never got to tell you she loved you. Just come back with me and tell Lucía that you're happy and you'll be here when she gets here someday." I stepped forward. "She needs someone to tell her that everything will be okay. She needs *you*, Marie."

Her eyes moved around the room, not staying on any spot for too long. "What can I do? I made the mistake. If I hadn't gone to that party, I wouldn't have died. I know I left my family behind by my poor choices. I don't want her to do the same."

I kept closing the gap between us until my stomach got in the way. "You're the one who can get through to her. She misses you. She trusts you. I want to see Lucía find peace, and I know you want the same."

She closed her eyes, the gears in her head turning.

"Okay," she whispered.

"Okay?" I asked.

Marie opened her eyes, nodding. "Okay. I'll see her. I'll go back to my sister and tell her it's okay for her to go on without me."

"Thank you."

She shook her head. "No, thank you for being there for her and caring. I want Lucía to live a full life, the one I didn't get to. I want her to live for both of us. I need to make her see how this hurts me when she hurts herself. I can't bear the thought of my own sister taking her life because she felt so utterly alone." She lowered her head.

Even therapists had *feelings*. They had families just as much as we did.

"That's what we're here for. Even after you talk to her, I won't go anywhere. I will be watching over her. I'll be her volunteer guardian angel until I can talk to the court and get one assigned to her. I'll make sure she gets the best." I rested my hand on her shoulder.

She laughed a bit. "You can't give her the best if it's not gonna be you. It would be second-best."

"All right, all right. I'll make sure Lucía gets the second-best guardian angel in the business. I will take care of your sister. I want nothing but pure happiness for her."

A single tear rolled down my cheek. Lucía was my responsibility now.

Scapegoat

Ayden, Selene, and I stood by the couch as Marie and Lucía held each other. Their tears were many, but they were that of missed hugs and laughs.

"You did well." Ayden kissed my cheek.

Selene smiled as she watched in awe.

They talked about everything that had happened over the past eight years. I was going to let these two have their moments before Marie would need to let Lucía know how much she was worth. Her soul was priceless.

"Let's leave them be. Ayden and I have a meeting with our lawyer," I said.

Selene nodded. "I'll see you two later." She flew out of the apartment before my husband and I headed off to meet up with Alex.

I sat in a comfy chair, mostly because I was pregnant.

I looked at her as she sat down, fixing her papers. "How have you two been doing?"

"Good." I nodded. I glanced at Ayden and he confirmed what I said with a thumbs up.

"I see you guys went behind our back and talked to Matthew about your plan?" she asked.

My face heated up. I lowered my head. "It seemed like the only way to save everyone."

Alex laughed as if she hadn't caught me in my law-breaking moment. "Relax, Eliana. Matthew talked to God. They said they approve."

My head snapped up and I covered my mouth. "Tell me you're serious. Oh my gosh. Holy sh—" I stopped before I said something I shouldn't have. "I mean, that's amazing!"

Ayden was smiling as if he knew this would be the outcome. Cocky assface.

"Yes, they said it was a great idea. It does make sense and they've started to set dates for every soul wronged. This is how the case will further proceed. With this plan going into effect, we are sure to win this. The last date is next week. We'll finally see the result of your case and it is looking to be very positive. Congratulations, you two." She smiled and leaned forward.

I squealed, unable to contain my excitement. "This is so perfect. Everything is coming together. We can finally tell Lucía we have great news. We can tell her without feeling like the bad guys because everyone is really getting what they want. I just can't believe this is going to work." I clapped.

He chuckled. "I knew it all along."

Looking at him, I hit his arm. He didn't feel it. "We get it, you're a genius. This is about everyone's happy ending and not how smart you are." I gave him a cocked eyebrow.

Alex looked between the both of us. "You guys want some privacy I presume?"

"Only if you wish to give it. This is just how we usually communicate," I joked.

Ayden leaned back and put his hands behind his head. "I'm just the best husband ever."

I shot him a glare. "Let's go. We're headed back to see Marie and Lucía. They must know the good news." I stood up and dragged Ayden behind me.

"I'm dead serious. They accepted our plan, and we will get a victory from all this." I covered my mouth, squealing some more.

The two sisters hugged one another, grins as apparent as ever. "Is this the light at the end of the tunnel?"

Marie smiled. "It seems so." She rubbed Lucía's back.

Despite allowing Connor to stay with her, the cravings still hit. Not enough to force me off this couch, but enough to make me wanna whine for something to snack on.

"Promise me you will love yourself. I want you to live a happy ending for the both of us." Marie grabbed Lucía's face in her hand. "Promise me."

Lucía frowned. "Are you leaving already?"

"I'll visit, but I still have a job in Heaven. I'll be there when your time comes. It just isn't now. I didn't get to follow my dreams or find love. This Thomas guy sounds amazing, so you should give him a chance. If he's another Liam, send him my way. I'll take care of him before he can beg for mercy." She embraced her one last time.

Lucía wrapped her arms around Marie. "Don't go. Please."

"What did I just say? You will make me happy by living your happiest life. Do that, for me." She pulled away.

With a nod, Lucía dropped her gaze.

"I have to go. I'll see you soon." Marie left a smile in her wake. "I love you."

"I love you, too," Lucía said in a quiet tone.

Then she was gone.

Lucía sat on the couch, trying to figure out her feelings. "She's already out of my life, again. She's gone just like that."

"She'll visit. She just can't be around all the time," I reassured her.

Ayden stood, clapping his hands together. "I'll make us some cake, yeah?"

I grinned. "Yes!"

He laughed and went to the kitchen. That was why I married him. He made me a cake whenever I wanted it. I could never ask for another husband. A baker was the best kind.

"What if Thomas is truly bad?" Lucía asked.

I faced her, shrugging. "How will you know if you don't try? He could be a great guy. How many guys will even try with a pregnant woman? Not many. Seriously, when I say this, I mean it. He could be the one and you'll never know until you give him a chance. Most guys won't even mess with a pregnant woman because of the burden on them. But Thomas doesn't seem to mind. He likes you regardless."

Her mouth twitched upward. "I just don't know. He's not just taking on someone else's baby. He's carrying my problems and my depression. That just doesn't just go away. This is eight years of pain and seeing Marie was great... But..."

I reached forward and grabbed her hand, giving a light squeeze. "I know. I'm not saying this will solve anything. You need time. But we will be here and support you through this process. Thomas can be another helping hand. There is never anything shameful about having extra support."

She nodded a bit. "All right... What do I even say?"

"It won't matter. Thomas has a big crush. Nothing can ruin that." I stood from the couch. "Ayden, we're going to the cafe. We'll be back in time for cake."

I helped Lucía up and she drove. It was strange being in a car after not having been in one for so long. Ayden died in his... It was the same place he had survived death and earned me in return.

Lucía parked and shook her head. "I can't do this."

"Yes, you can. You are Lucía Álvarez. You've been dealing with this pregnancy on your own. You're strong. I'll be with you." I got out of the car and helped her out. "Come on. I won't let you miss out on a great guy over fear."

We walked inside the cafe, the little bell above us dinging. The cafe smelled of fresh-baked pastries and bread—marvelous. I needed food., but I had no money, which stopped me from getting any.

Lucía was slow to approach the counter. I sat at a table by the corner. In case she needed back up, I was here to swoop in and save the day.

"Lucía, it's been a while. How have you been?" Thomas asked as he exited the employee door that led to the back.

She leaned against the counter for some balance. Her legs were shaking, anxiety starting to coat her bones. "I've been...okay."

After we had saved her from suicide, we had to make the decision whether to take her to a hospital. I was worried they would lock her up in a mental facility and take away her child if they knew what she'd done. She didn't need that. It would make the problem much worse. Humans weren't always the best at rehabilitation.

"Okay? Is something wrong?" Thomas' face filled with concern.

She nodded. "I've just been dealing with my own issues. Have you ever heard phrases about our heads being the main part of us? I know I'm not making much sense. The quote is vague in my memory. It was something about controlling the mind because wherever the head goes, the body follows. It's why a body can't survive without a head, but if someone is paralyzed or without limbs, they can still survive.

The head is the most important part to take care of."

Thomas' tension deflated. "You're talking about your mental health."

She pressed her lips together. "I am..."

"Is there anything I can do to help?" he asked.

Lucía wasn't sure how to answer that question. I wasn't even certain I could, either.

Only she could give him a response.

"Yes, there is something you can do." She straightened her posture. "I have to fix myself. It's my responsibility to heal my mind but I could always use more friends to have my back. Could you be that for me?"

Thomas didn't hesitate to soften his features, a smile tugging at his lips as he nodded. He'd be whatever she needed. Friend, or more someday, hopefully. For now, he'd just show her how much he cared even if she never reciprocated the romance.

"Of course. I'll be there when you need me to be." He nodded towards her belly. "Have you named your baby?" He pointed to her stomach.

She looked down at her belly and nodded a bit. "I have. I want to name him after my dad. I know my parents haven't been in my life in a long time, but they were always there before I pushed them away." Closing her eyes, she exhaled. "But I've found a more suitable name recently. Connor."

I swallowed, tempted to break down and cry.

"That's a great name." I could only hope he would be good for her. Lucía needed all the friends she could get.

I rested my chin on my hands held up by my elbows on the table I sat at. Life was beginning to look up. It had been the worst journey ever, but it was coming to an end. We had defeated Liam and put Hell back in its place. We were warriors. We were going to make it through this.

We had gone from broken people and rebuilt ourselves as soldiers. It was a hard path to conquer but we did it. I had fallen apart many times along the way, but I got back up. Connor would be her baby and Lucía was going to get her happy ending.

I smiled at the thought of Ayden. He had stuck with me through this entire journey, and I had to give him credit. I knew I made the right decision when I said yes to marrying him. Asking for a better husband wasn't an option. There was nobody who could fill the role as well. I truly believed in soulmates solely because he'd been so well-crafted as mine.

There had been a day when I used to say it was impossible for me to fall for a human. I knew it was supposed to happen, but I didn't believe it would. I didn't think Ayden would be the very person I would love. Yet, he was. He was the only man I could ever love. He would always be the one for me.

We had been opposites that first day we met but they always said opposites attract. He was a cold man. He'd hated everyone and everything. He would never think about taking orders from someone else. He tried hard to prove he was the alpha male.

Well, he was. He was the only male in our little group. Selene, Lucía, and I were all women. He was the exact alpha we needed. He was strong and compassionate. He cared about us. He cared about *me.*

Seeing him do something he loved was a delightful feeling. I was a content wife when Ayden was himself and he was filled with joy in what he did with his time. I vowed to succeed in my mission to be his guardian angel and I came through with my promise. I may have failed Justin, but I did not fail Ayden. I won the lottery, and the prize had been his heart.

"A little friend of ours is missing. Any idea where he might be?" a familiar voice asked.

I came face to face with Daniel, the man who'd once cursed my sexuality. "Not a clue." He called Liam a friend, as if keeping him in a cell was the same as crate-training. Was it?

"How has it been with your husband? Rocky?" A smirk tugged at his lips.

I gave him a cunning smile in return, as a favor. He couldn't scare me anymore. Now all that was left of his memory was pure bitterness. A taste only a mother could love, and I certainly wasn't one. "Better. Our sex has risen to new heights."

"May I be the judge of that?"

"Are you asking me for a blowjob?"

Daniel's presence had once forced my body to cower. To recoil. To shudder.

However, too much had changed—enough that now I was dying to brag about how much our relationship had changed since we last saw him. I was capable of so much more. He should fear me.

"I'm asking you if Liam is that tempting to be around. You're breaking rules and stealing him from Hell because Ayden can't give you want you crave."

With a scowl, I stepped closer. "Don't test me."

He closed more of the gap between us. "But that's where all the fun is."

Fun.

He wanted to talk about the things that made me tick. Fun was jumping in a bounce house. Fun was going to the fair. Those were enjoyable. Nothing about this—or Daniel—elicited positive feelings. All he brought me was poison.

Before I made a wrong move and did something that endangered the people I loved, I turned on my heel and began to head back.

"If he really wants to prove himself and keep you satisfied, he'll learn to ask you for your ideas," he paused, "—sexual ideas, that is. Goodnight, Angel, and don't let the bed bugs bite."

Noisome

The more I pondered the idea, the clearer it became. Why did I ever want a kid? It wasn't solely my decision, but it had been painted like it was. I thought I wanted kids because I was desperate to be the parent my parents never were, but now that I was pregnant and had my parents back, I knew better.

After a long sigh, I looked over at Liam. "How could I? How could I forget that my parents loved me? It doesn't make sense."

He shrugged. "When you broke your soul, maybe you lost the memory of love."

"But I didn't forget about Selene."

"I think Selene's love was too strong to slip through the cracks. But your love for your parents may never have been strong enough. They were always around. Selene was your first real friend and then she wasn't there anymore. You're traumatized by her death, not your parents' death. They're still alive. I'm not a therapist or psychologist so take my words with a grain of salt." He cleared his throat. "I think by being broken, you craved more emotional pain. And with a piece missing, you forgot what it was like to love people, initially adding more trauma. But forgetting Selene would have been too easy of a way out, and too nice of an ending for you. So, you remembered the biggest trauma of all but forgot about those who made you happy. In the end, it left you with nothing but the feeling of being completely unwanted and alone. The ultimate eternal suffering."

Oddly enough, his words made total sense. As a broken soul, I had become addicted to the discomfort and so it made sense to add more on top of that. It was going to be a struggle to continue my afterlife without desiring to hurt myself emotionally, but I'd need to do it. I had to take care of my mental health now.

Ayden sat up, his eyes darting between the two of us. "Angel, is there anything I can help you with?"

"What do you mean?"

"I don't know. I don't like the idea of Liam knowing you better than I do."

Poor bubble. "I'm going to burst it, Ayden, but Liam was my friend before he murdered me. He's going to know me more than you'd like him to. Selene had been my roommate for about three or four months, and Liam had been dating her around the same length of time. We all became friends. I was there when they started dating. I was there when they said they loved each other. I was there even after she cheated on him. I never knew, of course, but I was there. And then, I wasn't. She was murdered and that was it. It became just Liam and I, solving a murder that he knew the answer to."

"I know, I know. He still murdered all of us. That doesn't change anything, and I don't trust him. I don't like him. This whole buddy thing you have going on with him is stupid and uncalled for." He gestured to Liam.

Yeah, Liam had slit my throat. He slit all our throats. What was I supposed to do though? "Do you suggest we take him back to Hell? I brought him up to help me find my soul and I suppose that's no longer in the question. Our focus is having this baby for Lucía and getting the other souls into a permanent destination."

Ayden looked at Liam. "That's not a terrible idea."

However, Liam wasn't so thrilled by it. "No, no. No." He got off the couch. "I don't want to go back there."

"Liam, it isn't a choice. You're going back. I never took you out with the intention to keep you out. You're dead and you certainly don't deserve to be in Heaven. Take offense, please, because you're not worth fighting for."

He shot me a glare. "Just kill me, will ya?"

"I already did." I followed him into the kitchen. "And I won't lie to you. I took great pleasure in it. At the end of the night, you killed me. You killed Selene. You killed Ayden. You don't deserve to go to Heaven now. You lost your chance. It's back to Hell."

"Just give me one more week. One," he begged.

Why was I considering it? "Fine. One more." And part of me feared he was trying to stick around long enough to see Connor be born. Was he planning something? I needed to be prepared for anything that could tear the fabric of our souls.

Ayden grabbed my wrist and pulled me into another room. "Angel, we can't."

"Ayden, I know what I'm doing. Trust me." I gave him a peck. *"Trust me."*

But as soon as I went to the bathroom for a second to make sure I did have it under control, I heard yelling.

Oh no.

Running to the kitchen, I grabbed hold of the wall before I ran into someone and fell. "What the hell are you two doing?" I shouted.

Ayden looked at me, giving me his best innocent look. Yet, he had Liam's stomach against the edge of the counter, arm around his neck to keep him stabilized. "This is not what it looks like."

"It looks like you're trying to fight Liam."

He nodded a bit. "You'd be correct. But in my defense, he killed me. This is my revenge."

"Really? Revenge?" I pulled him away from Liam. "You don't need revenge anymore."

But Ayden crossed his arms to prove otherwise. "You don't know what I need. Revenge is the best way out of this. He killed you and I want to rip his fucking head off." He scowled. "And who was it that tortured you when you were in Hell? He's a bloody monster. A *demon*. He doesn't deserve your compassion."

I forgot I'd mentioned that Liam had tortured me personally the second time.

"It's not compassion."

"Then what is this? Because you would never invite a rapist into our home! Sam, huh? That would be a no. But *Liam* is okay? What's the difference between murder and rape, Angel? Nothing! You told me that all sins are equal, and these two are no different." He slammed his hand on the counter, making Liam jump.

A sigh. "I'm sorry, but he killed me. I'm allowed to react however I need to."

Ayden laughed without any humor present. "And I'm allowed the same since he killed *me*, too." He left the cabin, slamming the door behind him.

I chased after him, afraid this could only get worse if I didn't try. "Ayden, stop! Wait! I can't keep up!"

He came to an abrupt halt and spun around, looking me dead in the eye. "You have no idea. You have no idea what it's like to watch the one person you love allow themselves to get hurt over and over again. You know how terrible this idea is and yet you don't stop," his voice cracked. "You told me how you felt when Selene and I were becoming friends, and you admitted you were afraid we would hurt you. But what are you doing now?"

"I do not love Liam! This is different!"

"How?" He yelled. "How the fuck is this any different? Those two broke up through death, and we stayed together and now we have been allowing them to come between us!" He banged his fist against a tree trunk. "I can't keep doing this."

My chest weighed heavily. "What are you saying?" I swallowed. "Please, stay. Don't go." I stepped forward, reaching out. "I fell in love with you and I don't regret it."

He didn't say another word. Instead, he walked off into the woods, and to deter me from chasing him again, he pushed off the ground and flew north.

I fell against the tree as the tears poured down my cheeks. Why was I keeping Liam around? What was I gaining from it? Nothing. But I was beginning to lose *everything* in return. Ayden. Sunny. Selene. Connor. No matter how hard I tried to win, I always lost.

I never wanted to fall in love. Despite everyone else's obsession with romance and settling down, I never worried about such things. My heart only ached for a friend, and Selene had been exactly that.

Ayden had come and tore my world into two. He stepped inside it, then stitched it back together. But it never looked the same after that moment, and instead the skin fused back as best as it could, leaving behind a scar to show the world what had really happened that fateful day.

Wicked—the only way to describe the way Ayden lured me in. It all became a game to him, one where he'd win, and I'd never have a chance at all. I'd never been the best at winning any games.

Did Ayden regret everything that transpired between us?

Liam helped me off the ground. "He'll realize his mistakes." He took me inside, but I could barely pay attention through all the tears. I was afraid that he would never love me again.

He'd given up on us. He'd given up on me.

"Angel?" Liam asked.

I looked at him, sniffling. "I'm sorry." Angel? No. That was abhorrent. "Don't call me that. You have no right."

"I tried Eliana, but you wouldn't listen."

Angel. Ayden nicknamed me that when I refused to tell him my real name. Since then, he's called me that ever since. I'd be a fool to not admit I loved the term of endearment. Coming from him, it was the sweetest thing, and that was why I never wanted anyone else to use it. It was for Ayden's tongue only.

"He will come back."

"He won't, Liam. Ayden isn't coming back." Those words stabbed my heart and ripped it open like a wolf tearing apart flesh. Saying them aloud made me realize how true they were, and just how terrifying they blogged about our love.

Our love had been false.

I retreated to the one place that gave me comfort. The closet.

The closet wrapped me up in its arms and whispered sweet nothings. It provided me the haven I needed. I hadn't fully processed the pain of losing him, and I couldn't be sure if I ever would. Maybe it was a good idea that we decided not to keep Connor. Or...it was because of that that Ayden had the last straw with me.

Leaning my head back, I choked on a sob. "Ayden, why would you do this to me? I thought you loved me. You promised." I placed the back of my hand against my mouth to quiet my cries. "Just tell me the truth. Tell me that you regret marrying me. Kissing me. Saying you love me. Tell me that you regret having me as your guardian angel."

Despite no body, chills shook my soul to the core. So, having nothing else to do, I lay on the floor and closed my eyes, dreaming of a reality where everything worked out for the better. All I had to coax me to sleep were the dreams in my mind. They certainly did their best and succeeded.

"You should be rotting in Hell. Ayden has the right idea," Selene said. "Why don't you go back there? It's your job to fix this mess."

Liam scoffed. "You cheated on me. And according to your God, cheating is just as bad as murder. You and I are on the same level."

"We are not the same! You know for a fact—" Selene paused. "She's waking up. I heard something." She came to the closet door and slid it open. "Oh, Elli. Honey." She frowned as she bent down and helped me up. "You're a mess. Let me help you."

I let her fix my face, and she attempted to make me cookies, but it wasn't the same. Selene despised Liam, but they shared one thing in common without realizing it. They both gave me the same pitiful look.

Ayden walked out on us. Was that all I'd be reduced to? The wife whose husband left her?

"He's never coming back, Selene. He said he couldn't keep doing this."

"Sometimes men say those things and still come back. They don't realize how their words sound to us." She lifted my chin. "But no matter what happens, I will always be here for you." And I began to doubt if she meant it.

Careless

"I'm afraid that we won't make it," I whispered into the early morning. The sun was barely rising above the horizon, leaving the sky a dark blue.

I took a walk back to my old college, watching the students find their way through the mess. It all had begun here, and yet I couldn't remember why I chose this college to begin with. Maybe if I had never come here, my life could be normal.

Turning on my heel, I left my footprints behind in the snow, letting everyone know my presence had been here. A few people gave me looks, pointing directly at me. They recognized me from my memorial set up in the main hall.

My next stop was the library Ayden broke into years ago. It looked almost the same. They chose not to change much, and I didn't blame them. I wouldn't have changed much, either.

Except maybe the locks.

My final stop was Ayden's apartment. "Would you still have loved me if you hadn't died?" Maybe it was all wrong. Maybe, just maybe...

"I thought I'd find you here," someone said in a quiet voice.

I whipped around too fast, losing my balance and catching myself against the wall. "I... What..." I couldn't get the words out. "I never thought I'd see you again."

Ayden stepped forward and released a sigh. "I'd never do that. I just needed time to sort out my thoughts. I guess... After what my grandpa did to me, I never got full closure. I never got to tell him off and make him pay. I just don't understand why you don't feel that way toward Liam."

"We killed him. We already got our revenge. His soul is tethered to Hell no matter what. There's nothing more I need to do now." I leaned my back against the wall.

He decided not to respond to that. Instead, he said, "I heard you. When I flew off, I decided to go up to Heaven. I heard your little prayer." He looked off in the distance. "I'm angry because you've been giving all this time and attention to Liam instead of me. What am I doing wrong? Do I need to drag you to Hell and torture you myself? Didn't I already do that when I told you I'd never love you?"

"Why are you so jealous of him? You know I would never love Liam."

His head turned and he locked eyes with me. He stepped forward again, closing the gap between us, and then he placed his hands on either side of my head. "I am not jealous of him. Something isn't right with him, and you can't see it. I just don't want to see you get hurt again."

"Why can't you trust me?"

"I do, Angel. It's *him* I don't trust," he mumbled, leaning closer. But he never let me have a little taste. He pushed off. "I'll see you at home."

"Wait," I said. It was too late by then. Ayden had already flown away.

By the time I made it back to the cabin, I was ready to slap him for leaving me behind. My thoughts were scrambled as I walked through the door. He had the music blasting, and it was none other than rock music.

Ayden came out of the kitchen, no shirt. "Took you long enough."

"What..." I narrowed my eyes. "You left me behind."

He shrugged, plopping down on the couch and laying his arm across the back. "I gave you time. Why don't you sit beside me?"

"No."

"No?"

"No."

"Sit down."

"No."

"Suit yourself." He undid the buckle to his belt, unzipping his jeans with it. But that was as far as he went. I knew what his game was. He was attempting to seduce me by being the same man he was before he had died.

Folding my arms across my chest, I sat beside him. "It's not going to work. You're sick."

With a chuckle, he asked, "What isn't?"

The V shape dipped down below his boxer briefs. What was it about men and that dip that made them so attractive? "Seducing me with this bad boy charm you have."

"Is that what I'm doing?" He grabbed my feet and pulled them into his lap, removing my heels.

"You know exactly what you're doing." The muscles in my body relaxed.

He began massaging my feet, digging right into the good spots. "I'm not doing anything. I believe you're just looking to cause trouble."

"Me? Trouble? Never. I'm the good girl. I'm nicknamed Angel for a reason." And that was no lie. I lay back on the other arm, closing my eyes. This was the perfect time to take a nap.

He put my feet down, sliding his hands right up my legs. "You are always trouble," he whispered into my ear.

I grabbed his hands and lifted them off me. "If you say so, then I suppose I must live up to the reputation." I slipped out from under him and got off the couch. "Trouble does exactly as she's meant to, and that includes not giving you what you want."

Ayden groaned, face planting into the seat cushion.

It was satisfying to watch him suffer after how I felt the past few days. If he had just made it easy on me, this wouldn't have been a problem.

"Angel, please come back."

Now in the kitchen, I began to make myself something to eat to feed the cravings. "You made me feel like I wasn't good enough. You left me here by myself. If Liam can't be trusted, why was I alone with him?"

A sigh escaped his lips. "I see how it is. You're mad at me."

"Am I not supposed to be? You're the one who left. You walked out on us. I never thought you were coming back. That is a hidden fear for a girl like me. I've given you everything. I have given you my entire heart and I've never done that before, and what did you do? You walked away."

"I told you already, I never planned to leave. I just needed extra time before I did something really stupid." He sat up and looked at me.

"It was stupid to leave me."

"I was trying to give myself some space and let my anger disappear. It bothers me that people think taking time to cool off is the same as ignoring someone. I could still hear you. If something was really wrong, I would have come running."

It wasn't good enough. "I can't look at you right now."

Ayden came to the kitchen, but he was missing pants. "How can I make it up to you?"

That wasn't something I had the answer to. I wanted him to figure it out himself. When was the pivotal moment I had truly fallen in love with him?

He moved behind me, moving all my hair to one side. He planted a few kisses along my neck. As much as I loved it, it wasn't putting me in the mood. "Ayden, please stop."

He lifted his head and turned me around to face him. "Did I really hurt you?"

"Yes. I told you. You *really* hurt me."

"Let me bake you something. What's your favorite kind of dessert?" He brushed his thumb over my cheek.

He expected me to answer that, and I couldn't do so right away. I took a minute to think about it, but then that confused me some more. I enjoyed fruits in desserts, but I also enjoyed just pastries themselves.

"Cheesecake? Cake? Pie? Cookies? Cupcakes? Name it."

"Ice cream cake with fruit."

"What?"

I nodded. "That's what I want."

Ayden chuckled. "I don't do that well, but I'll see what I can whip up." He circled the island and began to gather ingredients. Within minutes, he already had a mixture going.

Once the cake was in the oven, he gave me the bowl. "Want to lick it?"

I grabbed a spoon and scooped some up, flinging it at his face. Laughter burst from me as I threw another spoonful at his face. Ayden's eyes went wide, and he reached over and pulled it from my hands. My smile began to fade as he turned to put it in the sink. Seconds later, he spun around, and the batter clung to my lips.

"Rude!" And then I was running.

For the next few minutes, I chased him around the counter, getting caught every now and then when he reversed it on me. Finally, I swiped my foot under his and he went down face first, rolling onto his back. As soon as he did, I tripped over his foot and fell right on top. No words could describe how much I longed for this moment again. It was one of the first happy memories I had with him and getting a chance to recreate it after marriage eased all my worries.

When Ayden and Selene got into the same fight with flour, my jealousy hit its peak. Oh how the tables had turned...

Chuckling, he licked my lips and up the bridge of my nose. "You had batter all over you."

A small smile flickered before it was gone. "Do you remember the moment you first fell for me?"

"That's impossible. There wasn't a single moment. It was a collective of memories put together. The way you laugh. Your smile. Your determination to make everyone happy with themselves. You came into my life and flipped it upside down."

"I know it's hard for you to believe I could love the man you were, but that's it. I did. I fell for you at your worst, and I would do it over again. You didn't like me very much...but you were never violent towards me. You never called me names. You were never the bad guy," I uttered.

Ayden grabbed my thighs, pulling my legs up until they straddled his waist. "But I was. I hurt you many times, and maybe it wasn't physical or verbal abuse, but it was wrong. You deserved so much better. I tried to make you feel less like a person and for that, I am so sorry."

I relaxed my soul. "You changed. You changed for yourself and that's what matters most." I kissed him softly, sucking the batter off his lip. "Had to clean that."

"Why don't you clean the rest?"

With a laugh, I nodded and licked the rest of it off his face. "Better?"

"Mm, so much better." He pushed hair behind my ear and ran his knuckle across my cheek. "I love you, Eliana Dyer."

Somehow, that was what mended my heart. How could he manage to pull me back in? It was effortless for him, almost as if he had done it all before. And he had...the first time we fell in love.

"I think I'm falling for you all over again," I said.

Ayden pulled me in for a kiss, caressing my lips with his own. "I don't doubt it. I'm that irresistible." Before I could argue, he deepened the kiss, keeping me hostage for as long as we needed.

The timer beeped and I pulled away with a sigh. "Go ahead." I rolled off and let him get his cake from the oven.

By the time I fixed my clothes, Ayden pulled me to the bedroom. "Cake needs to cool now." He reeled me in for another kiss and I happily obliged. There'd been plenty of times when the clothes didn't come off in seconds, but this was not one of those moments. After the awful way we left things this past week, we needed to make up for it, and soul-to-soul had been the cure. It served its purpose.

I couldn't complain about being pregnant *after* death, because my boobs had managed to get a bit bigger, and I was thankful not to feel that kind of torture.

And in an odd way, I was even more grateful that Ayden's focus was never on my breasts. I had never been too happy with them and knowing he wasn't paying much attention to them now made me feel less self-conscious about it.

No, instead, that night his focus was on me—and just our needs alone.

My stomach would have been doing flips if I had one. This was by far the scariest day of my life, worse than being tortured in Hell.

The judge sat on her stand, already having conversed with God, the decision being made for each soul. Alex was nervous for both of us which just added to how we already felt.

Today was the day on which we would find out where everyone went after their bodies had been chopped up.

Our parents were at home so they could hear the final decision when this court session was over. Selene was inside the room, sitting in the back row. Lucía was at her own home, waiting. We needed to bring her good news. We had to.

"We have discussed the situation in which Lucía will need a guardian angel, and it has been approved. Lucía Álvarez will get our top guardian angel as soon as possible. With her latest suicide attempt, it is clear that she needs our best to help her in the long run. She has agreed to take on Lucía and help her with the depression that has been growing inside her for eight years and counting. As Lucía's sister is Marie Álvarez, it gave us even more incentive to grant her the best in our business," the judge said.

The judge looked at Ayden and I, clearing her throat. "Ayden and Eliana Dyer, God had given permission for us to grant you your wishes to let Lucía keep her child with his soul and all."

I covered my mouth as a ringing echoed in my ears. Connor was officially her child, and there was no going back now.

"Now, we will move forward with the final decision on the souls of," she said, continuing to list off every name of the souls here to go somewhere.

She went through about ten souls before Becky came up, each of those ten mostly getting into Heaven while a few were sent down to Hell.

Becky stepped forward.

"Becky Maslow. Based upon your life on earth, we have determined that now as a soul no longer attached to your body, your eternal home will be in Heaven."

Becky started to cry, emotions blended between pure joy and a longing to see her daughter again. Now, she'd have a chance to watch over her.

Everyone cheered until a few more were placed in Heaven or Hell, and Sunny was saved for last.

"Sunny Smith. Based upon your life on earth, we have determined that now as a soul no longer attached to your body, your eternal home will be in Heaven."

We all jumped up and clapped, screaming woos and more. To hear that another one of my charges made it to Heaven just filled my heavy heart. I dared to never go back and do it over. Maybe...

Ayden and I stood up, walking to the sides of the rows where we met up with Selene and Sunny. She gave us one big hug. "Congratulations! I am so happy for all of you. You guys truly deserve this."

Selene stepped away and nodded towards the person behind us. We turned around to face Alex, our lawyer. "I'm so glad to have fought for you and I'm proud to say you won. I hope you two will be very happy. You deserve so much more. And Eliana, we are so glad to have you back as a guardian angel."

"Thank you, Alex. Truly, thank you so much." I gave her my best hug before Ayden shook her hand. Selene, Ayden, Sunny, and I left the room and headed to Lucía's for a celebration.

Ayden gripped my wrist, kissing my knuckles. "You chose to become a guardian angel?"

I smiled, glancing his way. "Did I not tell you? I wanted to find some security, and this was right up my alley. I might not be whole, but I'm whole being surrounded by all of you." I hadn't even told him the best part yet. But that was for later.

When we arrived at her apartment, we told her everything we knew about the case, from the fact that she would get a guardian angel and she was going to keep their baby. What more could we ask for? She had confirmed knowledge that Connor was completely her own son to raise.

I stood, getting everyone's attention by clinking a fork against a glass. I'd always wanted to try that. "I have some important news to make here. We are all aware now that Lucía is getting a guardian angel, and I have joined the business again."

Selene gasped, figuring it out before anyone else.

"Lucia's guardian angel has been chosen, named top guardian angel and someone who has rightfully earned her position." As selfish as that sounded... "Lucía," I said as I smiled at her, "I'm going to be your new guardian angel."

Lucía screamed before she started to cry. She came over and hugged me from the side, whispering, "Thank you. Thank you so much. I promise I will do my best not to let you down."

"And I will *not* let you die." I pulled away from our hug.

She invited Thomas over, and not because she wanted to tell him when she couldn't, but because she wanted to enjoy this evening of good news with more friends.

He arrived and Ayden baked a bunch of cupcakes for everyone. While Lucía couldn't celebrate with any kind of alcohol, she could still have sweets. That had to make up for it.

"You guys are way too sweet for doing this. I am so proud to be the one who knows you." She devoured the cupcake she had in her hands.

Selene sat back, giving Ayden and I the eye. "Tell us, Ayden. I know Elli won't do it. What is your sex life like since Connor came along? I know that women still want to do stuff. I'm sure you give her what she wants."

I glanced at Ayden, my eyes wide. Did I want him telling Selene our sex life? Absolutely not.

"Of course. What kind of husband would I be if I didn't take care of my wife in every way?" Ayden gave me a smirk. "We almost had sex on Christmas, in her old bedroom."

I choked on my words. "We did not almost have sex. You wanted to but I told you we couldn't. Almost having sex is when we get half-naked. We didn't even get anywhere near that."

Ayden crossed his arms.

"I'll be right back." I walked to the bathroom and took a moment to breathe. Metaphorically speaking, of course.

I nearly jumped when Ayden appeared in the doorway as I looked in the mirror. "Don't scare me like that."

He gave me a look. "Is something wrong?"

"Yes." I nodded as I unbuttoned my shirt. "You do this to me. You make me want you. Let's have sex, right now." Between winning the case and seeing Ayden in his black attire that made his green eyes pop,

I was craving what he had to offer.

He laughed. “Angel, I love you, but we are at Lucía’s. Everyone can hear us. You were the one who told me we can’t do it in front of others. You have to listen to your own advice.” He lifted an eyebrow.

I grabbed his shirt, pulling him close. “Screw my advice. I want to see you naked.”

He kissed my head and removed my hands from his shirt. “As much as I want to see you naked as well, I can’t. A wise woman once told me that we have to spend our time with friends as much as we can. We have eternity to have sex.” He grabbed my hand. “Let’s go eat my cupcakes.”

“And have sex?” I asked.

He shook his head. “No, we are going to talk and be with our friends. Why do you want me?” He stopped. “Why so sudden?”

“I don’t control the hormones. They control me. It comes at random moments.” My eyes lowered to his pants. “I want that.” I pointed between his legs.

“I know. Why do you think we’re providing Connor’s soul?” He gave me a sly smile.

I let out a gasp. “Excuse me, I’m not the only one who wants sex all the time. It takes two to make a baby, buddy. I was a virgin before you. You were not. It’s safe to say you want sex more.”

He shrugged and pursed his lips for a second, buttoning my shirt back up. “Sure, sex is good. But I’ve been fulfilling my needs for years now. You suppressed yours before me. Now that you have me, your wild side is loose. And that is why your sex drive is getting higher.” He walked to the living room with a proud smile.

That assface.

I was left in the hall with my mouth hanging open. I crossed my arms and went back to the living room.

My mood died down eventually, thanks to Ayden so rudely

rejecting me. It did tick me off, and maybe I'd get over it. Or maybe I'd punish him later...

I brought my attention to the window, watching the city coat itself in snow. Winter was a compassionate season. People saw it as cold, but Ayden had been frozen, too. Here he was, filled with so much compassion.

In the past, winter had always comforted me in my time of need. Selene's death was no accident, but it was just as heartbreaking. The snow had fallen gently, mourning for the lost.

Something so frigid could still hold so much warmth inside, and that was how fireplaces and hot chocolate were born. They kept us warm when the outside left us freezing. Winter was always mistaken for the cold and heartless season, and yet it seemed the most romantic and joyful of them all. Despite beliefs, it was by far the deadliest as blood splattered the walls.

A kiss in the snow was something a girl could dream of. It was more romantic than steamy, whereas rain made a kiss seem steamier as both parties got soaked. In the snow, people had to bundle up and cuddle to keep warm. That was romance at its finest hour. We could cuddle by the fireplace, drinking our hot cocoa.

Christmas was a season of giving, one that people seemed to love more than others despite their ill intentions the rest of the year. After all, there was a song that said it was the most wonderful time. Customers may have gotten meaner, but most people would get merrier. Families came together. Everyone shared the holidays.

I had lost so much during this season and yet, it was still the most loving of them all. Winter had been there through all the pain. Summer wasn't there for me when Selene died. Spring wasn't there when I got my parents back. Autumn was nowhere to be found when Ayden took me into his family for the first time when I was still just his guardian angel.

Winter was the witness to my pain, and it could empathize with how I felt. Winter was a natural occurrence of Ayden's presence.

People baked more sweets around winter. People cooked more food. People got closer to keep warm. It looked icy on the outside, but it was so comforting on the inside. Safe, even. There was nothing in this world that reminded me of Ayden Dyer more than winter had.

What did Selene remind me of? Selene reminded me of the summertime. She was a happy-go-lucky girl, someone who was so selfless and made sure everyone else was just okay. Selene was the only friend I had on earth before my death, and summer was the one season that made friends with everyone.

Summer was a lovable season, who could deny that? Selene was a social human being. She was the walking version of the hottest season of the year. The sunshine was out all the time, and Selene had always looked on the brighter side of things.

I had yet to find a walking person of spring. That season seemed to be the hardest. It had to be someone who was pretty to look at yet could be cold one day and warm the next. They would be unpredictable. They would have real feelings, and I didn't mean that in a way that the other seasons didn't. I just meant that the feelings for spring would be intense, as intense as a cold and hot day.

It could resemble Sunny. Like the warm spring day when I'd sat with her outside the rehab after her mental health break.

What was I comparable to? Autumn. Autumn, a season that could be anything. It could be as cold as winter or as warm as the summer. Autumn chose its own path. Autumn was the season that got people ready for the best season of the year, winter. I was the one who paved the road for Ayden to shine his brightest. I was the spotlight that beamed *on* him, to show the world what this man could be.

Autumn was colorful. It was a season that changed its colors, just as I'd changed mine. I wasn't the same Eliana before I met Ayden.

Things were different. I was going to be a guardian angel again. I was a wife. I was a woman in love with a man who had once been the bad boy. Hell had tried to tear me down, but I came back. I may have changed and died as Autumn leaves did, but I came back every year. I never gave up on humanity.

It was the season of eating. It was the season of scares. It was a season that had many different pieces and Ayden had helped me recognize parts of myself that I never knew existed. Autumn wasn't always the same every year. Sometimes winter came early and pushed me away. There were days where summer overstayed its welcome and I was barely making it through. What mattered was that I always came back to myself.

I may have been a month long or three months, but I would always do my job. I would change. I would allow the earlier version of me to rot for Ayden to come in and bring something near—to start over for a better future. In the end, I came back stronger, refusing to give up my position in this world.

Winter was the most compassionate season of them all. People froze to death, yet winter would keep their bodies preserved longer until they were found. Winter gave kids snow days. It gave us a wonderland. It gave us hope because it brought humanity together in ways no other season could.

Ayden Dyer brought people together in his own ways. He brought me together with my parents, and with Selene and Lucía. He brought me to him with the way he had acted. Had he not been in danger, I never would have had the chance to be his guardian angel. I could never have met him if things didn't end up the way they did. Winter looked dead on the outside but was very alive on the inside. It was part of nature's course with the seasons. It had a purpose to be here.

Winter saved me from a miserable eternity.

His white wings were bigger than Ayden's. "It is nice to meet you, Lucía," the angel said. He was a blonde boy, one with brown eyes and a smile that could save the day. This was her *other* guardian angel. The one they didn't tell me was going to help me. Rarely did people get two guardian angels, but it was more important for a pregnant woman with suicidal tendencies. Two bodies at stake.

I knew where I had to be. I walked right up to him and crossed my arms, giving both Lucía and Ayden a look. "Tell me, Nameless, what you intend to do to help Lucía." Oh yeah, I was going to interrogate him. From one guardian angel to another, I had to make sure he was right for her. Lucía needed guaranteed redemption from the darkness.

He gave me a smile, not a fake nor a smirk. It'd been genuine. "I understand your concern. My name is Xander. I intend to get to the root of the problem. Lucía attempted suicide for a reason, and we can't magically make that go away. It's a problem that has been sitting inside her for a long time. I will look at her mental health and go from there. I will address every area that she needs help with to make sure she gets the best care there is. I want her to be happy as much as you do. That *is* my job."

I huffed. "Fine. Fine. Sounds good enough to me, Xander. Be careful, please. She has a child with her, and I want to ensure the best outcome. I love her. Love her as I do, and we won't have any issues. I'm having her baby's soul after all." I rubbed my belly.

"Ah, yes, everyone heard about the good news. Congratulations on your new baby. I hope Connor realizes how blessed he is to have you as a mother," he told her while holding his grin the entire time. It was beginning to drive me crazy.

"All right, so, if you want to lose the smile and relate more to the little humans, that would be fantastic. Even Jesus ate with sinners."

I lifted my eyebrows and watched his smile fade as he tilted his head. "Yes, I must be more relatable for Lucía to take me advice and accept my help. Thank you for correcting me."

I gritted my teeth and turned around. I moved towards Ayden, leaning in close. "This guy is way too happy and perfect for his own good. I hope Lucía doesn't mind that. I sure as hell do."

My husband chuckled. "I don't think most people like their guardian angels at first. I never did. I couldn't stand you."

I cleared my throat. "Oh, I see."

"What? It's the truth. Don't pretend you didn't know. We were enemies at first. I didn't want you around and I didn't try to hide how I felt." He crossed his arms, not afraid to argue with me.

"But you like me now, right?" I asked.

He let out a laugh that caused me to frown. "Angel, I married you. I think it's safe to say I like you."

"That doesn't mean anything. Vows aren't important to everyone. Plenty of married couples hate each other. They cheat. They lie. They steal from each other. I don't want that to be us." I looked at the floor, unable to see my feet. My stomach had reached full size.

"It won't be. I do not feel like that toward you. I love you so much. Every day I see you and I know I am the luckiest man to have married you. I see your smile and it makes me so happy to know that you're happy. I could never hate you. I would never cheat on you or lie to you. You are my wife, and you always will be." He kissed me with passion—a craving I hadn't experienced in a long time.

I pulled away, our foreheads touching. "I'm so happy that you've said that. You mean the world to me. You drove me nuts when I first got assigned to you but somehow, you showed me who you were. I saw the real Ayden. I fell in love with you. That is all that truly matters."

"Excuse me, are you guys going to leave me with Xander? I can't deal with his happy personality all at the damn time." Lucía asked us. As we turned to face her, she pointed at Xander who was watching us.

I laughed. "Trust me, you will get used to him. Ayden had to deal with me before he accepted me as his guardian angel. I don't like Xander but if he does good, that's what matters. You wanted to die but we couldn't let you. We can't always give you what you want. You have Connor and that is amazing news. If Xander ever bugs you, just go to Thomas to vent. He's a good listener. I'm also here."

She groaned, giving Xander a hard-to-miss glare. "Fine."

I shook my head and looked at Ayden with a smile. "She'll be okay. I know she will be."

"I know, Angel," he said.

"Well, Lucía, we should go back to our cabin now. Xander will be here to look after you in the meantime." I grabbed Ayden's hand to drag him out of the apartment.

Ayden waved goodbye, leaving them with his big, goofy smile. He could never be too serious all the time or that would erase a big part of who he was.

We walked down the stairs, getting to the bottom of the building. The parking lot was almost empty since most people worked during the daytime. I'd never had a job. My parents worked too much so I just used their money instead.

Maybe I shouldn't have, but if they said they loved me, they could pay for my tuition. It was a fair trade. I sure as hell didn't want to pay for it and be in debt for the rest of my life because I was too young to make enough to pay off a huge loan.

Pain shot into my uterus, and I knew what this was. Ayden caught me before I fell to the ground.

Intense, too much for me to stand on my own. I always had a sensitive body. Of course, I didn't actually have a uterus, but it had been sensitive when I had one before my death. This made *no* difference.

"Lucía's going into labor. The baby's coming," I said. Ayden watched Xander come out of the apartment with Lucía hanging onto him. I couldn't focus on how nervous I was because of the contractions she was getting.

Xander took her to the hospital. We followed behind but had to keep ourselves invisible. Doctors didn't need to witness an angel give birth, or how a soul came to be.

They came over, getting Lucía to the maternity floor. They found her a room and we followed, but Ayden sat me in a chair right away. I was tired of standing.

She changed into a hospital gown in the bathroom before sitting on her bed. "The contractions are still far apart. I can tell he won't be coming for a while."

Ayden looked at me as if he was waiting for my response to this.

I shook my head. "It means we must be in labor longer than we want to be. Our babies are ready, but we aren't dilated enough. It's not time to push. *This* is going to suck." I groaned. I did not want to wait forever to see Connor, but I had no choice.

"What do you do about you? How will you give birth? Does it

push as Lucía does?" Ayden asked.

I scrunched my face at the thought of that. That was an awful image. "No, no. I think I just need to push when she does. As soon as both babies are out, the soul enters the body."

Lucía peered over at Xander. "Do you have to be here for this?"

"I do, Lucía. I have to be here because this will be tough on you." He gave her a sorrowful smile.

Lucía looked at her stomach. "Of course, but which woman isn't in pain? Birth is painful. Thank Eve for that."

I chuckled. "She's right. Eve ate from the tree first, thus cursing all women with more pain than men. She screwed us all over." I looked at Ayden. "Unless I've told you this before. My mind is jumbled. I can't even remember what I've said and what I haven't."

He didn't say anything to me.

"Ayden, you okay?" I rubbed his shoulder.

He nodded a little. "I'm just nervous. I mean, this is a big deal for me. I know you're not going to be a mother but... I guess I'm just now realizing what's happening. Connor is still part of us. Will he come out looking exactly like your baby?" he asked Lucía.

She shrugged. "I would guess since souls look like their physical bodies and if this is Connor's physical body, he would look like mine."

"She's right." I chewed my lip. "I look exactly like my physical body did."

Ayden stood up, grabbing himself a cup of water. He didn't need it, but it calmed his nerves.

Xander sat in the chair but his eyes held a secret. He knew something we didn't. He wasn't keeping the secret on purpose, but he knew.

The doctors came in and measured her cervix. They did this several times through many contractions before they finally gave her the green light. Ayden had lay me back on the floor. It wasn't comfortable but I wasn't a human, so the hard floor made no difference to how I felt.

"Bloody hell, I'm delivering my own baby!" Ayden yelled.

"Ayden, just do what the doctor does. She's going to push, and you just grab Connor when he comes out. There won't be any blood or cord for you to remove. He will just be a clean little soul," Xander whispered.

Regardless, my husband scrunched his face in disgust. "This looks so gross from my view."

I rubbed my face. "Shut up, Ayden. Just do your damn job."

As soon as Lucía began pushing, I did the same. It was no walk in the park. The pain was well over the normal pain threshold, and I was surprised living women could survive this.

I had to push multiple times before Connor came out and it was over. Ayden grabbed him, speechless.

Sitting up, I peeked over to see Connor. He was quiet but precious. He was perfect.

"Why isn't he crying? Why isn't he crying?" Lucía yelled.

Ayden and I turned our attention to her while the doctors were doing everything they could to get some air into his lungs while his skin turned blue. No, this couldn't be.

After a few minutes, the doctors stopped trying. "I'm so sorry," the male said.

"Ayden, quick! Get him into the body!" I threw my arms in Connor's body's direction.

He jumped up, carrying the soul to his body and trying to push him in. "He won't go in! I can't get him into the body!"

"Keep trying!"

He kept pushing, using every angle and method he could before stepping back. "Fuck... Angel, what have we done?" He cradled the soul of Connor Álvarez while his little body lay lifeless in the clear box.

Lucía screamed at him and started crying, shaking in an uncontrolled manner. Xander's eyes landed on us and I looked at Connor. He knew Lucía would lose her child. They had promised to let her baby be hers, but they didn't come through. She had to lose her baby and for what purpose? How was I supposed to be able to live with myself, knowing that we took her son away from her by starting this court case in the first place?

And at the end of the night, winter was the only season to witness this devastating loss.

"You knew that Connor wasn't going to make it and you never said anything." I clenched my jaw, eyes locked on the wall directly behind Xander.

He rubbed his neck. "I couldn't. I was under oath."

"They promised that she would get to keep him! Why did they lie? She is absolutely shattered." I looked over at Lucía as she clutched his body to her chest. She couldn't believe her own baby was already gone.

Xander watched her and lowered his head. "You have to understand that something happened in court, something that nobody else knew about. Things have been decided. Liam is missing from Hell, and they couldn't risk him hurting the baby."

"So they killed Connor instead?"

"That was the only way, Eliana. That is why Lucía got two guardian angels. The baby was safer in Heaven, and solid bodies cannot make it up past the clouds. We couldn't protect her from him."

When I looked at her, shame gnawed at my insides. I brought Liam out. I was the reason that they feared the worst and made the most indefinite decision about a helpless child.

"Stay with her. Don't leave her side. I have something I need to do," I told him.

I left Ayden with Xander and Lucía, knowing she needed the extra support. Nothing had torn me apart more than knowing I was the reason behind all of this. Why had I made such a rash decision? Why did I never consider how it may have affected anyone else?

I returned to the cabin and pulled Liam from the floorboards. As soon as he saw my bump return to its normal size, he knew Lucía had given birth. Swallowing the torment inside my soul, I choked out, "I fucked up. I really fucked up."

Liam didn't say a word.

"The Heavenly Court found out you got out. They feared you'd come after Lucía and Connor. They killed Connor, Liam. He's not coming back." I broke down, stumbling into the counter. "Connor is dead."

Liam grabbed my wrist, but I ripped it away. "I'm sorry."

"No you're not!" I spun around, spitting in his face. "You were never sorry. You have spent years tearing our lives apart until we were nothing. You couldn't stop. You are what's wrong with this world, Liam. You. Are. The. Problem."

Despite how angry I was, I let him pull me in for a hug. I wanted to kill him all over again. I wanted to get justice, but there was nothing left I could do. I'd saved the souls. I saw to the end of our case. It was over now.

"I'm sorry it has to end this way," he whispered against my hair.

I pressed my face against his shoulder, peeking over it only when something odd began to glow. I shoved him away and stared at the ball, moving it between my fingers.

I saw my face in it, and immediately it called to me. "My missing piece…"

"Eliana, please, don't."

"It's mine, Liam. I must."

"Eliana, no," he reached forward, trying to grasp it. However, he couldn't because it wasn't his to hold.

Just as I shoved the ball back into my chest, Ayden came barging in. Terror filled his eyes.

Memories flooded back, flashing by so fast I barely had time to pick them apart. I focused, and they found their place like a gear fitting in with another gear. Then, like a movie, they played.

A knock came through my door and I opened it up to reveal his face. Letting him inside, a sigh escaped my lips. "I was just getting ready for bed."

Liam shut the door behind him, throwing me a sorrow-filled smile. He wore leather gloves with a jacket, getting ready to head back out into the wintery night. "Times are getting tough. It's Christmas and it doesn't at all feel like it." He leaned his back against the wall, burying his hands in his pockets. "She would have made it all better."

Something fluttered inside me. "She would have."

He fiddled with something in his pocket. "I was saving this for her. It was supposed to be romantic." He pulled out a mistletoe. "It's not very romantic when she's got no heartbeat to race for me."

For some strange reason unbeknownst to me, mine started to race. Why was I feeling this way?

"Christmas was her favorite. It was the one holiday where she could be wholly herself." He twirled it between his fingers. Hurt—pain—settled where it shouldn't have. Like it'd been locked in a box, waiting for someone with the key to open it.

My heart began to beat louder, and my mind moved at the speed of light. Maybe it was grief, acceptance, or even just having a shoulder—but whatever it was, it was forcing its way into my skin like a demon possessing a body.

I wish I could have blamed my desires on a demon.

Liam continued to twirl it between his fingers, mesmerized by its vibrant colors. He was well unaware of my presence now. He was unaware of the look in my eyes.

I reached out and grabbed hold of the collar of his jacket, pulling him against me. Our lips were millimeters apart, and I wanted to feel so shameful for wanting Selene's boyfriend, but I didn't.

With our hot breaths coinciding as one, I brought our lips together until we were no longer hesitating. My hunger grew stronger and my breaths shallower. My need spread through my body, aching and screaming for more.

Liam reached down, grabbing my thigh and pulling it up towards his waist. "Eliana, you and I both know this is wrong on so many levels," he spit out. Yet, he never pulled away.

Selene had always gotten the first pick of the barrel, and I was left to dry. Liam was always around, always there to have my back and this past week, we grew closer over our shared trauma. He never had a clue, and maybe I never had either... But I was falling for Liam, and I wanted him in ways I had never craved another man before.

He brought his hand up to my lips, parting them with his thumb. "I always knew you felt some sort of way about me."

I closed my lips around his thumb, using my teeth to pull the glove off. "And you never said anything? How could you? Selene was your girlfriend and my roommate." My best friend.

Liam leaned down to kiss me again, but my throat began to close, and then it had cut off all airflow. He snaked his arm around my waist, grabbing hold of my wrist. "I'm sorry it has to end this way." He tugged, and a sharp pain shot up through my arm until my entire body was screaming in agony. Tugging again, I stumbled away and choked while holding onto my throat. My lungs couldn't inflate. My throat wouldn't open back up.

He let out a small sigh as he tossed the mistletoe. "I suppose you should be careful of what object you allow into your mouth. You made it too perfect, Eliana." He grabbed my wrist before I collapsed, pulling on my fingers. Before I had the chance to wonder what he was doing, my entire body became as light as a feather and the burning sensation in my lungs dissipated.

Something thumped against the floor, and when I looked back, my body lay on the hardwood, as lifeless as Selene's.

I faced Liam once more, yelling out as he stared me in the eye. "You're coming with me." He yanked me along, but my hand slipped from his and I began to drift higher and higher. "Damnit! One day I'll get this right." He hurried and pulled his glove off the ground. "And one day, I'll be running the show."

"Angel?" Ayden whispered as he pressed the side of my head into his chest.

I had remembered it all wrong. Everything... My entire death had been a lie. "You..." I faced Liam. "You knew?"

Liam shrugged it off as if lying about my entire demise had been no big deal. "Hey, I had an important role to play, and I take that very seriously."

After pulling myself from Ayden's grip, I yelled, "You fucking bastard!" I lunged at him, but Ayden pulled me back.

Liam leaned against the counter and threw his arms up. "I told you not to, but you didn't listen to me. I'm sorry, but you were my easiest target. I couldn't say no. No family to miss you. No friends. And the best part? You were already in love with me, Eliana! I didn't even have to charm you."

My husband tightened his arm on my waist. "What the fuck?"

Liam rubbed his face. "I'm sorry you both had to find out this way, but yes, there was a time when Eliana Wilson—"

"Dyer."

"—was in love with the villain. Look, okay, it wasn't supposed to happen the way it did but then you kissed me, and you practically asked me to kill you then and there."

I wiggled in Ayden's arms. If he'd just let me rip his fucking face off... "When a girl expresses herself physically, she is not asking to be murdered."

"Okay, that's a bit harsh." He put his hand up in defense. "I simply ripped your soul from your body. Unfortunately, I didn't have the art of holding onto a soul quite mastered yet. That is how you slipped away and became an angel instead."

Tears pushed at my eyelids like water pressed against a dam. "You killed Selene and I to do what—practice ripping souls from bodies? Why would you? How?"

Liam traced his finger along the edge of the counter. "It was too easy. When you sell your soul, you get these amazing abilities. I wanted to master those abilities. So, I did."

All these years I thought I knew everything. When Ayden told me my soul was broken, I knew a memory was missing. However, I never knew it was the biggest memory of all. I had loved Liam, and he had used that to pull my soul straight from my body.

And Liam? He'd sold his soul well before I'd ever been aware of it. Before he met Selene and I.

Because of him, Sunny and Becky lost their lives for good, against their will, too.

If only I'd been intelligent enough to see the answers right in front of me. It always boiled back down to Liam Brown, didn't it?

Ayden asked me once who I loved more, and I thought he had lost his mind. I never loved Liam, or I thought I hadn't. It was all a mirage then. The answer became as clear as day.

I ached for Ayden the most. Without his soul intertwined with mine, I'd be nothing.

"Shall we?" he asked.

Straightening my back, I narrowed my eyes as the rage began to bubble over. "We shall." Liam's immediate response was to run out the door. Ayden went after him first, tackling him to the ground. I caught up to them and shook my head. "You knew this day was coming. You knew you'd have to go back there."

He hissed at me, struggling against my husband who held Liam's hands behind his back. "I'm not going back. That place is torture. I sold my soul to be an ally—a ruler. Lucifer fucked me over and threw me into a cell to rot."

"I warned you about that, but you refused to listen to me," I said while squatting to his level. "And that is no longer my problem. I'm a guardian angel for the living. You, Liam, have been dead for over six months. You destroyed lives. You destroyed *mine*."

Liam threw Ayden off, but I pushed his face into the dirt before he could take off again. He almost got free from my grasp, until I reached under his hips and shoved my hand into his jeans, yanking where he hurt most. His second head.

It seemed to keep him under my control.

"Eliana, please, don't do this," he begged.

"Did you show me that kind of mercy when I was fighting for my life?" I pulled harder and he cried out in pain. "Ayden, grab the handcuffs."

He did as I said and put them on. He helped me pull Liam up off the ground, forcing him back to the portal. Lucifer stood at the entrance, arms across his chest. "We've been waiting for our special guest."

"Eliana, no. Please." He gave me a puppy look, which had no effect on me. "I didn't leave on purpose. She made me!" he told Lucifer.

I threw Liam down at Lucifer's feet. "He's all yours."

"No, Eliana, no." He turned back to look at me, fear forever etched into his face. "No!" he screamed as Lucifer closed the portal for good.

Maybe it had been harsh—and even uncalled for to let Liam suffer a fate much worse than death. There'd been a day when that would have shaken me to my core, drenching me with remorse. That day had long passed and now I wore nothing but justice. Liam had been the victim of it all. There was no returning to the past. All that laid before me now was my future.

Ayden Dyer.

ABOUT THE AUTHOR

Monica Shantel has always had an interest in artistic and creative hobbies of sorts, including but not limited to: drawing, crafting, graphic design, and painting. Although all she has is a high school diploma under her belt, she is not new to the writing community. At the age of twelve, she began building stories to escape reality and find hope in life once again. Her debut novel is Beauty of a Crimson Soul. Along the same genre, she writes dark tales of mythical romance which only add more to the growing fantasy worlds inside her head.

ACKNOWLEDGEMENTS

Thanks to my mom for always supporting my writing, even as a valid career. Thanks to my brother who's asked questions and made me think about my plots, and to the other family members who have picked up my books just to say they were proud of me.

To Ashly for always supporting me.

And thank you to Cass for pointing out the rights and wrongs of this book to help me make it the best it would be. This book needed all your help. You brought this trilogy to life.

www.ingramcontent.com/pod-product-compliance
Lightning Source LLC
Chambersburg PA
CBHW020338310726
48979CB00015B/2421/J

* 9 7 8 1 9 6 0 6 9 6 1 2 0 *